FAIRY TALES OF THE WORLD

FAIRY TALES OF THE WORLD

Galley Press

FAIRY TALES OF THE WORLD

Published in this edition 1985 by Orbis Publishing Limited for Galley Press,
an imprint of W. H. Smith and Son Limited, Registered No. 237811 England.
Trading as WHS Distributors, St John's House, East Street, Leicester, LE1 6NE.
© Artia, Prague, 1985
Graphic design by Bohuslav Blažej

Texts by: M. Novák, Z. Černá, D. and M. Šťovíčková, M. Kosová, V. Hulpach,
M. Tvrdíková, J. Horák, O. Sirovátka, V. Šťovíček, Z. Dubovská, M. Malý, J. Tichý
Illustrations by: J. Šerých, E. Bednářová, K. Teissig, M. Troup, V. Brehovszký,
J. Trnka, M. Želibská, J. Liesler, L. Maňásek
Translated by: O. Kuthanová, V. Gissing, J. Eisler, S. Finn

ISBN 0-86136-742-1
Printed in Czechoslovakia by Severografia, Liberec
1/99/22/51 – 01

CONTENTS

JAPAN
7 ~ *The Badger and the Fox*
14 ~ *Yukiko and the Little Black Cat*
25 ~ *The Tea House in the Forest*

CHINA
32 ~ *San-lang and the Dragon Princess*
41 ~ *The Maids in the Mirror*
50 ~ *The Herb Fairy*

AFRICA
60 ~ *The Two Brothers*
65 ~ *The Magic Mirror*
70 ~ *The Bird Who Gave Milk*

NORTH AMERICA (INDIAN)
76 ~ *The White Water-lily*
81 ~ *The Gift of the Totems*
88 ~ *The Otter's Friendship*

RUSSIA
94 ~ *Ivan Bull*
100 ~ *The Greedy Fox and Kuzma Getrich*
107 ~ *The Dazzling Falcon Finister*

BOHEMIA
114 ~ *Flagstaff, Fatso and Big-eyes*
122 ~ *Toby and the Wolf*
126 ~ *The Clever Cobbler*
131 ~ *The Disobedient Princess*
138 ~ *The Devil and Kate*

SLOVAKIA, POLAND AND BULGARIA
144 ~ *Golden-curls and How She Kept Silent*
151 ~ *The Calf's Skin*
157 ~ *The Grateful Animals*

INDONESIA
164 ~ *Princess Purbasari*
172 ~ *The Prince Who Became a Demon*
176 ~ *The Story of a Certain Hae-hae*

TIBET
180 ~ *The Lama and the Carpenter*
182 ~ *The Story of Broadheart*
188 ~ *The Talking Buddha*

SCANDINAVIA
194 ~ *The Capricious Princess*
202 ~ *The Priest Know-All*
210 ~ *Lazy Lars*
218 ~ *The King's Rabbits*

PERSIA
228 ~ *The Adventures of Bidjan and the Fair Princess*
238 ~ *The Merchant's Son*
244 ~ *The Melon Child*
250 ~ *The Magic Caterpillar*

The Badger and the Fox

On distant Sado Island lived a badger called Denzaburo. Denzaburo was greatly admired by the animals on the island because he was well educated, as well as being young and goodlooking. But he was admired most of all for his ability to turn, at a moment's notice, into practically anything or anyone you could think of. For a long time Denzaburo was content in the knowledge that he was the cleverest person on the island; but gradually life began to bore him.

'I may be famous and respected on this island,' he told himself, 'but somewhere else there may be someone who is cleverer than I. After all, I am still young enough to learn.'

So he made up his mind to go out into the world. For even if he were not to meet his master, he thought, he could still learn something new. He decided to leave without delay, and soon turned his back on Sado Island. Up hill and down dale he walked, all over the land. He saw and heard many fascinating things; but, strange to tell, none of the people he met was famous in any way.

Then, one day, he came out of a forest and was wondering which way to go, when he met a glossy red fox. The fox greeted him very politely, wishing him the best of health on his journey. One word led to another, and Denzaburo introduced himself.

'I am the badger Denzaburo of Sado Island,' he said. 'I am going nowhere in particular; just travelling to complete my education.'

'Oh,' said the fox, 'so you are Mr Denzaburo, the famous badger of Sado Island? This is truly a great honour. I have heard so much about you.' The fox bowed very low to show his respect, and the badger then asked where the fox was going.

'I am Osan of Eha Province. The purpose of my journey is very much like yours. You see, where I come from I am absolutely unique. So I left home in the hope of meeting someone to teach me new lessons. How happy I am to have come across you, Mr Denzaburo!'

'Ah, Mr Osan of Eha Province,' beamed the badger. 'Your fame has spread far beyond your native land. I, too, have heard much about you. Indeed, I never dared to hope that I should meet you in person. What a lucky coincidence brought us together!'

The badger and the fox continued to exchange compliments. Finally they decided to show each other examples of their art, for this would be interesting and would also establish who was the greater master. They were each determined to show the other their best transformation tricks. The winner of the contest would be the one who succeeded in fooling the other.

'Let us continue along this road,' suggested the fox. 'Before we arrive at the nearest shrine, each will try to outwit the other.'

The badger agreed to this plan. They parted and the fox ran on ahead. The badger watched him until he was out of sight. Then he picked up his bundle and set out after the fox.

Denzaburo passed through a small wood and presently came to a road bordered by rice fields. He looked carefully about him but saw nothing suspicious. He decided that the fox must have run all the way to the shrine, where the presence of pilgrims bringing offerings would make it easier for him to blend into the scene.

The badger walked on until he came to a roadside statue of the god Jizo. The statue was sitting cross-legged with hands folded in its lap. The kindly eyes in the shaved head were fixed on the horizon.

'What superb sculpture,' thought Denzaburo, 'and how beautifully finished! There are no chisel marks at all. I shall sacrifice a rice ball to the god so he may bless my journey.' The badger took a rice ball from his bundle and placed it at the god's feet. He bowed low until his head touched the ground, and murmured a few words of prayer. When he straightened up again he was amazed to find that the rice ball had disappeared.

'I have never heard of Jizo accepting offerings in this way,' thought Denzaburo. 'Perhaps the wind has blown the rice ball away.' But though he searched all over the place, there was no trace of the rice ball.

'Ah well,' thought the badger, 'it must have rolled away somewhere. I will offer the god another one.'

So he placed another rice ball at Jizo's feet. Again he reverently bowed to the ground; and again, when he raised his head the rice ball had gone.

Denzaburo thought this very strange indeed. But he always liked to get to the root of a problem, and so he made up his mind to make an offering of a third rice ball, which he again placed at the statue's feet with all due reverence. This time he bent his head even lower, but from the corner of his eye he watched the statue closely. He straightened up abruptly — and what did he see? The wooden statue was holding a half-eaten rice ball in its hand! Denzaburo laughed and grabbed Jizo's hand. An instant later the statue had disappeared and by the roadside stood the fox, shaking with laughter.

'That was excellent,' said the badger. 'It cost me three rice balls, but your greediness gave you away.'

It was hard to decide who had won the bet. The badger had been fooled for a while, he admitted, but not for very long. The fox argued that if he had not eaten the rice balls he would have got away with it. As they were unable to come to a decision, the fox suggested that he should have another turn.

'Mr Denzaburo,' he said, 'to change into a statue is child's play for me. I will show you a better trick. We are now approaching a village; keep your eyes open.'

Osan whisked his bushy tail and disappeared. The badger walked on towards the village; but first he turned into an old monk, so as not to startle the villagers.

After a while he saw a crowd of villagers running towards the main road which led to the shrine. He quickly joined them to see what was going on. What a spectacle met his eyes! A wedding procession was coming down the road. The bride was sitting in a beautiful palanquin behind red silk curtains, and the relatives and guests who accompanied her in the procession were dressed in magnificent black silk kimonos, with their coats-of-arms embroidered down the front and sleeves. A crowd of servants followed, carrying generous offerings in lacquer bowls.

The excited villagers told each other that they had not seen such a fine procession for a long time, and that the bride must be a very rich man's daughter. Denzaburo, in his monk's disguise, was watching too. He was just gazing with wonder at the beautifully embroidered kimonos, when a young monk came up to him and tugged his sleeve.

'You must be a stranger in these parts,' he said. 'I have not seen you before. Would you like to come to our shrine for a rest after your journey?'

The badger thanked the young monk and followed him to the shrine. The wedding party had just drawn up at the gates and the bride was getting out of the palanquin, when a rice ball, intended as an offering, rolled to her feet. Without a moment's hesitation she stooped and picked up the rice ball. Then, raising it to her lips, she was about to take a bite out of it, when the rice ball whispered, 'I have won!'

An instant later the procession had disappeared and at the temple gates stood the badger and the fox, face to face. They exchanged glances, and raced off to the woods at top speed to escape the villagers' anger.

When they had rested for a while and got their breath back, Denzaburo said, 'That was a wonderful job you did! You nearly fooled me, you know, except that you over-reached yourself. For one small fox to change into all those people — well, it just can't be done! Your tail peeped out of the last servant's clothes, and that is how I recognized your work.

'Tomorrow, you must let me show you what I can do,' continued the badger. 'If you don't mind, I should like you to come to the shrine two villages farther down the road. I am afraid we have outstayed our welcome here and must move on. I shall try to show you a prince's procession. Please watch closely, because I am sure you will not be able to notice my presence.'

Mr Osan politely expressed his doubts. He said he knew that Mr Denzaburo could easily turn into a small procession, but a prince with his entourage was a different matter altogether. Did the badger realize how many people were involved? The fox added that as badgers were larger than foxes, they were naturally able to produce more people, but even so . . .

The badger smiled in reply, saying, 'Please wait until tomorrow! You shall see for yourself.'

But the fox was by no means convinced.

'A prince's procession is very long,' he thought. 'Denzaburo will not be able to travel far without collapsing under the strain. He will probably start out as himself and do his transformation act near the shrine. If I go there early in the morning, I shall see everything.'

Mr Osan slept badly that night. At daybreak he got up and ran down the road to the big shrine the badger had mentioned.

He was there before sunrise, and hid in the bushes at the side of the road, eagerly watching for his friend's arrival. He lay there for a long time, while the sun rose high in the sky and the birds sang gaily. The road was empty but for an occasional pilgrim and a few villagers carrying home their baskets. But there was no trace of any prince's entourage anywhere to be seen.

The hours passed and the sun's heat increased. It was almost noon when the sound of hoof beats could be heard in the distance. The fox sat up and saw a great procession slowly drawing near.

Mr Osan wondered whether this could really be the badger. Was he able to walk such a distance in that heat? He quickly changed himself into a villager and stepped out into the road in order to see better.

The procession was certainly very impressive. In front walked a group of servants who cleared the way. Just behind them, at the head of the procession rode four samurai in full armour, sitting stiffly on glossy black horses.

'No,' decided the fox. 'This must be a real procession. The badger could never produce anything so magnificent.' He continued to watch, until the splendour of the procession so overawed him that he bowed low, with his forehead to the ground, as a peasant should do when a prince rides past. The richly lacquered palanquin drew nearer and nearer. Inside, the prince was resting on soft cushions, while the bearers walked carefully so as to keep the palanquin steady. Four more samurai, clad in armour, followed close behind, each girded with twin swords and sitting motionless on his proud black steed. The procession gave such an impression of stateliness and grandeur that Mr Osan hardly dared breathe. He stood with bowed head, waiting for it to pass.

How great then was his anger when the procession dissolved into thin air, leaving the road deserted but for the laughing badger, who called out cheerfully, 'Do straighten up, dear Mr Osan! A simple badger does not deserve so much respect.'

The fox blushed and began to tremble all over with fury for having fallen into the badger's trap. His humiliation was all the greater for having been told beforehand what the badger was going to do. Oh, the shame of it!

'Listen, Mr Denzaburo,' he said icily, 'tomorrow I will show you that I can do just as well. If you will trouble yourself to come back here at noon, you will see a PERFECT prince's procession. Please do not underrate my abilities.'

The badger said very pleasantly that he would be delighted.

Early the next morning he climbed a tree by the road and waited for the promised procession. He was absolutely certain that the fox would be able to produce nothing better than a very modest parade, which would be easy to see through.

After some time he heard hoof beats and saw a beautiful procession coming down the road. A crowd of servants walked at its head, followed by a group of dignified, fully-armoured samurai on horseback, riding two by two. The badger counted sixteen of them! Then came a gold-encrusted palanquin with embroidered silk curtains, between which the high-born prince could be seen relaxing on soft cushions. Behind followed sixteen more samurai riding in pairs on glossy horses, and at the tail of the procession came a large crowd of less important samurai, each girded with twin swords.

The badger could hardly believe his eyes. Could the fox have managed all this? He decided to make sure: changing quickly into a samurai, he stepped to the side of the road, and stood in a respectful attitude with head bowed — but not too low, so that he could keep an eye on the procession.

When the samurai on foot drew near, Mr Denzaburo burst out laughing and quickly went back to the palanquin. He drew the silk curtains apart, saying, 'An excellent job, Mr Osan! However, you took on a little more than you could handle. The tip of your tail is peeping out of the last samurai's cloak.'

The badger could hardly have been prepared for what happened next. The prince — for that is what he was — became extremely annoyed, and all the samurai attacked the poor badger with their swords. He managed to change back into his true self, slipped between their legs and raced back to the wood just in the nick of time; for if they had caught him, they would certainly have killed him.

He had been too sure of himself, and had acted on suspicion alone, mistaking the tip of a samurai's sword for the fox's tail. What Mr Denzaburo had not known, but what the fox had heard the day before while he was waiting for the badger was that a gala spectacle was to take place in the shrine the following day. It was the anniversary of the shrine's founding, and the monks had prepared a great feast to which the prince was invited. Mr Osan had played a trick on the badger which had succeeded, and Mr Denzaburo had never been so furious in all his life! He shouted with rage and stamped his feet; in fact it was a good thing that the fox was not there, because the badger quite forgot his manners.

A few days later, when Denzaburo had got over the worst of his shock, he decided that he had had enough of travelling. He returned to Sado Island, and the first thing he did after coming home was to drive all the foxes from the island. Ever since that time, foxes have avoided the island. Search as you may, you will not find a single fox on Sado.

Yukiko and the Little Black Cat

There lived once, in a village, a proud and wicked woman. She was rich enough to afford anything she wanted, and yet her heart was filled with envy of anyone who was rich, contented, good-looking or young. If she saw someone in a happy mood, or heard of a true friendship, this was enough to arouse her bitterness and anger; indeed she was annoyed each time a poor person dared to smile.

'How irresponsible those beggars are,' she would fume. 'They are too lazy even to worry! Yet here am I, higher born by far, with more problems than I can handle. Is there any justice?'

She would go on grumbling until she found a way of spoiling a cheerful person's day.

Among the wicked woman's many servants was a young girl called Yukiko, an orphan who had grown up in the rich household. Although she had hardly known anything but beatings and scoldings, she had managed to keep a pure, kind heart and a sweet temper.

Her special darling was a little black cat, who returned the girl's love in equal measure. She slept on Yukiko's bed, and when the girl came into the kitchen, the little black cat would gently rub against her legs, and purr. Yukiko would pick the cat up and stroke her smooth fur, forgetting her troubles in the thought that she had one good friend in the world.

Of course, the mistress of the house begrudged Yukiko the cat's affection. Woe to the girl when the woman caught her fondling the animal! She would immediately think up some urgent work. 'If you have time to play with the cat, you will surely have time to do something for your mistress,' was the call which usually came when Yukiko was already up to her eyes in work.

And the little black cat did not fare much better; the wicked woman would beat her, pull her whiskers or rub her fur the wrong way, saying with a cruel smile, 'Come, come, Pussy! You never hiss at Yukiko, so why should you hiss at me?'

It reached the stage when Yukiko only dared to play with the cat when they were alone. But she went on sharing scraps of food with her; if ever there was a bit of fresh fish left over from the mistress's table, Yukiko always saved it for her friend. The stolen moments she spent with the cat were her only consolation. It helped her to tell some living creature of her sorrows, even if she had to be on guard that nobody noticed her doing so.

Then came a day when Yukiko could not find her cat. The girl ran out into the yard a dozen times to search for her, but there was no trace of her darling.

'She is sure to be back in the evening,' Yukiko told herself. But an instant later, she caught herself thinking, 'What if some harm has come to Pussy?'

That evening Yukiko went to bed and waited for the cat to jump up and snuggle close to her. She lay wide awake all night, starting up at every rustle she heard in the house. In the morning she rose pale and heavy-eyed. The black cat did not turn up that day, or the next, and Yukiko's heart grew heavier with each passing day. She was unable to get over the loss of the only friend she had ever known.

The wicked woman enjoyed her servant girl's misery to the full. It pleased her so much to watch Yukiko's grief, that she almost forgave the cat for running away. She never missed an opportunity of taunting poor Yukiko. 'Serves you right, my girl, after all you did for that ungrateful creature,' she would say. 'She pretended to be fond of you, while all the time she was planning to run away. Don't ever expect any gratitude from man or beast.'

However, Yukiko refused to think badly of the cat. Although she was unable to answer her mistress, she said to herself, 'Something must have happened to the poor little thing. If only I knew where she was.' And so the days went by and Yukiko's grief did not grow any less.

Some time later, a travelling fortune-teller came to the village. He was a wise man, who did not only see into the future, but also answered many questions about the present. He stopped at every door, and eventually came to the wicked woman's house. She asked him a lot of questions, and kept him talking for hours because she wanted more than her money's worth.

It was getting very late when the fortune-teller finally left the house. Yukiko was waiting for him at the gate. She knew that if her mistress found out that she was talking to the stranger, she would be punished, but she just *had* to ask the wise man about her cat. So she blurted out her question.

The fortune-teller thought the matter over, and then spoke.

'Your cat has gone to Cat Hill in the Inaba Mountains on Kyushu Island,' he told Yukiko. 'If you long for her as much as you say, go to Kyushu Island and you will find her. But I have to warn you — the journey will be dangerous. You have no idea of what may be in store for you. Think it over, child; human beings ought to remain among their own kind.'

As soon as Yukiko learned that there was a place where she might find her little cat, her mind was made up. She was not afraid of hardship or danger. She pleaded with her mistress until she was given permission to go.

'Go if you must,' the wicked woman told her. 'But remember — you must work two days for every day you are away.' She imagined all the troubles Yukiko would run into, and was glad to think of the risks the girl was taking because of a cat.

Yukiko made up a small bundle containing a few dry cakes from the kitchen, and set out for Kyushu Island. For many, many days she walked, spending the cold nights curled up in bushes near the road, for she had no money to stay at an inn.

Before long she had worn out her straw sandals, and then the sharp stones made the soles of her feet sore.

At long last she arrived at Kyushu Island, and the sun was setting when Yukiko eventually came to a village on the island. She knocked at the door of a hut and asked the way to the Inaba Mountains.

'The Inaba Mountains lie across the river,' she was told. 'But you must not dream of going there. Only the bravest hunters dare to climb the slopes of the mountains, and even they stay close to the river bank and make sure they leave before nightfall. Beyond the river lies the Kingdom of the Cats, where human beings never go.'

Yukiko thanked the people politely for their advice, and firmly but graciously declined the villagers' invitation to spend the night in their hut.

'No thank you, I shall be all right,' she smiled. 'I have come a very long way in order to get to the Kingdom of the Cats, so I cannot turn back now, when I'm so close.'

So the village people let her go, shrugging their shoulders.

Yukiko left the village and turned towards the river. She found a shallow place and waded across. On the farther bank she was faced by a steep slope. She climbed up the slope, and at the top entered a thick forest. The girl took a deep breath and walked on courageously. Everything was quiet. Not a leaf moved on the trees. Yukiko was terribly tired; the climb up the slope had completely exhausted her. She began to wonder if she had better lie down and sleep where she was, when suddenly the trees thinned, and she came to a large clearing dotted with many high-gabled pavilions.

'There must be rich people living here,' she thought. 'Everything looks so neat and clean.'

Yukiko walked up to the fence and called out, asking politely whether there was anyone at home. At once a lovely girl appeared, whose body was as slender as a willow tree. She bowed gracefully and asked what she could do for the stranger.

'I am the serving girl, Yukiko,' explained the girl. 'My only friend was a little black cat. She disappeared without trace, and I asked a fortune-teller where she might be. He told me to come here to the Inaba Mountains, so I left home at once. Now I have arrived on Kyushu Island, but I do not know where to look for my little cat. I am tired and weary after my long journey; will you please let me spend the night under your roof? I can sleep in a corner, and I promise not to bother you at all. In the morning I will climb up to Cats' Hill and continue my search.'

The beautiful girl listened carefully to what Yukiko said. Then she bowed again, and said with a smile, 'So you have come to be eaten up?'

Yukiko was so frightened by these words that she would have turned on her heel and run, had not a little old woman come out of the adjoining pavilion at that moment and sternly sent the lovely girl away.

'Forgive me, my dear,' said the old woman kindly. 'I'm afraid the girl has no manners. I shall have to speak to her again. Oh dear, I'm sure she said something rude to you; you look quite pale. Please tell me what I can do for you!'

These kind words calmed Yukiko's fears. She again told her story, and gradually regained her confidence. The old woman listened politely and replied with a kind smile, 'Of course you can sleep here, my dear. Do come in. Don't you worry, you will be quite safe.'

She began to mumble then, as if speaking to herself, and Yukiko heard her say, 'What a long way to come only to be ea . . .' but she could not make out the rest.

However, the old woman graciously showed Yukiko inside, and gave the order for a bath to be prepared for the girl. After the bath, which Yukiko enjoyed very much, the old woman led her to a spotlessly clean and cosy little room where a bed had been made up on soft floor mats.

'Have a little rest, my dear,' she said encouragingly. 'I will go and bring you some food.' She again smiled at Yukiko and left the room.

Yukiko felt much better after the bath. She sat down and looked about her. 'What a strange house this is,' she thought. 'All these pavilions and rooms and everything so clean and tidy. What a lot of servants these people must keep. Yet I have seen none, and everything is so quiet and still.'

After a while Yukiko thought she heard voices in the next room. Her curiosity got the better of her; she tiptoed to the sliding door and quietly pushed it apart. Through the chink she saw two breathtakingly beautiful girls resting on mats. Their hair was elaborately arranged and decorated with finely carved ivory pins, and they were wearing heavy brocade kimonos in the most elegant style. Yukiko had never seen anyone so exquisitely lovely. The girls were talking in a soft, caressing way, which reminded her of a cat purring.

She quietly shut the sliding door and opened the one leading to the opposite

room. There she saw two equally beautiful girls kneeling in front of a mirror and making up their faces. Yukiko closed the door without making a sound and returned to her bed. Everything was as quiet as before.

She suddenly felt very nervous; the unnatural quiet depressed her and she longed for the sound of a human voice. She again rose and stealthily went back to the first door. Holding her breath, she slid the door open a crack, and leaned close to hear what the lovely girls were talking about.

After a while she could make out some words; then she clearly heard one of the girls saying, 'Did you know that the girl who came here today is looking for her friend, the little black cat? She seemed so worried about this cat, perhaps we had better not eat her . . . !'

Yukiko's knees began to tremble with fright. Teeth chattering, she returned to her bed. She was frantically trying to think of a way to escape, when the door opened and a slender girl entered the room. She was clad in a brown brocade kimono, embroidered with white chrysanthemums and held together with a wide brocade belt. She moved gracefully on softly padding feet. Yukiko overcame her fear and looked closely at the girl; to her relief she recognized her friend the cat, for on the slender human body was a cat's head.

'How happy I am to see you again, Yukiko,' purred the little black cat. 'I am grateful to you for all the love and care you lavished on me in the old days, and for coming all this way to visit me.

'You see,' she went on, 'I was getting old and ill, and it was time for me to come here to the Cat Palace. This is where cats come when they are chased out by people, or when they grow old. To us cats this is Paradise! But there is no room here for human beings; indeed, it would be dangerous for you to stay. Rest a while and then go home, Yukiko. At present there are only a few of my friends in the palace, and I will not let them hurt a hair on your head. However, the other cats will soon return from the hunt, and once they are here, I shall not be able to protect you. I will go now and bring you some refreshment, and after that it would be best if you left.'

The cat gave Yukiko a sweet smile and left the room. Before long she came back, carrying a tray with dishes of boiled rice, vegetables and fresh fish cooked in a spicy sauce. There was also a pot of scented tea. The cat put mats on a small table, placed it before Yukiko and knelt down to serve her meal.

Yukiko felt quite safe now. She had never eaten such choice food in so leisurely a manner. She told her friend everything that had happened in the village after the cat's departure, and about the travelling fortune-teller and his advice. The two friends giggled and laughed, and it was like old times being together again. The food and conversation brought the colour back to Yukiko's cheeks and she forgot all her worries.

After the meal, the cat carried away the tray and returned with a small parcel. This she handed to Yukiko, saying, 'Do not open this until you are home again. If any cats should bother you on the way, just raise the parcel, shake it in their faces, and they will leave you alone. Have no fear, Yukiko, and go in peace.'

'Thank you for everything, dear cat,' said Yukiko. 'I am glad I came, for now I know that you are well and happy.' The cat saw the girl to the garden gate, where they kissed goodbye. She stood watching Yukiko until the girl disappeared among the trees.

Yukiko entered the dark forest and had only taken a few steps when the wild cats came running towards her from every side. Their green eyes shone with an evil light in the darkness as, snarling and hissing, they tried to attack the girl. Yukiko raised the parcel high and shook it as hard as she could. The cats retreated angrily and she went on her way unharmed.

On she went, the parcel raised in both hands until she had climbed down the slope to the river, and carefully waded across the water. Once she had reached the other bank, the cats were powerless; so Yukiko tied up the parcel in her bundle and sat down to rest before starting on the return journey.

She hurried home as fast as she could, remembering her promise to work two days for each day she had been away.

The wicked woman was quite surprised to see her serving girl back, safe and sound.

'I can hardly believe my eyes!' she cried. 'Do you mean to tell me that no wild beast ate you up, after all? You must tell me exactly what sort of welcome you received from your grateful cat.'

Yukiko quietly told her mistress all about her adventures. She described the Cat Palace, stressing how clean and comfortable it was, and how happy the little black cat was, living among her own kind. She also told how the cat had given her a parcel as they parted and how she was to unpack it only after her return.

Yukiko brought the parcel and opened it in front of her mistress. How great was their surprise when Yukiko took from the parcel a painting of a savage dog with teeth bared, and out of its mouth fell ten real gold pieces! Yukiko was speechless with happiness. No longer was she a poor dependent orphan, at the mercy of her cruel mistress.

She immediately bought herself free from service and moved to the town. With the remaining money she bought a small shop, where she sold rice cakes and fried titbits. She lived there in comfort and happiness, and often thought gratefully of her friend, the little black cat.

While Yukiko at last enjoyed her life, her former mistress was consumed with envy. 'If that stupid servant girl got so much money just through visiting a miserable cat,' she thought, 'what riches would I receive if I went to see her — for wasn't I her mistress?' These thoughts kept her awake at night, and at last she made up her mind to go to the Inaba Mountains to claim the fortune she felt was owed to her.

She hired some litter bearers and had a large supply of choice food stored in lacquered cabinets. Then without telling anyone where she was going, she set out for the Inaba Mountains on Kyushu Island.

The journey passed quickly, but not quickly enough for the wicked woman, who kept screaming at the litter bearers to walk faster. At length they arrived in the first village on Kyushu Island. The wicked woman leant out of her litter and asked the village people the way to the Inaba Mountains.

'The Inaba Mountains lie over there beyond the river,' they told her, pointing out the direction. 'But you must not go there, lady, for even our bravest hunters never venture far from the other bank.'

The wicked woman dismissed their warnings with a haughty wave of her hand, and demanded that the ferryman be called. 'I want him to come immediately,' she called after the messenger. 'I am not going to waste any more time in this wretched place.'

The ferryman arrived and took the wicked woman and her party across the river. On the farther bank she alighted from her litter and sent the litter bearers and servants back, telling them to wait in the village for her return. To herself she thought, 'There's no need for them to be present when I take over the fortune due to me.'

The wicked woman quickly climbed the slope in the direction Yukiko had described to her. Having been carried so far in the litter she had no reason to feel tired; but she was soon out of breath, for she was not in the habit of walking anywhere. She wiped the perspiration from her brow and was relieved when she presently came to the large clearing dotted with high-gabled roofs.

'So this is the Cat Palace,' she said. 'I don't see anything grand about it; but a simple serving girl would find it impressive, I suppose.' She put on a bored expression as she walked up to the fence.

'I say, is there anyone at home?' she called loudly. 'Open up!'

From the main building appeared a lovely young girl, bowing so low that her back arched like a cat's.

'What can I do for you, madam?' she purred.

'I have come to pay a call on the black cat that used to serve me but ran away without any explanation. I am certain she will feel honoured when she learns that her mistress has made this long journey just to visit her. So let me in at once and have her brought before me,' said the wicked woman haughtily.

The lovely girl grinned like a cat. She was on the point of saying something rude, when a little old woman came out of the pavilion next door. She hobbled up to the fence, sending the girl away at the same time.

'Do come in, madam,' she said kindly. 'You must be tired after your long journey.' She stood aside to let the visitor enter the pavilion.

'Ah, that's more like it,' thought the wicked woman, as she stepped inside.

The old woman ordered a bath to be prepared for the guest. Afterwards she showed the guest into a cosy room where a bed had been made up on soft mats.

'I am hungry,' announced the wicked woman.

'I am having some refreshment prepared,' answered the old woman, bowing low. Very soon a serving girl brought a tray of choice titbits and the visitor ate her fill. After the meal she immediately lay down to sleep, for the unaccustomed walk up the steep slope had made her tired.

In the middle of the night the wicked woman was awakened by a strange scratching noise. She sat up and looked about her. Through chinks in the wall she saw a light in the next room. She walked quietly across the room and pushed back the sliding door. To her horror she saw two enormous tabby cats lying on mats, their eyes shining with an evil green light. The woman quickly shut the door and opened the one on the other side of her room. There, too, she saw two large cats with glittering eyes. The wicked woman's heart beat faster; now, thoroughly frightened, she recalled that Yukiko had spoken of beautiful girls in the adjoining rooms, but had made no mention of dangerous big cats.

At that moment another door opened and the little black cat entered the room.

'Ah! So you've come at last,' said the wicked woman angrily. 'It's high time you appeared; I don't like your precious Cat Palace one bit, I might add. Give me my parcel of gold pieces and let me go!'

When the little black cat heard these arrogant words, she saw that her former mistress had not changed. She blinked her green eyes and gave a loud hiss, whereupon the big cats from either side sprang into the room, tore the wicked woman to pieces, and gobbled her up there and then.

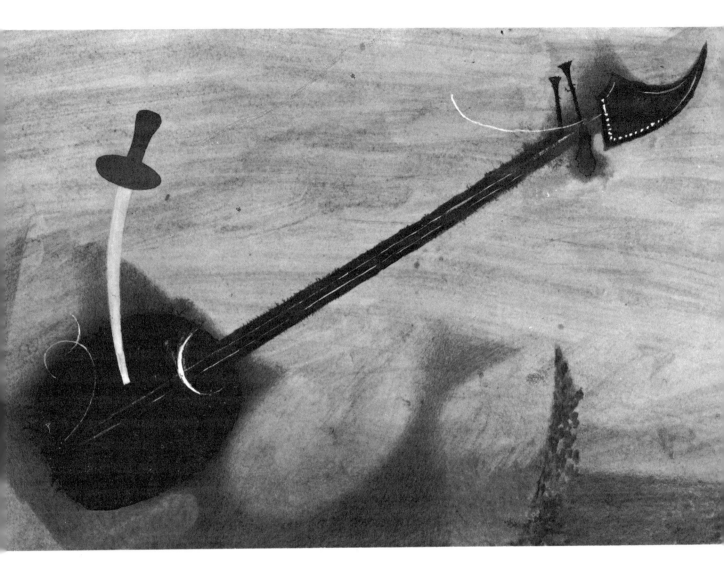

The Tea House in the Forest

In the town of Sakai lived three friends who were young salesmen called Kuemon, Sasuke and Chubei. One day they set out together for Sumiyoshi where a religious festival was held each spring. The friends started out early; they wanted to reach Sumiyoshi the evening before the day of the feast so that they would not miss the opening ceremony which began at sunrise.

However, the day was unusually hot for spring and the friends made much slower progress than expected; also they took frequent rests in tea houses along the road. They were resting at a tea house by the edge of the forest, when they noticed that the sun was already low in the western sky. Sasuke urged his friends to walk on again if they wished to cross the forest before dark; but Kuemon suggested that it would be better if they returned to the nearest village and spent the night there, going on to Sumiyoshi in the morning.

Sasuke would not hear of it. 'We agreed to see the festivities from the beginning,' he reminded his friends, 'and the best part is the procession at sunrise. Come along, you two; it will be cooler under the trees.'

But Chubei took Kuemon's side. 'Be sensible, Sasuke,' he said, 'we cannot reach Sumiyoshi in daylight, and I would much rather not walk through the forest in the dark. Kuemon is right; we had better turn back. If we get up early, we can still see the parade.'

'Oh, so you two are scared of ghosts, are you?' taunted Sasuke.

Kuemon calmly admitted that he was afraid. He reminded his friend that strange things could happen in lonely places, especially when it grew dark, and dared Sasuke to walk on alone.

'Of course I will!' cried Sasuke. 'I can look after myself.' He patted the short sword that hung from his belt.

In vain did his friends try to dissuade him from going on alone; Sasuke just laughed and said they were cowards. In the end, Kuemon and Chubei walked back to the last village they had been through, and Sasuke hitched up his belt and strode off into the forest without a backward glance.

He had not been walking long when it began to get dark in the forest. All of a sudden a black cloud blotted out the last weak rays of the sun, and it began to rain quietly but steadily. This was something that Sasuke had not thought of. He walked on under the dripping trees, looking for a place to shelter until the shower passed.

The forest was thinning out and before long Sasuke came to a clearing. He was reluctant to leave the shelter of the trees, but just then he noticed a house with lighted windows on the other side of the clearing. 'Good,' he thought to himself, 'this is just what I need! The people are sure to let me wait there until the rain passes.' The young man dashed out into the rain and across the clearing, making straight for the house with the lighted windows.

There was no fence round the house and the sliding verandah door was pushed back. So, without more ado, Sasuke slid out of his sodden sandals, swung himself up on to the verandah and entered the house.

In the light of an oil lamp, the young man saw a cosy room with a pretty recess of lacquered wood, and spotlessly clean matting on the floor. The hibashi, or charcoal brazier, was of porcelain with a spider's web pattern; on a finely carved tray stood a bottle of rice wine and a cup. Nothing moved in the house, and except for the noise of the rain outside, not a sound could be heard.

It did not occur to Sasuke to wonder where the owner was, or even what such a well-furnished house was doing in the middle of the forest. He was glad to be out of the wet, and wrung out his sopping sleeves and warmed his hands over the coals. He caught sight of the bottle of saké, which he thought would be the very thing to defeat the cold which was making him shiver.

Sasuke was wondering whether he might pour himself a cupful of sake, when he heard the stairs creaking. He listened carefully, and heard quiet steps coming down the passage accompanied by the soft rustle of silk. Then the door opened quietly and a girl came into the room. Her beauty took the young man's breath away and he quietly congratulated himself on his courage and determination, thanks to which he would be able to see the festivities in Sumiyoshi from the beginning, as well as spend an evening in such pleasant company.

The girl's delicately oval face, with ruby red lips and regular brows over expressive eyes, was set off by the exquisite red silk of her kimono embroidered with gold flowers. Her slender waist was encircled with a wide sash of rainbow-coloured brocade. Slim hands gleamed white against the crimson of the wide sleeves which nearly touched the floor; and in her right hand she held a long-necked samisen — a three-stringed musical instrument — which was covered with black leather.

The lovely girl knelt down in the middle of the room, moving as lightly as a blade of grass touched by the breeze. She laid her instrument aside and bowed low before Sasuke. The silver pins in her elaborately dressed hair sparkled as they caught the light.

Sasuke straightened up and made an answering bow, preparing to apologize for his presence. But before he could say a word, the girl shot him a dazzling smile and shook her head as a signal that Sasuke should not speak. She moved closer on her knees and silently offered him the cup.

Only now did it occur to Sasuke that she had not bade him welcome in her house. He decided that she must be dumb, and said nothing; but he accepted the cup with a smile and allowed the girl to fill it with the wine which, strangely enough, was still pleasantly warm. He drank it all down; and the girl must have been pleased that her guest enjoyed the offering, for she refilled his cup again and again. Sasuke tried to pour some wine for his hostess, but she shook her head.

At last the slender porcelain bottle was empty and Sasuke did not know whether he was intoxicated with the saké or with the beauty of the silent girl. Gesturing to him to make himself comfortable, she picked up the instrument and took the plectrum from her sash, suggesting by her smile and delicately raised eyebrows that she would now play for her guest.

Sasuke failed to notice that the rain had stopped long ago. He leaned against a lacquered pillar in the recess, watching his beautiful hostess and thinking how much he would enjoy telling his friends about the experience they had missed because of their cowardice.

The girl tuned up her samisen and started to play a strange melody which Sasuke had never heard before. The music was quiet and soothing, loud and exciting in turn.

During the loud, wild passages, the melody seemed to attack the listener from every side and the musician gazed at Sasuke, her dark eyes glowing like coals. The young man felt himself grow numb, as though the music was bewitching him. He sat spellbound, seeing nothing but those shining black eyes.

Every now and then the girl plucked the middle string extra strongly, and each time Sasuke felt a strange sensation, as though something smooth and cold was tightening round his neck. However, as soon as he ran his hand over his neck the feeling stopped, and it was as though he had torn away an invisible cord which had bound him. Whenever this happened the girl would frown — but an instant later she would play on with a smiling face.

Time passed and she plucked the centre string more and more often, until Sasuke felt himself being bound by invisible cords. 'What magic is this?' he thought, horrified, summoning all his strength and drawing his short, sharp sword in self defence.

The girl gave him a vicious look and plucked the middle string so hard that it snapped with a twang. It shot out from the instrument and twisted round and round Sasuke's body. He lashed out with his sword, but it was too late; the string bound him firmly to the pillar, while the sword flew out of his hand, piercing the leather-covered round body of the samisen.

At that moment the girl stopped frowning. She gave Sasuke a long, sad look and there was a shadow of pain on her lovely features. Then she rose and left as quietly as she had appeared, the samisen cradled in her arms.

An oppressive quiet spread through the house. The cold night air crept in through the walls, the fire died down, and the flame in the oil lamp trembled, grew weaker and went out. Sasuke lay there in complete darkness, unable to move. 'I'll never survive this night,' he thought. 'My sword has gone and I am tied up, unable to raise a finger to save my life.'

But nothing happened and before long the dawn came. In the first light of the day Sasuke noticed in amazement that the beautifully clean mats on the floor were now torn and frayed. Everything in the room was covered with dust and the verandah door was not open but had fallen out. In place of the china brazier there was now a pile of rubbish, and where the bottle and the cup had stood lay a big and a small stone.

Could it all have been a dream? Sasuke was inclined to think so, but the string that bound him to the pillar was real enough. Then his eyes opened wide as he stared at the floor where drops of blood formed a trail to the door. No, this was no dream. Trying to find a solution to the puzzle, Sasuke thought long and hard until at length he fell asleep.

The morning sunlight was flooding the room, when Sasuke woke up with a start at the sound of Kuemon's voice outside. 'Come here, Chubei! Look at this inscription: The Three Strings Tea House. Whoever thought of having a tea house in the forest? No wonder it went to rack and ruin!'

'Kuemon, Chubei! Come here! Help me!' shouted Sasuke at the top of his voice.

'It's Sasuke!' cried Chubei. 'For heaven's sake, what have they done to you?'

The two young men quickly cut through the string binding Sasuke to the pillar. He gave them a brief account of what had happened the previous night, saying that he would tell them everything later, but now he had to find the girl and make sure he had not hurt her by mistake with his sword.

The three friends followed the trail of blood up the rotten staircase. In a corner under the eaves they came upon a huge torn spider's web, underneath which lay an immense dead spider, stabbed through its body with Sasuke's sword.

'Now you can see that we were right,' observed Chubei triumphantly. 'Strange things do happen, and it is unwise to walk through the forest at night — as you have found out to your own cost.'

'But at least I wasn't afraid,' countered Sasuke proudly, replacing his sword in its sheath; but he was secretly thankful to get away from the place as quickly as possible.

And so the three friends hurried on to Sumiyoshi in order to arrive before noon and at least be in time to watch some of the festivities.

San-lang and the Dragon Princess

Once upon a time there lived a young man by the name of San-lang who had a heart of gold. Now this young man was engaged to marry a certain girl who lived near by, but her father, who had grown rich, thought: 'I'm wealthy now, so why should I give my daughter to a pauper?' And he made it known that the engagement was off.

When San-lang heard the news, he cradled his head in his hands and cried. But then he remembered his faithful flute. This flute had been given to San-lang by his father. It accompanied the young man everywhere and had often brought him joy and solace. He knew how to lure all kinds of tunes from the instrument, some so happy and gay that the peacocks came near to do a little jig, others so sad and mournful that they brought a lump to every throat and tears to every eye. Even the stone lions would weep when San-lang played his sad tunes.

One day the young man again played his flute and a crowd of listeners collected. It so happened that the farmer who had not wanted San-lang for a son-in-law passed by.

'Ah,' cried one of the people, 'there goes the man who refused his daughter to San-lang because he is poor!'

The farmer was so enraged by these words that he ordered his two bailiffs to throw San-lang into the sea that very night. Late that evening there was a knock on San-lang's door. He went to open it and before he knew what was happening, the bailiffs grabbed him, pulled a sack over his head and carried him to the shore.

They were just about to throw him in the sea when he cried:

'Kind men, please let me play the flute one last time before I die.'

The bailiffs looked at each other and decided it was safe to grant the young man's request.

'All right,' they said. 'But you must play the kind of tune that will make the peacocks dance!'

San-lang raised the flute to his lips and all his pain and anguish flowed into the melody; the flute sang and wailed, wept and lamented. The bailiffs were unable to bear it and they cried:

'Stop that accursed music at once! You can play that sort of thing to the Dragon King at the bottom of the sea!'

But the flute went on sighing and moaning. It was too much for the bailiffs who picked San-lang up and . . .

You think they threw him into the sea? Well, they didn't — because just then a strange thing happened. There was a blinding flash of lightning and a great thunder clap, and the earth quivered as huge waves piled up in the sea and the moon hid behind the clouds.

A black object appeared on the distant sea; it drew nearer and nearer and when it approached the shore, the bailiffs and San-lang saw that it was none other than Mrs Octopus, the Dragon Princesses' nurse.

Mrs Octopus stretched out a long black arm, wound it round the first bailiff and flung him far out to sea. Then she stretched out another long black arm, and the second bailiff went the same way.

'I have been sent by the Dragon King,' the Octopus told San-lang. 'He heard your playing and liked it so much that he wants you to be his guest. Don't be afraid,' she continued at the sight of the young man's startled expression, 'just climb on my back and before you know it we'll be in the palace.'

San-lang did as he was told and the Octopus was off. The waves parted to let her pass and closed again behind her. Very soon they arrived at a magnificent crystal palace. Inside the palace on an ivory throne sat the Ruler of the Ocean, the mighty Dragon King.

'What is your name, young man?' he asked. 'The sound of your flute is so powerfully enchanting that it made my palace sway on its foundations. Indeed, it cracked one of the coral pillars. Play me one more, young man, and make it sad or cheerful, as you wish. As for you, Mrs Octopus,' he went on, 'go and bring my daughters here. It may teach them a lesson to listen to this young man.'

San-lang did not need any urging; he put the flute to his lips and began to play.

At that moment a door opened and the Dragon King's three daughters entered. Their beauty almost took San-lang's breath away. The eldest, who walked in first, was as lovely as a dream, the middle sister was lovelier still and the youngest, who came last, was the most beautiful of all. San-lang nearly dropped his flute in his excitement at her beauty. The three Princesses were also carrying flutes. The young man struck up a happy tune and after a little while the Dragon King began to twist on his throne, Mrs Octopus tapped her foot in time to the music and the Princesses began to sway until they were fluttering about the royal chamber like butterflies. Their father got so carried away that he jumped off his throne and put his arms round the old nurse, Mrs Octopus, waltzing her round and round. They were all enjoying themselves hugely. In fact, they had not had such a good time since the crystal palace had been built.

Finally the flute fell silent and the dancers looked at one another like people waking from a dream. The first to regain his dignity was the Dragon King.

'Children,' he declared, with a solemn glance at his daughters, 'what we have just heard may be earthly music, but I liked it. From now on this young man shall be your teacher. Now it's your turn to play for him.'

At first the Princesses were a little shy, but then the eldest began to play. The

Dragon King sat back in his throne and began to doze. Soon he was fast asleep. The eldest Princess looked at him, turned on her heel and walked out of the chamber.

Then it was the second daughter's turn. She began to play and Mrs Octopus fluttered her lids once or twice and also fell into a deep slumber. That annoyed the Princess so much that she followed her sister out of the room.

The youngest Princess played last and she had hardly begun when first the Dragon King and then the old nurse woke up. Their eyes sparkled and their cheeks glowed, and before long their feet began to dance of their own volition.

When the youngest Princess finished, her father said to her:

'Very nice, my dear, but your playing cannot compare with this young earthling's. When you play the flute the palace doesn't sway, nor do the pillars crack. Let him be your tutor, child!'

From that day on the youngest Dragon Princess spent all her time taking lessons from San-lang. When some time later she again played the flute for her father, believe it or not, the crystal palace swayed on its foundations and the pillars bent this way and that.

'Enough!' cried the King. 'You play most beautifully, my dear.'

Now the elder Princesses turned green with envy to hear their sister praised. The next day, when the youngest Princess was again having a lesson with San-lang, they went to the King and said:

'You must be blind, Father, not to see what's going on. Your youngest daughter is going to elope to Earth with San-lang!'

'Are you serious?' roared the Dragon King, his face turning red with anger. 'Call her at once. And send her nurse along as well. I can't imagine how Mrs Octopus could have let this happen.'

A little later the youngest Dragon Princess arrived, accompanied by the terrified nurse.

'O you undutiful child,' thundered the Dragon King. 'Is it true that you want to elope to Earth with the earthling San-lang?'

'Yes, Father,' said the Princess proudly. 'I love him and want to spend all my life with him.'

'You foolish girl, you're throwing your life away! You are descended from Dragons and have a life span of five hundred years, whereas this wretched earthling will barely live to be a hundred.'

'I know,' said the Princess quietly. 'But I cannot live without him.'

'Woe and misery, your cold Dragon heart has changed to a hot human heart, or you would never say such words!' He turned to Mrs Octopus, saying: 'Nurse, the child is your responsibility. Keep your eye on her and don't let her out of the palace!'

Then the Dragon King called for General Crab and ordered him to take San-lang to an island in the Western Ocean.

'The island sits in the middle of the sea,' said the King. 'He would need wings to get away from there. He will be stranded for as long as we wish.'

He pulled one hair from his beard and told General Crab to sew San-lang's lips together.

'The Princess has fallen in love with him because of his playing,' he thought. 'We shall see what happens if he cannot play.'

The King's orders were promptly carried out. General Crab sewed up San-lang's lips, placed the young man on his back and transported him to the island in the Western Ocean.

A little later the Dragon Princess said to Mrs Octopus: 'Nurse, I want to be with San-lang.'

'What good would that do?' said the nurse reasonably. 'Come, child, let me feel your heart. Gracious, your father was right! Your heart is as hot as a human one. Be sensible, child! That earthling can barely live a hundred years and you can live to be five hundred.'

'I don't want to live another day, unless you take me to San-lang right away,' said the Princess stubbornly. 'If you don't take me, I'll go by myself!'

That was too much for Mrs Octopus. The youngest Princess was the apple of her eye and she would have done anything for her.

So she only sighed and said: 'All right, my dear, have it your own way. You know you can always rely on me.'

At that moment a palace servant arrived with the news that the Dragon King had promised his youngest daughter to the Dragon Prince Proudfoot, who was approaching with his retinue to the sound of drums and gongs.

'Oh dear,' cried the Princess. 'We've got to get out by the back door. I could not bear to meet the Prince. He feeds on octopuses and goldfish. How loathsome! Think of spending five hundred years with a husband like that. Never!'

So the Princess and her faithful nurse slipped out of the back door. They had not gone far when the calm waters began to boil to the sound of thunder.

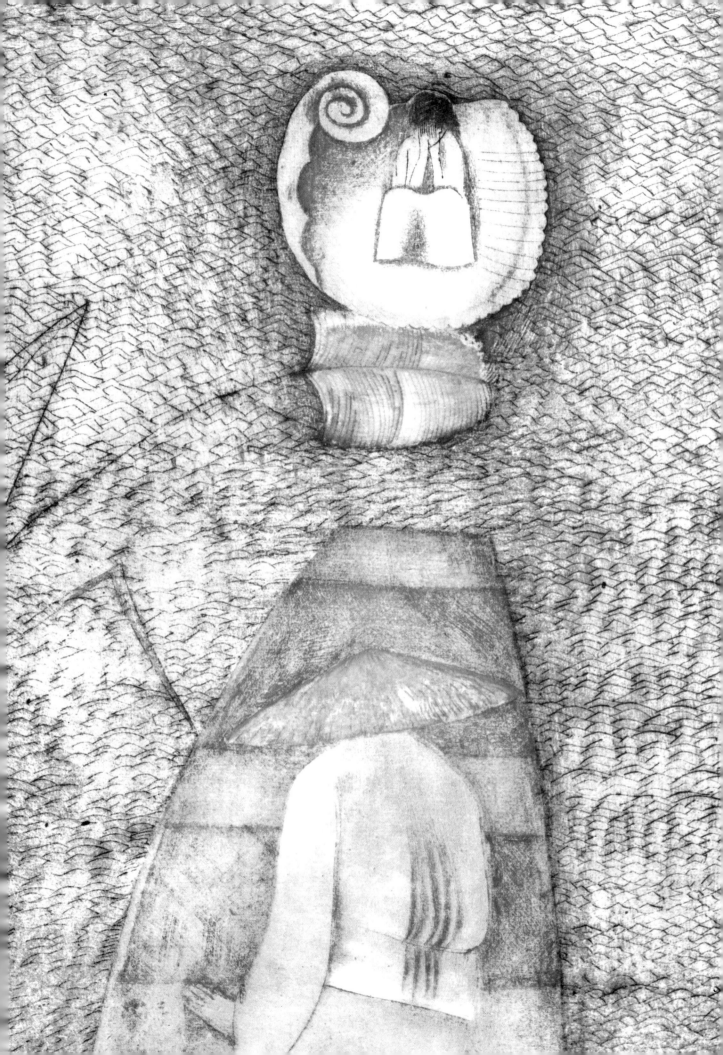

Old Mrs Octopus knew at once that they were in danger. Prince Proudfoot knew of their escape and was after them.

Mrs Octopus quickly hid her darling in a small coral reef at the bottom of the sea and summoned her large circle of relatives, one thousand, one hundred and one octopuses. When they arrived, she addressed them in these words:

'Dear members of my family, you all know Prince Proudfoot, the Dragon. Each morning he breakfasts off octopus; indeed he has killed more than one of my own children. Now he is after my dear charge, the youngest Dragon Princess, whom he wants for his bride. Shall we octopuses let him get away with it?'

'No, no, no,' shouted one thousand, one hundred and one octopuses. And they placed themselves in position and emitted one thousand, one hundred and one ink-black clouds. Prince Proudfoot and his retinue were suddenly faced with impenetrable darkness, under whose cover the old nurse swam to the island in the Western Ocean where San-lang lived in exile. There she placed the young man on her back and transported him to the Princess. Then she took both to the mainland.

The three had hardly arrived on the shore, when the Princess's two sisters appeared.

'Your royal father sends his love,' they began, 'and he will allow you to live on Earth on the condition that you return home when San-lang dies. Your fiancé, Prince Proudfoot, will be waiting for you.' They held out handfuls of agates, rubies, pearls and other treasures, adding: 'Your father sends these to help you manage on Earth.'

'Give Father my thanks,' said the Princess, 'and tell him that I can never return home. I will stay with San-lang for ever, and I don't want these!' And she flipped her sisters' hands, so that all the agates, rubies, pearls and other treasures fell into the sea. Her sisters covered their faces in horror and disappeared into the water.

Then the Dragon Princess bent over San-lang and pulled the hair from her father's beard out of the young man's lips. She dropped it in the sea, but Mrs Octopus gave a cry of alarm.

'Don't throw the hair away!' she shrieked. 'It is sprinkled with San-lang's blood and can be put to good use.'

But the deed had been done. So the old nurse flung herself into the waves and recovered the hair.

San-lang, the Princess and Mrs Octopus settled down in a lovely garden. It was most idyllic but soon he began to worry. How was he to keep the three of them?

'Don't you worry,' Mrs Octopus assured him cheerfully. 'Just bring a tub and fill it with water.'

When San-lang had put up the tub and filled it with water, the old nurse took the hair from the Dragon King's beard and threw it into the tub, and the instant the hair touched the water, the surface began to ripple with hundreds of little goldfish. Now all San-lang's cares were gone because the story of the goldfish got around and crowds of people started coming to the garden and buying the lively little fish to brighten up their homes.

One day there came to the garden the rich farmer who had turned down San-lang as a son-in-law. When he saw the golden fish, he was filled with envy.

'Where did you get these lovely fish?' he asked innocently.

'Oh, from a hair of the Dragon King's beard,' said San-lang casually.

'The Dragon King?' repeated the farmer, scratching his head. 'I don't suppose it's very easy to get such a hair...'

'Well,' said San-lang pleasantly, 'it doesn't have to be from the Dragon King's beard. I'm sure they could be bred from your beard too. If you like, I'll send our nurse, Mrs Octopus, over to your place. She's expert at pulling hairs out of beards.'

Now the farmer was not really anxious to have his beard pulled, but he did want the goldfish, and so he asked Mrs Octopus to come to his house.

The old nurse came, put on her spectacles and — phht! — pulled out a hair.

'This one won't do,' she mumbled and — phht! — pulled out another one.

'Not a very good one, either,' she grumbled and pulled a third hair out.

The farmer made faces and blinked with the pain, but Mrs Octopus was still dissatisfied. She went on tearing and plucking until she had pulled every last hair from the farmer's beard.

'Ah, this one might do,' she finally decided, holding the last hair up to the light. 'Now let us sprinkle a drop of blood on it!'

'Not mine, I hope!' squealed the farmer, adding in a wheedling voice: 'Oh, Mrs Octopus, won't you use a drop of your blood? I'm a little scared.'

'Very well,' agreed the old nurse, 'but my blood is black, you know.'

She squirted out a few drops of ink-black liquid on the hair.

'Place this hair in a tub of water, cover the tub and keep it covered for a few days,' the old nurse said, and with that instruction she left.

The farmer did as he was told and waited several days, although with mounting impatience. He could hardly wait for the moment when he would find goldfish swimming in the tub. He gave a big party, inviting all his friends and neighbours, and at the height of the party, he proudly took the lid off the tub. But what horror! The tub was crawling with snakes. The guests all roared with laughter, but hardest of all laughed Mrs Octopus, who had also been asked to the party.

'You shall pay dearly for that little joke!' hissed the farmer and immediately ordered his two bailiffs to give the old nurse a whipping.

'You'd better think again,' Mrs Octopus told the farmer, 'or you'll regret it.'

'Whip her hard,' he screamed, beside himself with rage. 'Whip her until she turns white!'

The bailiffs pounced upon Mrs Octopus, but she gave a jerk and squirted inky liquid in the farmer's face. He flung up his hands, but not in time; his face was as black as ink, and remained black, however hard he washed it. So the greedy farmer was well punished for his envious and miserly nature.

San-lang, the Dragon Princess and Mrs Octopus went on living in their garden. They bred goldfish in tubs and played the flute and their contentment knew no bounds.

The Maids in the Mirror

There was once a country which was as flat as a pancake, and so large that even the fastest horse would have needed more than ten days to travel round its borders. From that country you could dimly see the outline of a distant mountain range rising from the mist. Somewhere in that flat country there was a village and at its edge a tiny cottage. In the cottage lived an old woman and her two sons. Both the sons were very handsome and lively young men. The only thing that bothered their mother was that neither wanted to get married, and she longed so much for a grandchild. The matchmaker made many a futile attempt to find brides for the young men, who turned down every offer.

Late one evening when her sons were asleep, the old woman went out to her backyard. The stars glittered high in the sky, and the yard was full of dark shadows.

'Oh, my boys, my boys,' sighed the unhappy woman, 'will any girl ever find favour in your eyes?' She said this in a whisper, yet her voice flew up to the stars.

As she stood there in the dark, she suddenly saw a ball of fire rising in the south-west and flying towards her. The ball was bigger even than the moon and it came nearer, floating, rising and sinking until it quietly landed at the woman's feet. She had to shut her eyes before the ball's dazzling light.

What could it be? The woman rubbed her eyes and wondered whether she was dreaming, because there in the circle of light stood an old man with a long, white beard and smiling, rosy face.

'I have come to bring your sons a pair of brides,' he said, and his voice reminded the woman of the tinkle of heavenly bells.

'Oh, kind spirit,' she sighed, 'you've troubled yourself in vain. Those sons of mine are so hard to please, I cannot think of any girl they would like. Where are the brides, then?' she added inquisitively.

'Your sons shall see them in these looking-glasses,' said the old man, offering the woman two small, round mirrors. 'At first they will see only an image, but if at midnight on the third day of the third month they point the mirrors in a south-westerly direction, they will find the road along which they may travel to their brides.'

The woman took the mirrors and before she could recover her wits, the ball of light had risen in the air and was drifting away towards the south-west.

She woke her sons, told them what had happened, and gave them the mirrors.

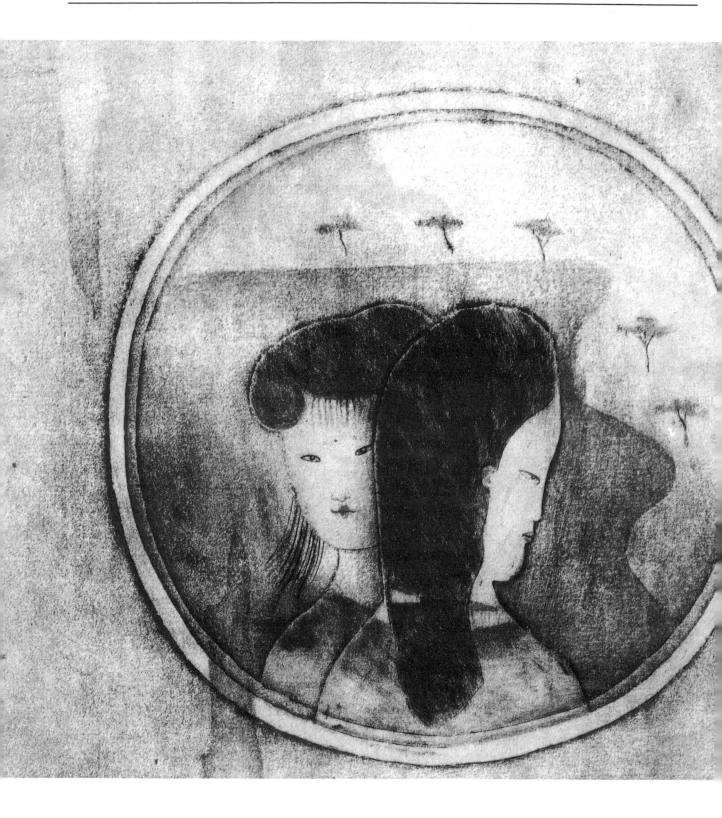

The elder son looked into his mirror and held his breath. Looking at him was a beautiful girl in a rose-coloured dress, and as he went on staring, she gave him the loveliest smile. His heart began to throb and a lump rose in his throat.

'Oh, Mother,' he cried, 'I want this one and no other! Tell me where to find her!'

The woman said nothing and looked at her other son.

He too was gazing into the mirror, and looking in delight at a girl as exquisite as a flower, in a dress of emerald green. He kept on looking as she blushingly nodded her head.

'Oh, Mother,' cried the younger son, 'I want this one and no other. Tell me where to find her!'

The woman stood looking at her sons with tears in her eyes.

'Oh, you unhappy children,' she sighed, 'your brides are only an illusion. I wonder whether you will ever find them.' And she went on to tell her sons the old man's instructions.

When the third day of the third month came, the boys told their mother: 'We are going to seek our brides tonight.'

'Children,' said the woman in an anguished voice, 'listen to me and stay at home. There may be some awful danger lurking along the way.' But when she saw that their minds were made up, she cried: 'At least one of you must stay at home!'

So the elder son said he would go first, and the younger offered to stay at home until his mother would allow him to go too.

At midnight the elder son went out into the yard and directed the light in the mirror towards the south-west. The next instant a white flash broke from the mirror and flew in a south-westerly direction like a white thread. Where formerly the outline of the mountains had risen dimly from the mist, there now stood thick forests and steep cliffs; footpaths criss-crossed the mountainsides.

On and on he walked until in the evening of the second day he stood at the foot of the mountains, where the road came to an end. Suddenly he saw a bright light shining from a cave nearby. At the entrance to the cave sat an old man with a long, white beard. The young man remembered his mother's story, and realized that this was the old man who had sent him the mirror.

So he walked up to him and said politely:

'Kind spirit, this is the end of the road. Please tell me which way I must go in order to find my bride.'

'I am glad that you have come,' said the old man, stroking his beard. 'Your bride is being held captive by a wicked witch who has turned her into a pink peony, in a garden which lies beyond a high hill to the west. If you shine the light from your mirror on the peony, it will regain its human shape. But the road to that garden is hard, my son. It leads across the Dragon Hill and the Gorge of the Spirits, and only he whose heart is brave can reach the garden. Are you still certain that you want to go?'

'I'm not afraid of anything,' said the young man.

The kind spirit promised his help; he gave the boy a whip and a ball of wool and told him what to do. The young man thanked him and went his way.

For a long time he walked along a path that twisted like a snake, now rising, now falling. And then a steep mountain rose before him, all covered with a thick, black fog.

The boy stood still to rest for a while. Suddenly a pair of glittering green eyes met his.

He guessed at once that it was a tiger. The beast was crouching on a rock. Now it gave a great roar and pounced, but the boy was undaunted. Mindful of the kind spirit's words, he cracked the whip over his head, shouting:

'Tiger, mighty lord of these mountains, let me pass, for I am on my way to my bride, the lovely Rose Maid!'

As if by a miracle, the tiger became docile. It wagged its tail and rubbed against the young man's leg, then it slowly stalked away into the brushwood.

Almost too exhausted to go on, the boy still struggled up to the top of the mountain. Before him lay the witch's hill with its peony garden at the top, but in between lay a deep gorge, at the bottom of which torrents of water hissed and swirled. The young man unravelled the ball of wool, and dropped one end into the foaming waters.

'Spirits of these waters,' he whispered, 'whether you're evil or good, help me, for I am on my way to my bride, the lovely Rose Maid.'

He had hardly finished speaking when from the water rose a mermaid, half woman and half fish, who caught the thread and pulled it to the far bank. And wonder of wonders, as soon as the thread touched the bank, it turned into a narrow footbridge spanning the roaring water.

The boy stepped out and began to cross the bridge. But halfway across he happened to glance at the depths and what he saw made his blood run cold. From

the hissing waters the red eyes of many spirits were staring at him. He hesitated, to fight down the fear that rose in him, and that short moment was sufficient to change the safe bridge back into a thread. Horrified, he staggered on a step or two, gripping at the air, and then he was falling — falling straight into the turbulent waters which closed above his head.

A year went by and once more it was the third day of the third month.

'Mother,' said the younger son, 'let me go and find my bride.'

The old woman began to weep. 'Stay home, my son,' she begged. 'Your brother didn't come back. I couldn't bear to lose you too.'

'Don't worry, Mother,' said the boy. 'You'll see that I will find my bride and bring my brother home as well.'

When the woman saw that his mind was made up, she said no more.

At midnight the boy went out into the yard and shone his mirror towards the south-west. A flash of light shot out of the mirror and showed the young man the road he must take. He walked for a long time until he came to the cave where the old man was waiting for him. The boy went up to him.

'I'm glad that you have come,' said the kind spirit. 'Your brother did not follow my advice, and he fell into the Gorge of the Spirits.'

'I'm not afraid,' said the boy. 'I'm going to find my bride and bring my brother back.'

The old man presented him with a whip and a ball of wool and explained their uses, and the young man continued on his way. After a long and wearisome journey he too came to the gorge in which the water hissed and whirled.

'Spirits of this gorge, whether evil or good, help me,' he whispered, and threw the thread into the water.

As if by magic the torrents calmed, and a mermaid appeared who was half woman, half fish. She caught the thread and pulled it to the other bank, whereupon it turned into a narrow bridge. The young man stepped on to the bridge and at once there rose a chorus of squeals and wails. But he shut his ears and kept the vision of the maid in the emerald green dress before his eyes. Across the bridge he ran until he reached the other bank in safety. Again he walked on, until he came to the wall of a garden from which there wafted a strong and heavenly scent.

'This must be the witch's garden,' thought the boy. He began to look for an entrance, but the wall was high and smooth and offered no foothold. So he cracked the whip against the wall, and the whip changed into a ladder which the young man climbed to the top.

What a beautiful sight he saw then! There were so many strange and lovely flowers that he did not know where to look. 'Not this one, not that one,' he told himself, until he stopped in front of two peonies. One was rose-coloured and the other emerald green.

The boy shone his mirror on the emerald green peony and the next instant the whole garden swam before his eyes. Before him stood the lovely girl in the emerald green dress and there was the sweetest smile on her lips.

'Emerald Maid,' cried the boy, 'I have come to rescue you. Will you come with me?'

'Yes,' said the girl, her eyes sparkling with joy, but then she turned back to the rose-coloured peony and her face grew sad.

'That must be my unhappy brother's bride,' though the boy. 'How can I help her when the mirror, which alone can transform her, lies at the bottom of the Gorge of the Spirits along with my brother's body?' At the thought, hot tears welled up in the young man's eyes.

And the rose-coloured peony — as if in understanding — bowed its head and silver dew drops glistened on its petals.

And then the Emerald Maid called out in alarm. 'Quick, come away!' she cried. 'The witch is coming!'

She drew the boy along to a small cottage. The door had barely closed behind them when the witch arrived.

'Who gave you back your human shape?' she screamed. 'Whom are you hiding in there? Open up at once!' Her angry breath came through the keyhole in hot gusts, but she was unable to hurt the maid any longer.

When the witch saw that threats would not work, she tried another way.

'My boy,' she said in honeyed tones, 'I was only testing your will power. I'm happy to let you have the Emerald Maid for your wife because I know that you are brave. But first you must do me one small favour. On the top of the hill I have a herd of horses and I'm worried lest someone steal them from me. Will you stand watch up there tonight?'

'Don't go!' said the Emerald Maid urgently. 'Those aren't horses but tigers and scorpions and they will kill you.'

'Never fear,' answered the boy. 'My whip will defend me.'

He allowed the witch to take him to the top of the hill, but when he got there, he could not see any horses. So he sat down on the ground and waited. When darkness fell, he saw green eyes glinting in the thicket and after a while tigers, scorpions and other dangerous creatures came crawling out.

Crack! went the young man's whip and the beasts beat a hasty retreat. When the witch saw that her ruse had not worked, she began to wail: 'My boy, take me with you, I'm so used to the Emerald Maid, I'd be lost without her.'

Now the Emerald Maid knew very well that this was only another ruse, so she said: 'You can come with us if you wish, but it's a long journey which would surely tire you. Why don't you make yourself small, so that we can carry you in a bottle?'

The witch thought that was a good idea. She immediately shrank in size until she fitted into a bottle, which the young man sealed tightly. Then they started on the return journey.

When they passed the Gorge of the Spirits, the young man hurled the bottle into the foaming water. The Emerald Maid had grown sadder with every step. Now she sat down at the edge of the gorge, crying:

'Oh, my poor, poor sister! What shall I do without her? How can I leave her all by herself in the bare and hostile mountains?'

And as she sat and wept, rain began to fall from the clouds and dripped off the pine needles. The whole land was weeping and the young man could not endure the thought of his brother lying at the bottom of the gorge, so he too burst into tears.

Suddenly a glow pierced the black clouds and the dark fog parted to let through a shining ball of light, inside which stood the smiling kind spirit. The ball of light came sailing nearer until it descended to the edge of the gorge.

'Spirits of the gorge, whether good or evil,' called the old man in a voice sounding like the tinkling of heavenly bells, 'deliver up from the water the young man who went to find his bride and failed!'

And the torrents calmed down and parted to make way for the mermaid, half woman and half fish, who was carrying the elder brother on her back. She placed him gently on the ground and he opened his eyes and asked:

'Is this a dream or am I awake?'

'You are awake after a bad dream,' smiled his younger brother, brushing the tears away. Then the brothers embraced.

The ball of light ascended into the air and rose ever higher until it disappeared in the clouds.

The two young men and the Emerald Maid went back to the witch's garden. There the elder brother shone his mirror on the rose-coloured peony, which stood wilted with its leaves drooping. But when the flash of light fell on its petals, the peony gave a shiver and before them stood the maid in the rose-coloured dress.

The four young people were overjoyed. Together they returned to the brothers' mother, who had lost all hope of ever seeing her sons again. There was no end to the rejoicing as they all settled down together.

The Herb Fairy

People in the south-west province talk of the Herb Fairy who lives in the distant mountain wilderness and looks after the herbs that grow there. She sees to it that they flower and thrive, that they bear fruit in time and that there are no fewer and no more than there should be. She is always willing to help poor people who come to the mountains to gather herbs, but she will often punish the wicked and the mean.

They say that the Herb Fairy was once a beautiful young girl who was called Ability. Not only was Ability lovelier than the white lotus blossom, but she could sing so sweetly it brought a lump to every throat. Her laughter rang out like the bells of heaven, and when she walked it was as though a fleecy cloud had floated to the earth. The girl possessed uncounted skills. She could embroider a flower that would put a living flower to shame; she could embroider a bird that no living bird could rival. But she was fondest of all of gathering healing herbs and knew all their names and properties. In short, she was so clever and bright that everyone called her Ability until her real name had been forgotten.

Ability was a maid at the royal court. The King of the land was subject to the Chinese Emperor, but he was a very rich man, so that even after surrendering his high taxes, he was left with plenty of gold for his own needs. The royal court was full of servants and the Queen and the King's other wives all wore silk and brocade and gold and silver flowers in their hair.

The King was a cruel man, as kings often are. Anyone failing to carry out a royal order was hanged at once. But Ability was as free as a bird. If she did not feel like making tea, she would not make it for three days and three nights. If she was not in the mood to bake, she would not bake for seven days and seven nights. Not even the cruel King could make her do anything against her wishes. However, Ability knew how to make the most delicious tea and bake the most delicious cakes for the King. None of the many palace servants could wait on the King as she could, so she stood under His Majesty's special protection. She walked about the palace in a roughly woven skirt, with a wild flower in her hair and her beauty outshone all the golden flowers and brocade gowns of the King's many wives and the Queen herself.

Court entertainments did not attract Ability. Instead of listening to the jade flute at banquets, she would run from the palace to the mountain wilderness to listen to the crickets chirping and to gather herbs with which she would cure sick people and animals.

The poor people loved Ability for her kind heart, but the Queen's ladies-in-waiting and the King's courtiers laughed at her and secretly called her the Wild Woman of the Woods. Ability did not mind that; only before the royal sorcerer, who was a particularly wicked man, did her laughter and song fall silent, and she never looked him in the eye.

Thus time went by, until one year when the harvest was unusually good. People were enjoying their new prosperity when suddenly the south wind brought a plague to the land. The disease spread and killed many old people and children.

Everyone was terrified of becoming ill; not even the King felt safe, because the plague made no distinction between rich and poor. So the King summoned his sorcerer and together they devised a plan. Little did they care about others, as long as the royal court was not invaded by the plague. They had the city gates closed and a deep ditch dug outside the walls, while guards patrolled the ramparts to ensure that no one came near. Indeed, they did not even let the birds fly in over the walls.

Ability chose that time to plan a trip to the mountains. Once she had made up her mind to do something, not even the King's strictest order could dissuade her.

She knew that all the exits were guarded, so she made a plan of escape. In the palace garden she picked flowers, and decorated a wooden washtub with them to make it look like a bower of blossoms. Finally she hid beneath the flowers and sailed down the palace canal, and out of the royal city.

The royal canal flowed into waters as deep as a well and as large as a lake. A fresh breeze raised high waves and drove the washtub ever farther, until at last Ability came to the Miracle Mountain whose slopes were a mass of wild flowers. She guided her craft to the shore and jumped out. As she walked up the slope, she found lots of strange herbs growing in the clefts of the rock. Some had long pointed or twisted leaves, others had leaves that were green at the bottom and red at the top. The girl gathered all these herbs until her basket was full.

Suddenly, Ability noticed peeping from under a stone the root of life, *jen-sheng;* she was about to get it when a snow-white heron descended from the sky and alighted on an overhanging cliff, turning into a fine stag before the girl's eyes. The stag leapt off the cliff to where the girl was standing and vanished. In his place there stood a young man as slim as a poplar and with eyes that shone like jewels.

Ability gazed at him and forgot all about the root of life. For a while the two young people looked at each other without speaking.

It was the young man who broke the silence.

'Why are you gathering herbs?' he asked. 'Poor people gather them because they need them, greedy people gather them for profit. Why are you gathering them?'

The girl did not have to ponder over her answer.

'Herbs have the most delicate leaves in the world and the sweetest fragrance,' she said. 'If you smell their scent, you forget that you're tired. If you taste them, you revive. I have loved herbs all my life.'

The young man smiled. 'The scent of herbs is sweet only to special people. As soon as I saw you, I realized that you were no ordinary girl. I am the Spirit of the Herbs and I live in these wild mountains, as the Flower Spirit lives among the flowers, and the Tree Spirit in the forest. If you like, I'll show you a place where every kind of herb grows.'

'I know that hundreds of kinds grow all over the mountain,' said the girl, 'but I have not seen many myself. I should love to see them all, but not today. The kind of herbs I must gather now are those which will save thousands from the plague.'

The young man nodded. 'I can see that you are good and brave,' he said. 'So I will give you some of the rarest herbs.'

He took her hand and together they climbed to the top of the Miracle Mountain. It is said that the clouds are the nearest thing to the sky, but the Spirit of the Herbs guided the girl through seven layers of white clouds to his home at the top of the Miracle Mountain.

Ability looked about her. Wherever the eye could see, clouds floated like a whitely shining sea. The Spirit of the Herbs scattered handfuls of seeds on the clouds, and the seeds dropped through the clouds and were picked up by the breeze and carried to cracks in the rocky slopes. They immediately took root and sent up little green shoots.

Wherever Ability looked, she saw the strangest and most precious herbs. There were those which bear fruit every year and those which flower only every few years, and there were those which sink little roots only after many years of growth.

The Spirit of the Herbs spoke again. 'These herbs bring happiness to the person who finds them,' he said. 'They grow on the steepest slope, so that they can be gathered only by the brave.'

Ability gathered a basketful of the precious herbs. When the time came for her to leave, she sighed deeply because she was sorry to part from the handsome Spirit of the Herbs. The young man smiled down at her. Handing her a delicate blue flower, he said softly:

'Won't you come back to me, and to the Miracle Mountain? We could live happily here for ever and ever on the mountain. For now, keep your freedom and do whatever you please. I won't try to force you, but if you want to come back to me, you must first eat this blue flower. I shall wait day and night in the hope of seeing you again.'

Ability could not tear her eyes from the young man's face. With an effort she broke the spell and accepted the blue flowering herb from his hands.

'I should be happy to spend my life here with you on top of the clouds,' she said. 'When I have cured the victims of the plague, I will come back.'

The young people parted and Ability returned home to help the sick. Meanwhile, a search for Ability had been taking place in the palace. Since her absence had been discovered the King had been restless, impatient and furious in turn. He went off his food and drink, because he enjoyed only what Ability prepared.

'Ability's job in life is to serve me,' screamed the King. 'Find her at once!'

Servants ran off in every direction, and when they could find no trace of the girl, they began making up stories about her. The night-watchman had seen her doing the laundry in the brook, and the cook had seen her drying herbs in the sun; the gardener had heard her singing in the garden, and the sentries knew that she had gone to the town for cotton. When the King had had enough of these rumours, he sent out a troop of soldiers with orders to find the girl and bring her back.

After seven days the soldiers were back, joyfully reporting that the plague had passed and the sick were recovering.

'Is that what I sent you to find out?' thundered the King. He ordered that the soldiers be executed, and sent out another troop to find Ability.

Seven days later the second lot of soldiers were back, with the report that the harvest was good and people were readily paying their taxes. The King was beside himself.

'Where is Ability?' he roared.

'Your Majesty,' said the soldiers, 'everyone has seen her, but no one knows where she is now. They say that she has cured dozens of plague victims with some herbs she carried in a basket.'

The King had the soldiers thrown into prison and decided to find the girl himself. He had his favourite horse saddled, and soon he was riding out of the city gates at the head of his army. They rode through many villages and killed great numbers of pigs and fowl, and finally they came to a wood at whose edge girls were gathering mushrooms. From them the King heard some news of Ability.

When the girl had cured all the sick people, the girls reported, she ate a small blue flower and immediately turned into a white heron. She then flew off towards the mountains, to meet the Spirit of the Herbs who was waiting to take her for his bride.

That was all the King needed to know. He whipped his horse and galloped back to his palace. There he summoned his sorcerer, a man familiar with all manner of evil spells, who promptly thought of a way to punish the girl.

Meanwhile Ability lived happily on the Miracle Mountain with the Spirit of the Herbs. As free as the birds they were, and as gay as two butterflies.

Every morning the Herb Spirit would sing a little song for Ability which went like this:

'My darling bride,
Open your eyes.
The night is gone,
The sun will rise.
The white clouds shine
In the morning light.
The fragrant pine
Wears dewdrops bright.
The scent of herbs
Sweetens the air.
Wake up, wake up,
My bride so fair.'

Ability would sit up with a smile and catch hold of her husband's hand, and together they would fly down from the summit. As they glided past the birds awoke, the flowers raised their heads, and the poplar trees softly moved their branches. Deer would leap along with them and rabbits turn somersaults in the grass.

In this happy way the spring passed and the summer. Autumn came to the mountains, and after it the cruel winter. The birds went to hide in their nests, and the animals retired to their warrens and holes. Ice and snow covered the mountain-sides and the North Wind froze the sea of clouds. Ability suffered intensely in the bitter cold; the icy wind blew night and day, and she had nothing to ward off the cold.

The Spirit of the Herbs was above human frailties, but he suffered with his wife and tried to help her. He collected feathery downs and animal pelts from all over the mountains, but they did not keep the frost out. Before long poor Ability was chilled to the bone, so that she could hardly speak. When the Herb Spirit saw her pitiful state, he went out among the people and brought back a fur coat, as light as a feather and beautifully warm.

'No human being can sew a fur coat so warm and light,' he happily explained. 'This is a magic coat that I bought from the King's sorcerer.'

The girl shuddered.

'I'd rather die than accept anything from the King's sorcerer,' she said.

But the Herb Spirit was unable to endure Ability's suffering any longer; he gently put the coat on her, pleading with her to try it on at least. Ability felt a delicious warmth invading her numb body. The coat was so wonderfully snug that she forgot her fears. Smilingly, she placed it round her husband's shoulders, to show him how warm yet light it was.

At that instant there came a deafening roar, and the frozen rock cracked open from the summit to the valley. The Spirit of the Herbs turned into a shell, which sailed through the sea of clouds and fell into the water at the bottom of the deep, deep gorge.

Ability stretched out her arms to save him, but her hands clutched thin air. Blindly, she groped along the edge of the abyss, calling for her husband. And the lonely wind wept tears of compassion for her, which engraved runnels in the snow and turned to ice in the cold air.

The Herb Spirit could not bear to hear his wife weeping in misery. From the bottom of the gorge, he called in a voice full of pain: 'Oh, my poor wife, let my friends help you bear your loneliness. The Spirit of the Mountain will protect you, the Spirit of the Wind will assist you, and every living and growing thing in the mountains will serve you well. Each year when the spring awakes the flowers from their sleep, let the Spirit of the Wind guide you down to this gorge. The breeze will ruffle the surface of the water, and you will see me lying here. I can give you no better comfort, but I entreat you to remain in the mountains. It will help me to know that you are near. Your food will be herbs, but most of all the red-rooted herb with the white flowers which grows at the top of the Miracle Mountain. Continue to care for the mountain herbs, as we have cared for them together.'

At these words, Ability suppressed her sorrow and said: 'I will remember all you have said, my dear. I promise to care for the herbs, and when the spring arrives, the Spirit of the Wind shall take me down to see you. But first I must punish the King.'

So Ability returned to the palace. Her arrival came as a great surprise to everyone, and there was a great deal of speculation about her reasons for coming back of her own free will.

The King mistook her return for submission. He called her to his side and said: 'You are my slave, dependent on me for your freedom and welfare, your life and death. From now on you shall do my bidding or die.'

Ability looked at him in silence.

When the King saw that threats did not work, he added: 'But if you serve me as well as before, I will command the sorcerer to set free the Spirit of the Herbs.'

'The wheel cannot turn back and the river does not flow back to its source,' answered Ability, 'just as a woman who has been free all her life will not bow to violence.'

'Tell me what you want!' cried the King. 'If you have any wish, I shall see that it is fulfilled. No one shall harm a hair of your head!'

Ability shook her head. She held out to the King a strange-looking herb, saying: 'I have no more wishes; I have no more hope. Take this herb, King, for remembrance. He who eats it remains young and strong for ever.'

The King was so pleased that he ate the herb immediately. The next moment his tongue began to hurt. He wanted to speak, but not a word came out, for the cruel King had been stricken dumb for the rest of his life.

No one in the palace ever saw Ability again, although a search was held all over the land. Some said they had seen a white heron fly off to the distant mountains with a mournful cry.

Village maidens gathering herbs on the slopes sometimes hear the Herb Fairy sing in a sweet voice, though few have seen her. But every year when spring returns to the mountains Ability asks the Spirit of the Wind to take her down to the gorge.

There the breeze ruffles the surface of the water, and she can see the Spirit of the Herbs.

It has been said that if a good and honest person follows the warm springtime breeze to the mountains on that day, he will bring home some precious herb.

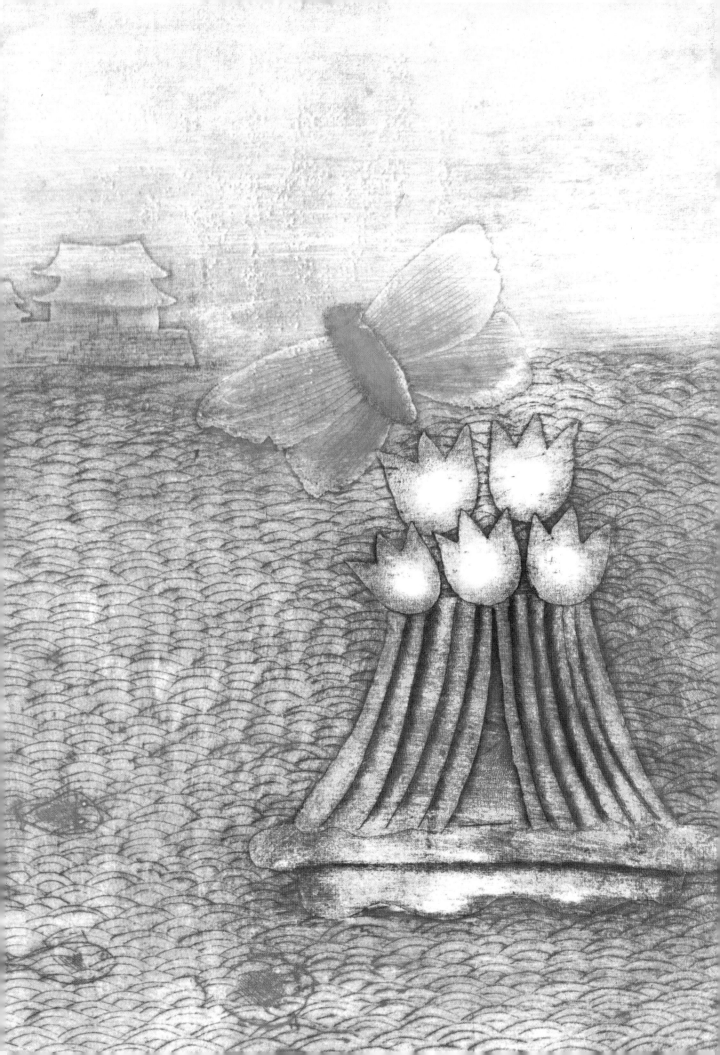

The Two Brothers

Once upon a time there was a poor man who had two sons. The man was very poor indeed and, as the boys grew up and their appetites increased, he found it more and more difficult to support them.

Eventually he had to say to his sons, 'My sons, you are grown up now and, as I have no way of supporting you, you must go out into the world and fend for yourselves.'

So saying, he gave each of them twelve chunks of bread the size of a fist, and a piece of meat.

The boys set out and when they had gone a short way, the elder said, 'Come, let's rest a while and have a bite to eat. First we'll eat your food and then mine. You are smaller and weaker than I am, and would soon be tired if you had to carry all that food.'

So they ate from the younger brother's bundle, and after a few days they had eaten all his bread and meat.

When he next became hungry, the younger brother turned to the elder and said, 'Give me some of your bread and meat; we've eaten all of mine now.'

'Not on your life. I won't give you a thing,' replied the elder brother.

'But you promised we'd both eat your food after we'd eaten mine,' the younger brother protested.

'What I said stands,' said the elder brother curtly. 'I'll give you something to eat, but you will have to suffer for it. It will cost you the sight of one of your eyes.'

The younger brother gasped. He cried and pleaded with his brother to be reasonable, but all was in vain.

In the end he said, 'All right then, do what you want. I'm weak with hunger.'

So the elder brother took a handful of the dust and grit on the path and threw it in his brother's eye. The boy screamed with agony as the grit scratched his eye and damaged it so badly that he could no longer see out of it. Then the elder brother gave him a piece of bread, and the two continued on their way.

The younger brother kept moaning, for the wound pained him and he was still hungry. The piece of bread he'd received had done little to satisfy his hunger. When his brother stopped and sat down for a meal he couldn't stand it any longer.

'Please, brother, give me something to eat from your bundle,' he begged. 'You gave me only a small piece of bread and I'm still hungry.'

'I'll let you have something to eat; but only if you will let me do the same to your other eye,' replied the cruel brother.

What could the younger boy do? No matter how much he begged and pleaded, the elder brother remained adamant. In the end he decided it was better to be blind than to die of hunger.

'All right then, blind me in my other eye too,' he said.

At that the elder brother threw grit into his brother's other eye, so he could not see at all. He felt no pity for the younger boy, who was writhing on the ground in pain. He just packed his meat and bread without even giving him a bite as he had promised, and set off without him. The younger brother called after him, and begged him not to leave him alone in the woods where he was sure to die of hunger or be devoured by some wild beast. But his brother went off without even a parting glance.

Presently, as two women passed near by, they heard strange moans and sighs. They found the blind boy sitting on the ground where his brother had left him, and asked why he was crying.

'You'd cry too if your own brother had blinded you so that he wouldn't have to give you anything to eat, and then abandoned you in the woods,' he sobbed.

'Don't cry!' the two women consoled him. 'We'll give you something that will make you see again.'

They went to the edge of the woods and picked a plant growing there, squeezed the juice from it and spread it on the boy's eyes. But his eyes began to hurt even more than before. The pain became so great that he fainted. When he came round a few minutes later, his eyes no longer hurt and he was able to see as well as before. His gratitude knew no bounds, and he thanked the two women from the bottom of his heart. Before taking their leave the women gave him one more piece of advice.

'Follow this path till you come to the village where a rich and powerful king lives. He, too, is blind. Go to him and restore his sight with this plant. You will be well rewarded.'

The boy thanked them once again and set out for the village. When he came to the king's house he said to the guards, 'I wish to see the master of this house.'

But the guards wouldn't let him pass. They told him, 'You're still too young and not yet worthy of seeing our master.'

The boy, however, wouldn't be put off.

'I have a remedy that will make him well,' he said.

'Then come in,' said the guards.

He had barely stepped inside when they seized him and beat him until he no longer had the strength to get up from the ground. The queen happened to walk by

just then and, seeing the boy on the ground, asked, 'Why are you beating this boy?'

Before they could reply, the boy cried, 'I want to be taken to the king because I have a remedy for his blindness.'

'Then take him to the king immediately!' ordered the queen. So the guards took the boy before the king after all.

'I came here to cure your blindness, Your Majesty,' said the boy, bowing low.

The king was quite surprised at these words, for he had been blind for the past thirty years and had given up hope long ago that he would ever see again. Though doubtful that the boy could fulfil his promise, he decided there was no harm in trying.

The boy told the guards to spread a rug on the floor and lay the king upon it. Then he took several leaves of the miraculous plant, squeezed out the juice and put some in one of the king's eyes. The king cried out in pain, and the guards immediately seized the boy and began beating him again. Soon, however, the pain passed and the king was able to see with one eye.

The first thing that met his gaze was the guards beating the boy, and he cried out, 'Stop that right away! Whoever lays a hand on that boy will have his head cut off!'

Then the boy put some of the juice into the king's other eye and the king again cried out in pain. Once more the guards knocked the boy down, and they began beating him even harder than before. They would have beaten him to death if the king hadn't opened his eyes and seen, with both of them, what was going on.

'Why are you beating that boy when he has restored my eyesight? Didn't I say that no one must lay a hand on him?' he shouted.

'We thought he was killing you, Your Majesty,' said the guards.

'That's not true. You knew very well that he wanted to restore my sight, but you preferred a blind king who couldn't see what you were up to. So, as I said, off with your heads!'

When the guards had been taken away the king thanked the boy and gave him two ships, two boats, two furnished houses, thirty cupboards full of clothes, four horses and a magnificent royal throne. He also gave him his daughter's hand in marriage and one half of his kingdom. His daughter received as a dowry 240 gold pieces, a house, five horses, two servants and five wardrobes full of dresses. The boy was also given five servants to tend the ships. Then they all boarded one of the ships to go for a trip on the sea.

As they went up the gangway who should the royal son-in-law see on the shore but his brother. He was dressed in rags and was carrying heavy bundles on his back into the ship's hold. He gazed at the royal company with envy, but did not recognize his younger brother.

The Magic Mirror

Once upon a time there lived a man and his wife who were very unhappy because they had no children. They were so unhappy that finally they decided to go and see the great witch-doctor and ask if he could help them.

'Nothing could be easier,' said the witch-doctor after hearing their request. 'All you have to do is wait till the full moon, catch two fish, a male and a female, cook them and eat them. Then before the year is out you shall have a son.'

They did as they were told and within a year they had a son whom they named Tembo.

The boy grew fast and soon he was going into the forest to gather firewood, and then to hunt. Wherever he went he went alone, with only his friend the old black tomcat for a companion. He knew the countryside far and wide, except for the forest below the village where he was forbidden to go.

One day, however, he said to his parents, 'Now that I'm grown up, no matter what you say, today I'm going into that forest below the village.'

He took his hatchet, bow and arrows, whistled for the old tomcat, and off they went. Shortly after entering the forest he came across a large snake that had just swallowed a gazelle. The gazelle's head, however, had stuck in the snake's mouth and he could neither spit it out nor swallow it.

Seeing Tembo, he called out, 'Come here, boy, and cut off the gazelle's head. Otherwise I shall choke to death.'

'I won't! You will eat me,' replied Tembo.

'No I won't,' promised the snake. 'I'll even repay you.'

The tomcat put a word in then.

'Go ahead and help him, Tembo,' the cat suggested. 'It's sure to be worth your while.'

So Tembo took up his hatchet and cut off the gazelle's head.

The snake heaved a long sigh of relief, saying, 'Now hold on tight to my tail and I shall take you home where I shall repay you as I promised. But no matter what happens, don't let go of my tail.'

Tembo grasped the snake's tail firmly with both hands, the tomcat leaped up on his shoulders, and off they went. At long last they arrived at the snake's home. There, the host gave them something to eat and invited them to stay for three days.

After the three days had passed the snake said, 'I promised that I would repay you. Today I shall take you to the cave where I have my mirrors and you can choose the one you want.'

With that he led Tembo to a cave so full of mirrors that there was no room for anything else.

As they stood there, the tomcat whispered in Tembo's ear, 'Choose the one on which the fly will sit.'

Looking up, Tembo saw a fly buzzing about the cave, and soon it alighted on one of the mirrors.

'I'll take that one,' said Tembo, pointing with his finger to the mirror with the fly on it.

'You've made a good choice,' said the snake, as he gave him the mirror. Tembo thanked the snake; then they said goodbye and set off for home.

When they got back to the village, the tomcat said to Tembo, 'This is a magic mirror that will fulfil your every wish.'

'Really?' said Tembo in surprise. So he thought he would put it to the test without delay. 'Magic mirror,' he called out, 'I want a house with a red slate roof.

There was a flash, and then there before him stood a house with a red slate roof.'

Having seen how successful his mirror was, Tembo then went to his parents and told them, 'I am going to the governor to ask for his daughter's hand in marriage.'

Before setting out he put on a pair of sackcloth pants, a sackcloth shirt, an old hat, tattered shoes, and a tie of banana leaves. In his hand he carried an umbrella, also of banana leaves.

When he came to the governor's house he went up on the terrace, and the governor came out to meet him with his wife.

'What do you want?' he asked.

'Your daughter's hand in marriage,' replied Tembo.

The governor laughed and his wife joined in, adding, 'Our daughter shall be your wife, only on condition that you build a one-storey house here, in the middle of this river, in one minute flat.'

Tembo took out his mirror and called, 'Oh magic mirror, let there be a beautiful one-storey house in the middle of the river, filled with beds and chairs and tables and servants and with a big table laden with food.'

In the twinkling of an eye there was a flash, and then a house stood there in the river as Tembo had wished. The governor and his wife moaned and wailed at having to give their daughter to Tembo, but a promise is a promise and there was nothing they could do.

The governor's daughter was quite happy to be Tembo's wife, for she had

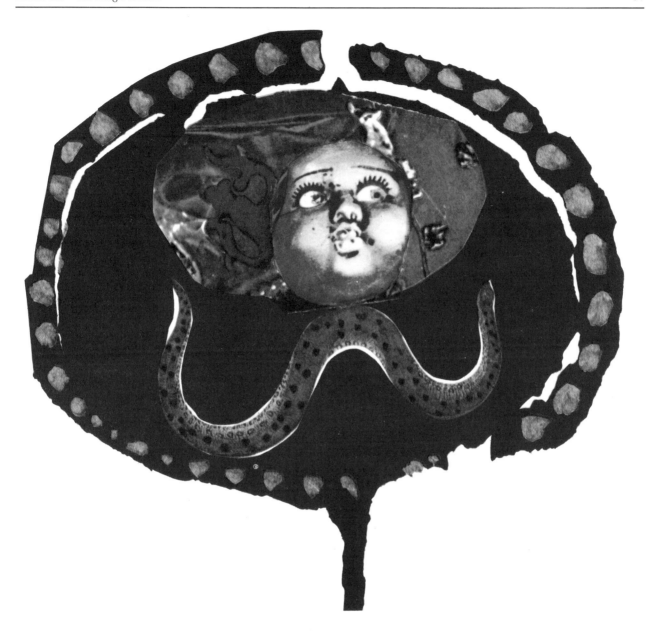

everything she wanted, more than she had ever had at home. All Tembo had to do was ask the magic mirror, and her every wish was fulfilled.

The governor, however, did not want to make his peace with Tembo, and so he sent out his army against him. As the soldiers approached the house in the middle of the river the rooster on the roof crowed:

Cock-a-doodle-doo!
What are we to do?
The soldiers are coming
To make an end of you.

The minute he heard this, Tembo ran to the mirror and said, 'Oh magic mirror, may the army be gone!'

When he looked outside there wasn't a soldier to be seen.

The governor, however, was not to be outdone, and so he sent out a larger army. As the soldiers approached, the cock on the roof crowed again:

Cock-a-doodle-doo!
What are we to do?
The soldiers are coming
To make an end of you.

The minute he heard this, Tembo ran to the mirror and said, 'Oh magic mirror, may the army be gone!'

When he looked outside there wasn't a soldier to be seen.

The governor soon realized that he would never get the better of Tembo as long as he had the magic mirror, however large an army he might send out against him. So he decided to send a clever old woman to Tembo to steal his magic mirror.

'Is it true that you have a magic mirror that grants you your every wish?' the old woman asked Tembo when she met him.

'Yes I have,' he said with a laugh, and went to fetch it so that he could show it off to her.

The old woman looked at the mirror from all sides, shaking her head in wonder. When Tembo glanced away for a moment she quickly hid it under her skirt and replaced it with another mirror. She took the magic mirror to the governor who put it under an overturned drum. Then he sent his army off once more.

Seeing the soldiers, the cock crowed for the third time:

Cock-a-doodle-doo!
What are we to do?
The soldiers are coming
To make an end of you.

'No!' cried Tembo taking the mirror in his hand. This time, however, no matter what he said the mirror did not come to his aid.

So the soldiers tore the house down, put Tembo and his tomcat in jail, and took his wife to the governor.

Tembo sat sadly in the dark prison, watching the rats scurrying about. He was still trying to think of a way to get out when his faithful tomcat came to his aid. The cat arched his back, watched for his chance and then pounced on the largest rat of all, digging his claws into the rat's neck.

'Let me go! Let me go!' cried the rat. 'I know where the magic mirror is. Let me go and I'll bring it to you.'

So the cat let him go, and in a short while the rat was back with the mirror as he had promised.

With a cry of joy Tembo took it in his hand and said, 'Oh magic mirror, let me be free and let my house stand in the middle of the river as before and with my wife there to welcome me.'

And so it came to pass, for Tembo had his magic mirror back. Never again would he let it out of his sight . . .

The Bird
Who Gave Milk

There was once a poor man named Tarla. One day he went to work in his field with his wife. All day they dug and turned the ground, and by nightfall everything was ready for sowing. The next morning, however, they arrived to find the field as it had been before they started. So Tarla and his wife spent the whole day digging and turning the ground again until late in the evening. The following day the same

sight met their eyes, and once more they set to work. They finished their task by nightfall, but this time Tarla turned to his wife and said, 'You go home. I'll stay here and keep watch.'

So the woman went home, and Tarla sat down in the bushes and kept watch. Suddenly a beautiful bird appeared out of nowhere. He was so beautiful that Tarla couldn't take his eyes off him. Alighting on the very bushes where Tarla was hiding he burst into song:

> *Widespreading field*
> *Turn round, turn round.*
> *Let what is on top*
> *Be down under ground.*

As the last note faded on the air, the field turned round and was as it had been before.

'So you're the one who's the cause of it all!' cried Tarla, and taking out a knife he made ready to cut the bird's head off. Frightened, the bird said, 'Don't harm me. If you let me live I'll give you so much milk that you'll have enough for the whole family.'

'All right,' said Tarla, 'but first the ground must be dug up and turned as it was.'

So the bird sang his song once again.

> *Widespreading field*
> *Turn round, turn round.*
> *Let what is on top*
> *Be down under ground.*

As the last note faded on the air the field turned and the ground was dug up again and ready for sowing.

Then Tarla said to the bird, 'Now give me the milk you promised.'

So the bird gave him so much milk that Tarla was almost unable to drink it all. Then he put the bird in a bag and set out for home. When he arrived he said to his wife, 'Wash all the largest pots and pans — the ones we use for brewing beer — and hurry.'

'I'd like to know what you are going to put in those pots,' said his wife. 'Why, we haven't one bit of food in the house.'

'Don't you worry,' Tarla replied with a laugh.

So his wife washed all the pots and pans there were, and then Tarla pulled the bird out of the bag and said to him, 'Now give us milk to fill all these pots.'

The bird did as he was told. He gave milk until all the pots were full. Tarla's wife drank her fill, the children drank their fill, and there was still lots of milk left.

Then Tarla put the bird back in the bag and said to the children, 'Not a word to anybody about the magic bird!'

And the children promised they would not tell a soul.

So the poor man's family began to prosper. The village people wondered why they were all so fat, but no one could discover why.

One day everyone went to work in the field, all except the village children who stayed at home and played games. While they were playing they started asking Tarla's children how it was they were so fat.

'But we're just the same as you are,' they replied.

'Don't be silly,' said the others. 'Tell us the secret.'

In the end Tarla's son Masemañamatug gave in.

'Let's go to our hut, then, and I'll show you something.'

The children went inside Tarla's hut where Masemañamatug pulled the bird out of the bag and said, 'Give us some milk.'

So the bird gave milk and the children drank and drank until they could drink no more. Then they said to the bird, 'Dance for us.'

So the bird began to dance, but the children cried, 'There's not enough room here; let's take the bird outside.'

So they took the bird outside, but as soon as they put him down he spread his wings and flew away.

Tarla's children began crying that they would be punished when their parents came home in the evening and found out what had happened, and so they all set off in pursuit. The bird flew from tree to tree and from bush to bush, but as soon as the children came close he flew off a bit farther. They kept on like this until the children suddenly discovered they were lost, whereupon they all began to cry.

'Don't be afraid,' Masemañamatug consoled them. 'Let's hide there in that cave. There's sure to be some dry wood inside, and we'll make a fire and cook ourselves some roots.'

The children entered the cave. Sure enough, they found some dry wood there, and so they made a fire. As they sat around it cooking roots a huge man-eating giant chanced to pass by and, looking inside, he cried, 'Give me some too!'

Masemañamatug threw him a few roasted roots, and while the giant was eating the children slipped out of the cave and ran as fast as they could. But the giant followed in their wake. Night had already fallen and it was very dark, and the girls were very tired.

'We can't run any more,' they wailed, so Masemañamatug called a halt and said, 'There's nothing to be done, then. Let's climb up on that tree and rest a while.'

The children had barely climbed into its branches when the giant caught up with them. Standing at the foot of the tree he roared, 'Give me some more roots.'

'We haven't any more,' said Masemañamatug in reply.

'Then I'll eat you!' cried the giant, and began sawing away at the tree trunk with his long nail.

Masemañamatug turned to the children and said, 'I'm going to sing a song, and you keep repeating, "Hold out! Hold out!" Maybe the tree will hold out and the giant won't eat us.'

So Masemañamatug began to sing:

Oh what have we done . . .

And the children chorused:

Hold out! Hold out!

and then they continued:

. . . after the bird we have run . . .
Hold out! Hold out!
. . . and with us the girls so frail . . .
Hold out! Hold out!
. . . they cannot keep on on the trail.
Hold out! Hold out!
We cooked roots and discussed our plight . . .
Hold out! Hold out!
. . . but then fell the blackness of night.
Hold out! Hold out!
We are lost, we are lost, we are lost . . .
Hold out! Hold out!
How are we to get out of this spot?
Hold out! Hold out!

At that instant they heard a rush of wings and the magic bird alighted on the tree.

'Catch hold of my legs,' he said. 'I'll carry you safely home.'

The children caught hold of the bird's legs, and in the twinkling of an eye back they were in the village. Tarla was overjoyed to see his children safe and sound, and with them the magic bird.

Now that the whole village knew what kind of bird Tarla had at home he had to give milk to the others too. But the bird gave so much of it that there was plenty for all. And so everyone in the village was fat and prosperous and happy.

The White Water-lily

In the days before the war drums sounded in the country of the Indians, a beautiful village stood at the edge of the prairie. The men went out to hunt every morning and returned every evening with rich booty, the women prepared their food and sewed clothing, and the children played from sunrise to sunset. Altogether they were all very happy and contented, happier than any other people in the world.

The Sun shone long into the afternoon, smiling down on the red men; the rain fell only when it was needed to replenish the wells and rivers and lakes with fresh water and to refresh the trees and flowers.

And now listen to what happened. The stars which every night flickered above the camp soon got to know about the Indians and, their lamps being so tiny that their light never reached the earth, they begged their chieftain to let them go and visit the village.

The Moon was the chieftain of the night sky, and he did not like to have his people wandering about and going to bed late in the morning, like the Morning Star. Whenever they did so, he had disagreements with the Sun. But that night he was in an exceptionally good mood, and so he granted the stars their request. They quickly got ready for their journey, laughing and chattering, so that they hardly heard the wise counsel given them by the Moon.

'You may go wherever you please, only take care not to touch the ground. If you did that, you'd have to stay there, and the Sun would burn you to death the next day, for his arrows are fatal to us.'

The stars journeyed long and far. It was lucky for them that the Moon was full that night, as otherwise they would surely have lost their way. At long last they reached the Indian village and, hovering above it, examined it from all sides. The Indians were asleep, only one little boy who lived on the very fringe of the camp was still awake. Hearing a strange whispering noise above his head, he listened carefully, then he looked out through the opening at the top of his wigwam — and his heart almost stopped beating at the sight that met his eyes. So many stars so very, very near! He climbed right up to the top of the tent and moved the pole to get a better view. The pole caught against something and crash! the smallest and most inquisitive of the stars came hurtling down. It had just been passing low over the wigwam and now dropped to the floor, where it changed at once into a beautiful, weeping girl.

'Now look what you've done!' she reproached the boy. 'I can't return with my sisters, and as soon as dawn comes, the Sun's arrows will find me and I shall die.'

The boy stared at her in astonishment. The other stars had in the meantime realized what had happened and they fled back home in panic, knowing they could do nothing to help their unfortunate sister.

The tears streamed down the girl's lovely face, and the boy was overcome with pity.

'I'll help you,' he said. 'When the Sun is out during the day, I'll close my wigwam and he'll not be able to see you. But what shall we do after that?'

'If only I survive the day, I'll change into a flower in the evening and I'll go and live on top of a high cliff from which I will watch you and your people, for I like your Indian ways.'

They did exactly as they had agreed to do. The boy stayed at home that day, taking care that not even the slightest and most curious ray penetrated the wigwam. And as soon as the day was gone, the girl slipped away through the smoke opening and hurried to a high cliff, on top of which a beautiful white rose grew the very next morning.

All the Indians admired the flower from a distance, but only the boy knew that it was actually the little star he had sheltered in his wigwam from the deadly rays of the Sun.

Before long the girl began to feel very lonely up there on her hilltop. Though she could gaze far out into the country and could watch life in the camp, no one ever climbed the sheer cliff to chat with her. Only the birds nesting thereabouts would sometimes fly up to her and keep her company.

One day a small wren came to talk to her.

'I am so lonely here,' the white rose complained. 'I miss human company. If only I could live down there on the prairie.'

'If that's what you want, I can easily help you,' the kind little bird replied. 'Just bend your head a little so that I can take you in my beak.'

The rose obediently bent her head, the wren picked her up in his beak and flew away with her to the prairie.

There life was far gayer. The Indians as well as all kinds of animals came to tell the white rose the news. But then one morning a deep rumble could be heard in the distance. 'Hurry, hurry!' everyone cried. 'We must hide, the buffaloes are coming!' And they all ran and hid as well as they could. A great cloud of dust soon appeared on the horizon, growing larger and larger all the time. The white rose was badly frightened and she hid her head under her leaves that had broadened out in horror. Like a hurricane the herds went past, their thousands of hooves making a noise like thunder.

When at last all was quiet again, the white rose peeped fearfully out from her sheltering leaves. The prairie had been laid waste, there was no sign of life anywhere.

'I mustn't stay here and put myself in such terrible danger,' the star said to herself. 'I'll be better off on the lake.'

Detaching herself from the ground she soon saw beneath her the glittering surface of a lake. Like an Indian canoe she glided gently into the water.

When, early the next morning, the Indians sailed out on to the lake they found to their surprise that there were beautiful white flowers on its surface.

'The night stars have put out blossoms,' said the little children, but the wise men shook their heads and said: 'It is the white star, come to live with us.' They were right.

Since that day, then, the star has lived on the lake in the shape of a white water-lily, and the Indians call her Wahbegwanee, or White Blossom.

The Gift of the Totems

Far beyond the four mountains and the four rivers, on the shores of a limitless ocean, there used to stand the Totem Village, called so on account of the tall, slender totem-posts standing behind each wigwam to give protection to the Indians as they sailed out to sea to hunt whales.

The fishermen believed that these carved and painted poles helped to ward off evil. They held them in high esteem, and whenever they came back from a successful trip they always held a *potlach,* or in other words a big feast, in their honour.

One night, just before one such *potlach,* a raven fell asleep in a tree near the totem grove. He must have had bad dreams or felt cold, for in the middle of the night he suddenly awoke; and as he listened there in the dark, trying to discover what it was that had disturbed his sleep, he heard soft, strange voices, as if the branches, buffeted by the wind, were conversing together.

The raven craned his neck a little, and the voices became more distinct. He had not been mistaken: the wooden totems were talking!

'What is thy opinion, O Highest of Totems?'

'The Spirit of the Great Cod-Fish tells me that the Indians are to receive a gift, and that this gift is to be a metal. A yellow, glittering metal like gold. Am I right, O Eldest of Totems?'

'The Spirit of the Wise Herring has told me in confidence that it must not be a metal as hard as gold, for that would harden the hearts of the red men. Dost thou agree, O Wisest of Totems?'

'Aye, for the Spirit of Mother Whale has informed me that out of this metal the Indians are to fashion the heads of their arrows, spears and lances.'

But though he listened as carefully as he could, the raven heard no more of the whispered conversation conducted by the totems.

'Anyway, I've heard enough,' he thought, making up his mind to watch very attentively at tomorrow's *potlach,* in order to gain some advantage for himself out of the gift the totems had mentioned. After all, he could not allow those stupid Indians to get everything while he went away empty-handed ...

The great *potlach* started even before the Sun had reached the middle of the sky. Ever since that morning, Indians from near and far had been arriving in their long boats with pointed prows, bringing precious gifts, such as coloured blankets, choice foods and beverages, and various weapons.

When all the guests had paid their respects to the totems in the grove and sat down in a circle, something quite unexpected and unforeseen happened: the air was suddenly agitated as if by the beating of thousands of birds' wings. The ocean rose up, and far in the distance, above the crests of the high-flung waves, a strange glittering object could be glimpsed, flying nearer and nearer.

And then, to the astonishment of the assembled Indians, the Highest of Totems addressed them in a human voice:

'The good spirits bring you a valuable gift. It is copper, from which you can make heads for your arrows, spears and lances. It will serve you far better than the flint you have been using hitherto.'

The Highest of Totems had not even finished speaking when, out of the blue, the raven appeared above the heads of the listening Indians and made straight for the brightly gleaming object in the sky, intending to carry it away with him. They looked up, dazzled by the glow and shocked by the raven's impudence. But the good spirits were vigilant and did not allow the bird to make off with their gift.

Now it seemed that all would be well, for the raven seemed to have realized the futility of his efforts and to be flying away. But then, taking everyone unawares, he returned in a flash, seized the glowing ball of copper from the surprised spirits, and was about to escape with it in his claws.

The copper proved too heavy for him, however. He managed to hold on to it for just a moment longer, but then had to let it drop into the sea, which buried the precious object in its depths.

'What's to be done now?' whispered the Indians, turning to the totems in the hope that they would give them some good advice. But the sacred poles stood there silent and motionless.

'Perhaps a clever and skilful fisherman can be found to salvage the precious gift with his harpoon,' said the chieftain, interrupting the profound silence that had settled over the assembly. 'If he succeeds, I shall give him my only daughter to be his wife.'

Hearing her father's words, the girl trembled and tears started to her eyes, for she had long ago pledged her troth to a brave hunter from their village; he had been gone for many days now, sailing distant seas to bring her a wedding present, and she had remained faithful to him all that time.

Yet, she could not oppose her father's decision. The others agreed with it, and some were indeed already casting off in their boats.

Lake Blossom — that was the name of the chieftain's beautiful young daughter — walked sadly to the totem grove, where she knelt in front of the Wisest of Totems.

'Oh, what am I to do? Please help me, O Wisest!' she pleaded.

Seeing that her heart was bursting with sorrow, the totem spoke to her in such low tones that only she was able to hear him:

'Put on a man's clothing. Then go along the seashore as far as the mouth of the Salmon Lake. There thou shalt find a canoe and inside it a harpoon. Put out to sea and take no notice of the waves which will play with the boat so boisterously that thou shalt learn the meaning of fear. The canoe will take thee to the spot where the ball of copper is to be found on the ocean bed. When it stops, pick up the harpoon and plunge it in so that it will pierce the copper. Then, having withdrawn the gift, sail back to the mouth of Salmon Lake. Shouldst thou not do exactly as I tell thee, know the waves will destroy thy boat and thou wilt perish in the sea. Now go and delay not.'

Not for a moment did the girl hesitate. Putting on the clothes of one of her brothers, she smeared her face with coloured clay so that no one should be able to recognize her and hurried to the mouth of Salmon Lake. There she found a boat and a harpoon, and bravely set out to sea.

She soon found that the ocean was very wild, with treacherous whirlpools sucking at the canoe and huge waves all but swamping it; yet still the boat travelled on towards its important goal.

As she went, the chieftain's daughter could see the overturned boats of those who had made the attempt before her. None of them had got very far, paying with their lives for their courage and their desire to marry Lake Blossom; in their last minutes they had come to realize that the ocean would never voluntarily yield what it had once taken for its own.

The canoe stopped. Raising the harpoon, the girl looked down into the turbulent waters. Her hand trembled, but the thought of her beloved transformed her despair into strength. With all her might she plunged the harpoon into the waters, and as soon as she felt it strike home, began to pull it out again.

The raging waves tossed the canoe about at their will; and when at last she had extracted the copper ball from the depths, the ocean lashed at her boat in real fury. It roared and bucked like a wild mustang, and the girl was certain she would be swallowed up by it at any moment. Yet she always emerged out of the tumbling waves, and before long had landed on the shore of Salmon Lake.

Shouts of joy greeted her on the shore, where all the people from her village had in the meantime assembled. The chieftain himself bent down to take the copper ball from the bottom of her canoe; but as he lifted it to show it to the crowd, the raven again swooped down on it, croaking prodigiously. Wrenching it out of the astonished chieftain's hands he flew with it to the top of the tallest pine, as if the evil spirits themselves had endowed him with strength.

'Now I've got your gift, and you needn't expect me to return it to you!' the raven shouted triumphantly. 'I shan't return it!' he croaked every time an arrow whistled through the air, as the desperate Indians tried to regain their treasure.

The girl, too, attempted to shoot the thieving raven. They all knew who she was by now, since her head-dress had slipped and her bluish-black hair had come tumbling down her back. But not even her arrows managed to reach the tree-top.

At that moment quick footfalls were heard coming from Salmon Lake. A young man came running, lightly as a deer. As soon as he was near enough to be recognized, the girl ran forward to meet him and fell into his arms.

'At last you've come, my dearest!' she cried. And as she embraced him, she told him what had happened. Wave Flier, as the young man was nicknamed because of the great skill with which he guided his canoe, took an arrow from his quiver, put it to his bow and, waiting for the insolent raven to show his head, sent it flying in the bird's direction.

In the tense silence all that could be heard was a fierce cry emitted by the raven and the whistling noise made by the arrow. Then came a crackling sound from the top of the tree as the raven dug his claws into the bark in his death throes — and the fiery ball of copper dropped down to earth.

The copper ball hit the ground and broke into a thousand small pieces. 'The raven was right,' thought the Indians — 'he stole our gift from us and now he has destroyed it and made it useless.'

'That is not so,' said a voice from the spot where stood the Wisest of Totems. 'It is from these very splinters that you will be able to make the sharpest arrow-heads and blades.'

And while the Indians were busy picking up the pieces of copper, the girl turned to the lucky marksman. Stretching out her hand to him, she asked:

'What gift have you brought me, dearest?'

'A small gift indeed,' the young man replied. 'I did catch a large whale, probably the largest whale in the world, but in Whale Bay I made a present of it to some Indians who were dying of hunger. This is all I kept — it is called ambergris.' And he handed the girl a wooden casket full of an ointment that gave off a heady scent.

Lake Blossom put the ointment on her hands and face and then she accompanied her betrothed to the totem grove. Behind the happy couple walked a crowd of Indians, led by their chieftain. He could not take his eyes off the two young people in front of him. And those nearest to him could hear him whisper:

'You have chosen wisely and well, my daughter. Wave Flier will be a good and faithful husband to you as long as you live.'

The Otter's Friendship

The snow fell unceasingly for many days and nights in the Month of Long Sleep. A wild blizzard galloped all over the country with the wind for a horse, obliterating the tracks of animals, which fled before it to the safety of their dens and hide-outs.

An unwelcome guest — hunger — made himself at home in the villages of the red men, forcing the hunters to go out into the storm; but they always returned empty-handed, weary with the unavailing search for the animal tracks which lay buried deep in the silent white snow.

The howling of hungry wolves could occasionally be heard above the clamour of the wind, chilling the blood of the hunters; nevertheless, the weeping of their hungry children dismayed them still more.

It was then that the tribe's shaman, the mighty Dadahwat, invoked the aid of his magic pouch.

'In it is a powerful charm,' he told the assembled hunters. 'All you have to do is to touch it and it will bring you whatever prey you wish to kill. But take care not to cut out the dead animal's heart and eat it, for then the magic would cease to work.'

The chieftain was the first to touch the magic pouch; he made a wish that he might next day kill a bear. All the other hunters followed suit, the youngest, Skage-di, being last. He wished to kill a lynx.

A frosty night set in. The snowstorm battered at the walls of the dwellings as if it meant to blow them away, and clouds of snow whirled and eddied through the countryside like white apparitions while the wind accompanied their wild dance by its fierce melodies in the tops of the trees.

Skagedi alone was awake that night. Unable to bear the pangs of hunger, he got up while it was still dark and went out into the forest trusting to his memory and hoping to find, in the first light of dawn, a fresh lynx track.

How great was his surprise, though, when he came across a lynx in the dark! The wild beast was holding down with his paw two young otters, which were still alive. They raised their heads on hearing Skagedi's footfall, looking up at him in the starlight with such beseeching expressions that his heart was moved to see them.

He killed the lynx with a single blow and was so overjoyed when the otters ran free that he quite forgot his hunger. But his stomach reasserted itself as soon as the otters vanished from sight. And now he felt so famished that he at once ate the heart of his prey, regardless of the shaman's prohibition. 'No one will know,' he said to himself as he returned home and lay down to sleep. And he dropped off at once into the deepest of slumbers.

In the meantime the men of the village had gone out to hunt, but the charm of the magic pouch had lost its efficacy. The bear got away, although the chieftain had almost caught him, nor did the others fare better.

There's something wrong, they decided, and they ran at once back to the village to consult Dadahwat, who at once guessed that someone must have disobeyed his instructions. They did not have to look far for the culprit — an unskinned lynx lay in front of Skagedi's wigwam, and when the shaman turned him over he saw that the heart had been taken. Skagedi had eaten it!

'The boy must be punished! He destroyed the charm of the pouch which was the envy of all the shamans throughout the Indian country. Manitou himself endowed it with its power.' Thus spoke the angry Dadahwat to the silent crowd of hunters. And he passed an instant verdict on the offender:

'We shall leave for another region, where we'll find hunting grounds rich in game, but you will stay here all alone in the village, without food and clothing, because you have sinned heavily against your friends.'

The punishment was harsh indeed, but Skagedi accepted it like a man. Not one of the hunters spoke a word in his defence, not a single woman gave him a compassionate look. Only little Wia's eyes filled with tears, which ran down her cheeks as she stood there looking at him.

They all left, and Skagedi was alone. He sat for a long time in his wigwam, shivering with cold; not even the fire could give him sufficient warmth any more. As he listened to the raging of the storm outside, it suddenly seemed to him that he heard someone's footfalls. Yes, there was no doubt about it — someone was approaching his wigwam. He looked out but could see no one, yet a soft, kind voice came to him through the blizzard:

'Skagedi, O Skagedi! A few paces away from your wigwam you'll find a bear hiding in the cave. Go and kill him, and you will be saved.'

The voice was heard no more — but Skagedi had heard enough. Next morning, when the wind had abated a little, he left his wigwam and soon reached a cave inside which he found a bear fast asleep. Killing him with a single arrow, Skagedi dragged the carcass to his tent, where he made new clothes and a pair of moccasins for himself from the bear's fur, cutting up and smoking the meat. And that evening, though he was very tired after his day's hard work, he could not go to sleep for a long time, thinking of his unknown benefactor, who had saved his life with his good and timely advice.

It was midnight by the time he was about to enter the land of dreams, and he again heard the now familiar voice:

'Skagedi, O Skagedi! When Dadahwat brings his pouch, take it in your hands. Then tell Dadahwat not to be annoyed with you any more, for you know how to restore the charm of his magic pouch.'

Skagedi ran out into the night, but he did not find the unknown adviser. Only the stars were there, silently glittering in the frosty night.

Wia really did come the following day. She had been afraid she would not find Skagedi alive, and her joy knew no bounds. And she was happier still when the boy told her that he could restore the charm of Dadahwat's magic pouch.

Skagedi had, however, made no mention of his strange adventure. And as soon as Wia had left, he resumed his work of the day before. In the evening he lay by the fire, impatient for the night, when he hoped to hear the kind voice again. And so he did.

'Skagedi, O Skagedi! When Dadahwat brings his pouch, take it in your hands. Then ask the hunters, one by one, what animal they wish to catch. Whenever they state their wish, just open the pouch and out will come the strong bear, the fleet-footed stag, or the snow hare—in short, the very animal they have asked for. You yourself make no wish, though. Just take whatever is left in the pouch and bring it to my wigwam. I shan't tell you where it is, but if you do as I tell you, you'll find the way yourself.'

Next day the Indians returned to the village, and the shaman, to whom Wia had given Skagedi's message, handed the boy his magic pouch.

'Very well, then — show us what you can do,' he said, watching the boy with very curious eyes.

Skagedi took the pouch and turned to the hunters.

'What animal do you wish to capture?' he asked the chieftain.

'The bear,' was the reply — and out of the pouch came a sleepy bear.

'And you?' Skagedi asked the chieftain's son.

'The stag,' replied he — but no sooner were the words out of his mouth than a fleet-footed stag jumped out of the pouch and lay down at his feet.

What followed was magical. One after the other the Indians called out their wishes, and Skagedi could hardly keep up with them in opening the pouch to let all the animals out.

Finally he himself put his hand inside. Deep down on the very bottom there lay something soft and furry, and when Skagedi pulled it out he discovered that it was an otter's paw. Quickly he put it back again and, slipping into his snowshoes, set out to find the wigwam of his unknown benefactor.

He did not know which way to go, but the snowshoes guided him in the right direction.

At the end of the forest he found a small round-topped hut. He had never seen it there before and therefore guessed it must be the abode of his unknown friend. He went in.

The hut was empty. Fish remains lay all over the floor, and the boy could smell an otter's scent. Laying the paw down on the ground he hurried out and turned back towards home. He was stopped by a voice calling his name:

'Skagedi!'

The boy turned round, and to his amazement saw that a great lake was now in the spot where the hut had stood just a moment ago.

'O Skagedi! As a reward for your having delivered my children from the lynx's clutches, Dadahwat's pouch will never again lose its magic power. The paw you brought was also mine.'

'Mine, mine, mine,' repeated the echo in the hills.

'But remember, none of you must ever lay otter traps, or you will lose my friendship.'

Only now did Skagedi hear a splash, and on the surface of the lake he saw rings such as are made when an otter jumps into the water.

He waited a little longer in case the otter might appear again, but the surface was calm and unruffled. And at the forest's edge he saw Wia, who hurried forward to meet him.

'Wia! Wia!' he called out, running towards her. He told her the whole story, and repeated it to the others when they got back home.

Never again did the village suffer want, for the red men lived in friendship with the otter, and so Dadahwat's pouch was always full.

Ivan Bull

Somewhere beyond the red sea, beyond the blue forest, beyond the glass mountain, and beyond the straw town where they sift water and pour sand, stood a mighty Czardom. The Czar and the Czarina ruled well, but they were most unhappy because they had no children.

One day, when the Czarina strolled through the royal gardens, she suddenly met a grey old woman who said to her, 'I know why you are so unhappy, your royal highness! But I know also how to chase away your sadness! Order your servant to catch the trout with the silver fin from the lake, then have soup made with the fish. When you have drunk this soup, you will have a son.'

As soon as the old woman had spoken, she disappeared as mysteriously as she had appeared.

The Czarina ordered the fishermen to catch the trout with the silver fin in the lake. Then her maid cooked the fish soup. The Czarina drank most of it, the maid finished the rest and took the slops to the bull in the sty. Some time afterwards the Czarina gave birth to little Ivan Czar; the maid gave birth to Ivan Maiden and the bull — to Ivan Bull.

The three boys grew and grew so rapidly, that at the end of twelve months they were as tall and as strong as others in their teens.

Then the three Ivans decided to roam the fields, and indeed to roam the wide world, so they would see other regions.

They entered the stables to choose their horses.

Ivan Czar and Ivan Maiden chose handsome, brave mares, but Ivan Bull was not so lucky. The moment he patted the back of any horse, it fell to the ground. Then he went into the deep cellar and there he found a horse the colour of the night; sparks flew from its eyes and steam puffed from its nostrils. When Ivan Bull patted this horse on its back, it did not fall down.

'This one is for me,' Ivan Bull said to himself and led the horse outside.

The three Ivans galloped over the fields; they rode on and on, till they reached the river Smorodina, at the spot where a stone bridge spanned it.

'Let us put up our tent here and stay overnight,' said Ivan Bull.

They pitched their tent right by the bridge and drew lots to see which one of them would stand guard that night. It happened to be Ivan Czar.

Ivan Maiden and Ivan Bull curled up in the tent, while Ivan Czar stood on guard by the stone bridge. But Ivan Bull just could not fall asleep. 'I'll have a look to see how Ivan Czar is guarding us,' he thought.

Ivan Bull strolled to the stone bridge and found Ivan Czar slumped on the shore, snoring so loudly the whole bridge was shaking.

Ivan Bull shook his head in disgust and then noticed that a terrible looking dragon with three heads was riding towards him along the bridge. His horse nervously stumbled.

'Why do you stumble, my mare?' asked the dragon.

The magnificent mare replied, 'I stumble and stumble because I am terrified.'

The dragon roared with laughter. 'What can you be afraid of?' he asked. 'There is only one creature on earth we have to fear, and that is Ivan Bull.'

'That's me!' cried Ivan Bull. And with one swift sweep of his sword he cut off the dragon's three heads. He threw the heads and the body into the river Smorodina, but let his horse gallop away into the pasture. Then he went to sleep.

In the morning Ivan Bull asked Ivan Czar, 'How did you get on, being on guard?'

'Very well, very well,' Ivan Czar nodded his head eagerly. 'Everything was so quiet all night, not a single leaf moved.'

The three of them then rode out into the wide open country. They rode and rode, but in the evening returned again to the stone bridge and their tent. It was Ivan Maiden's turn to stand guard.

Once again Ivan Bull could not go to sleep; he tossed and turned and in the end went to see how well Ivan Maiden was guarding them. He found him slumped on the shore, sleeping and snoring so loudly, that the stone bridge was shaking.

Ivan Bull shook his head in disgust and then noticed a six-headed, terrible looking dragon riding towards him along the bridge. His horse was stumbling nervously.

The dreadful dragon cried, 'Why do you stumble, my mare? Surely you are not afraid! There is only one creature on this earth we must fear, and that is Ivan Bull!' 'That's me!' cried Ivan Bull, brandishing his sword. With one swipe he cut off three heads, and with the second swipe he cut off the other three. He threw the dragon's body and all his heads into the river Smorodina, sent his horse into the open country and then went to sleep.

In the morning Ivan Bull asked Ivan Maiden, 'How did you enjoy being on guard, brother?'

'Very much, very much,' Ivan Maiden answered smugly. 'Everything was silent and still all night; not even a blade of grass moved.'

The three of them then rode out into the vast fields. They rode on and on, but in the evening returned once again to the stone bridge.

This time it was Ivan Bull's turn to stand guard. Before he left, he turned to his brothers.

'Tonight I will stand guard, but you, brothers, must also stay awake!' he said. 'When my horse begins to stamp let him loose!'

Ivan Bull went to the stone bridge and waited. After some time he saw a horrific nine-headed dragon riding along the bridge towards him. The dragon was merry, but his horse stumbled nervously.

'Why do you stumble, my mare? Surely you are not afraid!'

The horse answered, 'I am afraid, very much afraid, afraid of Ivan Bull.'

The dragon roared with laughter. 'You don't have to fear Ivan Bull,' he said. 'I'll sit him on the palm of my hand, and with the other hand squash him like a fly.'

'We shall see!' cried Ivan Bull.

Brandishing his sword, he swung it for the first time and sliced off three heads; he swung it for the second time and cut off three more heads; but before he had a chance to take the third swipe, the horrific nine-headed dragon glued the fallen heads back on again with its fiery finger, and it was as before with all the nine heads.

They fought on and on, but as quickly as Ivan Bull sliced off the dragon's heads, the dragon glued them back on with its fiery finger, before all nine were cut off. Ivan Bull realized that he could not beat the nine-headed dragon with its fiery finger.

Just then his horse began to stamp its feet wildly. It made such a noise with its hooves, that the stone bridge started to shake, and the water from the river Smorodina started to spill on to the shore.

But Ivan Czar and Ivan Maiden were so soundly asleep they did not hear the stamping, and did not let the horse go.

The dragon was now furiously attacking Ivan Bull, pinning him to the ground. Ivan Bull only just managed to slip off his boot, throw it into the white tent and break in two the reins of his horse. Quick as lightning the horse began to attack the dragon.

While it trampled on the dragon with its hooves, Ivan Bull swiftly cut off the monster's fiery finger, and after that it was easy to slice off all the heads. When all was done, Ivan retired to his tent and fell asleep.

The next morning he said to his brothers, 'Why didn't you release my horse, when he stamped his feet during the night?'

The brothers seemed surprised.

'We did not hear a thing,' they said. 'It was so quiet, not a single leaf rustled, not a blade of grass moved in the breeze.'

Ivan Bull led Ivan Czar and Ivan Maiden to the stone bridge, and, pointing to the dragons' eighteen heads and the three trunks in the river Smorodina, he told them everything that had happened.

Afterwards they journeyed on and on, till they arrived at a large, wooden house, knocked together carelessly from unpolished planks of oak. There were neither windows, nor doors, and a rough rock took the place of the roof.

'You go on ahead, brothers,' said Ivan Bull, 'I'll have a look round.'

The other two Ivans rode on, while Ivan Bull climbed the rough rock, peered inside and saw the three wives of the three horrific dragons complaining to an old hag.

The first was saying, 'Alas, mother, that confounded Ivan Bull killed my husband — your son — the three-headed dragon.'

The old hag replied, 'You can't bring him back to life, but you can avenge him! In a wide open field turn yourself into a feather-bed. Ivan Bull will lie on it and will burn to ashes.'

The second wife said, 'Alas, mother, that confounded Ivan Bull killed your son — my husband — the six-headed dragon.'

The old hag once again replied, 'You can't bring him back to life, but you can avenge him! Turn yourself into a well with a golden goblet. Ivan Bull will have a drink and will burn to ashes.'

The third wife complained, 'Alas, mother, that confounded Ivan Bull killed your son — my husband — the nine-headed dragon.'

The old hag replied, 'You too cannot bring him back to life, but you must avenge him. In a wide open field, turn yourself into an apple tree with red apples. When Ivan Bull picks one, he will burn to ashes. And even if all this fails, then I will avenge the death of my three sons.'

When Ivan Bull had listened to all this, he jumped astride his horse and caught up with his brothers.

The three Ivans rode on and on, and as they were tiring, they wanted to go to sleep. Suddenly they saw a large field with a lovely soft feather-bed in it.

'Let us rest!' Ivan Czar and Ivan Maiden shouted together.

Ivan Bull, however, took off his glove, tossed it on to the bed, and immediately it burned to ashes. Then he chopped up the bed with his sword and on they rode.

They rode on and on, until they became parched with thirst. All of a sudden a well stood before them, a golden goblet by its side.

'Let's have a drink!' cried Ivan Czar and Ivan Maiden.

But Ivan Bull took his other glove off, tossed it into the well, and the glove burned to ashes. He then chopped up the well with his sharp sword and on they rode.

They rode on and on, till they were very hungry. To their surprise they saw an apple tree laden with red apples in the middle of a field.

'Let's eat!' cried Ivan Czar and Ivan Maiden.

Ivan Bull, however, took off his cap, threw it into the tree branches, and the cap burned to ashes. Then he chopped up the apple tree with his sharp sword and on they rode.

Suddenly they realized someone was flying behind them.

It was the old hag, the mother of the dragons, flying in a huge bowl, propelling herself with a mallet. She was catching up with the brothers.

Then they saw a forge and the blacksmith Kuzma at work. He welcomed the brothers and closed the iron door behind them, and the old hag screeched to a halt outside.

'Open the door, blacksmith Kuzma!' the old hag screamed, banging on the door. 'I will gulp down Ivan Bull, as if he were a raspberry.'

'I will let you have Ivan Bull only when you have licked right through the iron door with your tongue!' blacksmith Kuzma shouted back.

The old hag licked the iron door; she licked and licked and licked and licked till her tongue came right through into the forge. That was what Ivan Bull was waiting for. He ran out and with one blow of his sword severed the old hag's head.

This is how Ivan Bull and his brothers got rid of the three horrific dragons and their mother—the old hag.

The Greedy Fox and Kuzma Getrich

Once upon a time, in a woodland meadow, there lived a young man called Kuzma Getrich. All he had in the world was a battered pair of trousers and five hens, nothing else.

One day Kuzma went to hunt in the wood. While he was out, a greedy fox ran into his cottage, killed one of the hens, roasted it and ate it, and then ran away.

When Kuzma returned, he counted the hens. One was missing; only four were left.

'The wolf must have taken it,' he sighed.

The next day he was off hunting again. On the way he met the fox.

'Where are you going, Kuzma?' it asked.

'To hunt in the forest!'

'I wish you luck,' cried the fox slyly and raced to the cottage.

It killed the second hen, roasted and ate it, then ran off.

When Kuzma returned, he counted the hens. Again one was missing. There were only three left.

'I bet it wasn't the wolf, but that sly fox!'

The next day, before he left for the forest, Kuzma closed all the windows firmly and locked the door. Again he met the fox.

'Where are you going, Kuzma?'

'To hunt in the forest!'

'The best of luck,' cried the fox, and raced towards the cottage.

But the cottage was locked and all windows firmly closed. The fox ran round the cottage, trying in vain to get in. Eventually it climbed onto the roof and slithered down the chimney. By the time it crawled into the kitchen, Kuzma was back again.

'What a fine thief you are! Just you wait, you won't get out of this alive!'

'Leave me alone, Kuzma,' cried the fox. 'Why don't you roast me another hen? I will help you to turn your luck.'

Kuzma roasted the hen, the fox gobbled it up, ran out into the clearing and lay down to rest. Just then the wolf ran past.

'Why are you sprawled here, fox?'

'You would be sprawled here too, if you had been with me at the Czar's palace for lunch. I ate so much I thought my stomach would burst; and I am going back tomorrow.'

'Listen, fox, can I come with you?' the wolf asked.

'Why not? The Czar has so much food; everything you could want. Why don't you bring with you forty times forty wolves, then our visit will be worth while.'

The wolf gathered together forty times forty wolves and the next morning they all ran to the Czar's palace with the fox. The fox left all the wolves in the courtyard and went to the Czar. 'Mighty Czar, I have come to you with a gift from my master Kuzma Getrich. He sends you forty times forty wolves.'

The Czar thanked the fox, ordered the wolves to be caught and skinned, and said to himself, 'That Kuzma Getrich must be a rich man.'

The fox returned to Kuzma and said, 'Please roast me yet another hen. I promise to turn your luck for the better.'

Kuzma roasted the bird, the fox gobbled it up and ran out into the clearing to rest. A bear passed by.

'Why are you lounging here, fox?'

'You wouldn't be able to move either, if you had been with me at the Czar's palace for lunch. I ate so much I thought my stomach would burst; and I am going again tomorrow.'

The bear asked, 'Listen, fox, can I come with you tomorrow?'

'Why not? The Czar has so much food and drink, there is everything you could want. Bring with you another forty times forty bears.'

The bear found forty times forty bears and the following morning they all went to the Czar. The fox left all the bears in the courtyard and went inside alone. 'Mighty Czar, I have come with a present from my master, Kuzma Getrich. He sends you forty times forty bears.'

The Czar thanked the fox warmly, had the bears skinned and thought to himself, 'This Kuzma Getrich must be a very rich fellow.'

The fox returned to Kuzma and said, 'Please roast me another hen, Kuzma. I really do promise to turn your luck.'

Kuzma roasted the very last chicken, the fox gobbled it up and ran into the clearing to rest. A sable and a pine marten walked by and remarked, 'Why are you sprawled here like this?'

'You too wouldn't be able to move, if you had been with me at the Czar's palace for lunch. I ate so much and drank so much, I thought my stomach would burst; and I am going again tomorrow.'

'Please take us with you, fox,' they pleaded.

'Why not? The Czar has more than enough food and drink; all you could want. Bring with you forty times forty sables and martens and we'll all go tomorrow.'

They gathered together forty times forty sables and martens and the next morning they all went to the palace.

The fox left all the sables and martens in the courtyard and went to the Czar alone. 'Mighty Czar, I have come to you with a gift from my master, Kuzma Getrich. The present he sends you is forty times forty sables and martens.'

The Czar thanked the fox warmly, had the sables and martens skinned and said to himself, 'This Kuzma Getrich must be a very, very rich fellow.'

Once again the fox ran back to Kuzma Getrich. 'Roast me another chicken, Kuzma,' he cried. 'I really promise to turn your luck.' Kuzma grew angry this time. 'You've already eaten my five hens. I have no more. And you haven't turned my luck!' he shouted.

'Stop worrying, Kuzma! I will keep my promise,' the fox assured him, and trotted away back to the Czar. 'Mighty Czar! My master, Kuzma Getrich, has sent me here to tell you he would like to court your daughter and ask for her hand in marriage.'

'Of course he can court her,' agreed the Czar. 'I should be happy to give my daughter to such a rich man, such a gentleman. Go back and tell him to join me for lunch tomorrow.'

The fox ran back to Kuzma Getrich. 'The Czar has invited you for lunch tomorrow, Kuzma. He wants to give you his daughter in marriage,' he said.

'But foxie, how can I go to the Czar's palace for lunch, when all I possess are these tatty old trousers?'

'Don't give that another thought, Kuzma. Just do what I tell you to, and you'll see, it will all come right,' the fox promised.

The next morning Kuzma and the fox set out for the palace. The fox ran on ahead, Kuzma walked slowly behind. He was moaning, 'How ashamed I shall be, when I get to the Czar in these tatty old pants.'

In the meantime the fox came to the river and used his paw to cut through the bridge which spanned it. The moment Kuzma set his foot upon it, the bridge collapsed and he fell into the water. He very nearly drowned.

The fox ran to the Czar, 'Oh, mighty Czar, what a dreadful thing has happened! The bridge has collapsed under Kuzma Getrich, all his golden coaches have floated away, and his servants have drowned. It is a miracle that Kuzma Getrich escaped with his bare life!'

The Czar immediately sent one of his gold coaches for Kuzma, putting inside an exquisite robe embroidered in gold, fashionable boots inlaid with silver and a sable hat strewn with pearls. When Kuzma put it all on, he looked just like a real prince. The Czar and his daughter could hardly take their eyes off him.

It seemed everything would end happily, for there was a great wedding of Kuzma Getrich and the Czar's daughter. The celebrations continued for three days. On the third day the Czar turned to Kuzma:

'Now, my dear son-in-law, we will go to your Czardom.'

Kuzma Getrich was terribly worried and he said to the fox, 'Alas, foxie, you promised to bring me good fortune, but it is turning into misfortune. Now the Czar will find out that all I possess is an old shack in the forest.'

'Stop worrying, Kuzma! It will all have a happy ending.'

The Czar, his daughter and Kuzma Getrich drove away from the palace in a gold carriage. The fox ran on ahead to show them the way. But instead of going towards Kuzma's shack in the woods, it went in the opposite direction.

The fox ran on and on, till it came to a green meadow, where shepherds were tending a huge flock of sheep.

'Tell me, shepherds,' the fox called out to them, 'whose flock are you tending?'

'It is Czar Viper's flock.'

'If you value your life, shepherds, say that this flock of sheep belongs to Kuzma Getrich. The Fiery Czar and his Flaming Czarina ride behind me and they could burn you to ashes.'

'Thank you, fox, for your good advice,' cried the shepherds.

By then the gold carriage with Kuzma, the Czar and Czarina had arrived, and the Czar was asking, 'Tell me, shepherds, to whom does this flock belong?'

'To Kuzma Getrich.'

'You have excellent sheep, son-in-law,' said the Czar with satisfaction, and they drove on.

In the meantime the fox came to some cowherds who were tending a huge herd of cows.

'Tell me, cowherds,' the fox called to them, 'whose herd are you looking after?'

'It is Czar Viper's herd.'

'If you value your life, cowherds, say that this herd of cows belongs to Kuzma Getrich. The Fiery Czar and his Flaming Czarina ride behind me and they could burn you to ashes.'

'Thank you, fox, for your good advice,' cried the cowherds.

By then the gold carriage with Kuzma, the Czar and Czarina had arrived, and then the Czar was asking, 'Tell me, cowherds, to whom does this herd belong?'

'To Kuzma Getrich.'

'You have excellent cows, son-in-law,' said the Czar with satisfaction, and they drove on.

In the meantime the fox came to some herdsmen who were tending a huge herd of horses.

'Tell me, herdsmen,' the fox called to them. 'Whose herd are you looking after?'

'It is Czar Viper's herd.'

'If you value your life, say that this herd of horses belongs to Kuzma Getrich. The Fiery Czar and his Flaming Czarina ride behind me and they could burn you to ashes.'

'Thank you, fox, for your good advice,' cried the herdsmen.

Already the gold carriage with Kuzma, the Czar and Czarina had arrived and the Czar was asking:

'Tell me, herdsmen, to whom does this herd belong?'

'To Kuzma Getrich.'

'You have fine horses, dear son-in-law.' The Czar smiled contentedly.

The fox at last ran into the gold palace of Czar Viper and knocked on the gates.

Czar Viper stuck out all his seven dragon's heads and cried, 'Who is knocking on my gates?'

The fox called loudly:

'Alas, Czar Viper, you're in trouble! The Fiery Czar and the Flaming Czarina ride behind me in a gold carriage. Run away as fast as you can, otherwise they will burn you to ashes.'

As soon as Czar Viper heard this, he ran out of the gold palace and ran and ran, as fast as his legs could carry him. No one ever saw him again.

Shortly after the Czar arrived with his daughter and Kuzma Getrich by the palace gates. The fox was waiting to welcome them and the Czar could not stop marvelling at the splendid palace his son-in-law owned.

From that day on Kuzma lived happily in the gold palace with the Czar's daughter, and foxie, too. They roasted a big fat hen each day for their friend, and the greedy fox stayed with them, full and content.

The Dazzling Falcon Finister

In Millionth Street of St. Petersburg there once lived a wealthy merchant Terenin who had three daughters. The two elder ones were good looking and proud, the youngest one, Maria, was modest, hardworking and a real beauty.

When one day merchant Terenin set out on his business travels, he asked his daughters, 'What would you like me to bring you back?'

The two elder sisters asked for expensive dresses, shoes and jewellery, but the youngest one said, 'Please, father, bring me a feather from the dazzling falcon Finister.'

The merchant was surprised to hear such a strange wish, but he promised to return with everything his daughters asked for.

Some time later the father was on his way home. He bought beautiful dresses, shoes and jewellery, but he had been unable to find the feather from the dazzling falcon Finister.

Just before he entered St. Petersburg he met an aged, bent man. The merchant said in greeting, 'Good health to you, grandfather!'

'Good health to you too, merchant Terenin! You are returning home, but you do not seem very happy.'

'That is true, grandfather! My youngest daughter, Maria, asked me to bring her a feather from the dazzling falcon Finister, but I could not find one anywhere.'

The old man nodded his head and said, 'I have such a feather, and it is a very rare feather. It is not for sale. As you are a kind man, however, I will give it to you for nothing.'

Then the old man gave the merchant an ordinary looking, tiny feather.

Merchant Terenin went on happily home. He gave his elder daughters the expensive dresses, shoes and jewellery; Maria's gift was the feather of the dazzling falcon Finister.

The elder sisters straight away dressed up in their new finery, preened themselves in the mirror and laughed at silly Maria. Maria did not care! She went into her own room, threw the feather on the floor and, lo and behold! The small feather first turned into a dazzling falcon and then into a handsome youth.

Maria and her Finister stayed together happily all night long; at break of day the handsome youth turned again into a falcon and flew away out of Maria's window.

From that day the dazzling falcon Finister visited Maria every night. He flew into her room in the evening, turned into the handsome youth, stayed all night and then flew away again at the crack of dawn, in the form of the falcon.

Her sisters soon noticed that a dazzling falcon was flying to Maria and they began to tell tales to their father. He said abruptly, 'Daughters, why don't you mind your own business?'

The elder sisters were jealous of Maria, so they set a snare for the falcon by glueing sharp fragments of glass on her window and gave Maria a large dose of a sleeping draught. The dazzling falcon Finister vainly tried to enter Maria's room that night; vainly tried to wake her up by knocking on the window with his beak. His chest was torn and bleeding from the sharp glass, but Maria was in a deep sleep.

In the end falcon Finister cried out, 'Whoever really needs me, will find me, but it will be difficult. He or she will have to look for me for a long, long time, until three pairs of iron shoes are worn out, three iron walking sticks are broken, and three iron hats are torn. Then I will be found.'

By then Maria was recovering from her drugged sleep and heard the falcon's words. She rushed to the window and flung it wide open, but her dear one had already flown away. A few drops of blood on the window-sill were all that was left of him. Maria cried bitterly and her tears washed away the drops of blood. Then she prepared herself for the long journey. She ordered three pairs of iron shoes,

three iron walking sticks and three iron hats, bade her father goodbye and left home.

Maria travelled a long, long time, over really rough ground. It may sound easy in a story, but in real life it was very hard. She had already worn out one pair of the iron shoes, broken one of the iron walking sticks and torn one of the iron hats, when she came to a clearing in the middle of a deep forest, where a small cottage stood. Maria entered and saw a white-haired old man sitting by the stove.

'What brings you here, maiden? I have been sitting by this stove for a hundred years now, and have not seen a single soul.'

'I am searching for my sweetheart, for my falcon Finister, dear grandfather,' answered Maria.

The old man nodded his head, but he knew nothing of such a falcon.

'Wait here till morning, young maiden. All the woodland creatures gather in this clearing at dawn; perhaps they may have news of your sweetheart.'

Maria spent the night in the cottage and at dawn, just like the old man had said, all the woodland creatures gathered in the clearing. There were bears, wolves, deer, even the tiniest ants, but they knew nothing about falcon Finister.

'I am sorry, Maria, that I cannot help you,' said the old man. 'But at least I will give you a present. Take this silver tray with the golden egg. When you put the tray down, the egg will start rolling on its own. You must not sell the tray for anything, except for one night with falcon Finister. Now one of the deer will lead you out of the forest. Follow the sun until you come to the blue sea. My elder brother lives there, maybe he will be able to help you.'

The deer led Maria out of the forest and she followed the sun, walking on and on, over rough ground. It was harder in real life than it sounds in a story.

When she had worn out the second pair of shoes, when she had broken the second iron walking stick, when she had torn the second iron hat, she came to the blue sea. A tiny cottage stood right on the shore. Maria entered and found an aged, white-haired man by the stove.

'Welcome to you, maiden,' he said in greeting. 'What brings you here? I have sat by this stove for three hundred years now, without seeing a living soul.'

Maria replied:

'I am looking for my sweetheart, falcon Finister, dear grandfather.'

But the old man had never heard of falcon Finister.

'Wait here till morning, young maiden. All the sea creatures gather by the shore at dawn; perhaps one of them might know something about your dearest one.'

Maria stayed in the cottage overnight and as the old man had said, all the sea creatures swam to the shore the following morning; there were big fish and little fish, seals, sea horses and even tiny sprats. But they knew nothing about the dazzling falcon Finister.

'I am afraid I cannot help you,' said the old man. 'I will at least give you a present. Take this gold loom with the silver spinning wheel. The wheel will weave a thin, gold thread on its own. But you must not sell it to anyone, not for anything, except for one night with falcon Finister. Now this whale will take you across the sea, then you must walk on and on until you climb the white mountain, where my eldest brother lives in his cottage. Maybe he will be able to help.'

Maria rode across the sea on the whale's back, and then walked on and on, over rough ground. It was much harder in real life than it is to tell in a fairy story. When she had worn out the third pair of iron shoes, when she had broken the third iron walking stick, when she had torn the third iron hat, she saw the tiny cottage on the white mountain. She went inside and found a white-haired old man resting by the stove. He said in greeting, 'Good health to you, young maiden! What brings you here? I have been resting by this stove for one thousand years now, and have not seen a single living soul.'

'I am searching for my beloved, for falcon Finister,' Maria replied.

Even the eldest old man knew nothing about Finister.

'Never mind, stay here till morning. All the birds assemble here then and maybe one of them will know something about your sweetheart.'

At dawn the next day all the birds really did gather in front of the cottage — eagles, hawks, and everything that flew, right down to the tiniest moth. They too knew nothing about falcon Finister. Suddenly a swish of wings was heard and an enormous falcon flew to the ground. He said, 'Falcon Finister is my brother and he is in a crystal castle a thousand miles from here. The countess who lives there has captured him and is feeding him with the wine of forgetfulness, for she wants to have him for a husband.'

When Maria heard that the countess from the crystal castle intended to wed her beloved, she began to weep bitterly. The old man tried to cheer her up:

'Do not grieve, dear maiden! You will see everything will end happily. The falcon will fly you down the mountain and you will go on to the castle. Take with you this silver frame with the gold needle. When you put the frame down, the needle will embroider a silk scarf all on its own. But do not sell the frame for anything but one night with falcon Finister.'

The falcon took Maria down the mountain and she walked on and on, over rough ground. She had no shoes left, no walking stick and no hat. Her bare feet were torn by sharp stones until they bled. She used her hands to support herself against the trees. The hot sun burnt her bare head. Then at last Maria came to the crystal castle.

The maiden sat on the crystal doorstep of the castle and took out of her bag the silver tray with the gold egg. When she put them on the floor, the egg began to roll all over the place. People gathered to see this strange sight.

The countess who reigned in this crystal castle saw the crowd of people, and sent her maid to find out what was going on. The maid soon returned with the tale about the magic egg made of gold, which rolled about all on its own and which with its silver tray belonged to a girl called Maria, who refused to sell it for anything but one night spent with falcon Finister.

The countess simply waved her hand and said to the maid, 'Run and fetch the silver tray with the gold egg! Tell the girl to come in the evening, then I will take her to falcon Finister. It won't bring her any joy, for after taking the wine of forgetfulness, falcon Finister sleeps like the dead and no one wakes him up.'

So Maria came to her beloved at last. She stood over him all night long, whispering sweet words of love, but Finister slept on, knowing and hearing nothing. The next morning Maria left in tears.

Once again she sat on the crystal step of the crystal castle. This time she took out the gold loom with the silver spinning wheel which spun a gold thread on its own. People crowded around to see this miracle. The countess sent her maid down again to find out what was happening. When afterwards the maid told her of the gold loom and the silver spinning wheel which spun a gold thread on its own, and that Maria would sell for nothing less than a night with falcon Finister, the countess sent her back with a wave of her hand, 'Go and fetch the loom and the wheel! Tell the girl to come here again this evening, but she won't wake Finister!'

Poor Maria once again tried all night in vain to wake her beloved with sweet words of love. He slept like the dead, without flickering even an eyelid.

The only thing Maria now had left was the silver frame and the gold needle. She sat on the crystal doorstep of the crystal castle, while the needle embroidered a silk scarf with a gold thread all on its own. People ran to her side to witness this miracle. The countess again sent her maid to see what all the commotion was about. When she was told that Maria now had a silver frame with a silk scarf, which a gold needle was embroidering with a silver thread all on its own, and that Maria refused to sell except for one night with falcon Finister, the countess laughed and said, 'Go and bring the silver frame and the gold needle! I will gladly leave her another night with Finister. After all, it will be the last time, for tomorrow is our wedding day.'

The unhappy Maria spent the last night with Finister. In vain she tried to wake her beloved with sweet words of love. Finister slept like the dead. When dawn was breaking and the night ending, Maria burst into tears and one of her tears dropped on Finister's forehead. Then something incredible and wonderful happened. As the tear touched his white forehead, Finister moved, opened his eyes and looked at Maria. And he cried joyfully, 'So you found me after all, darling Maria! You have worn out three pairs of iron shoes, broken three iron walking sticks, torn three iron hats, and now broken the evil, magic spell.'

With that he kissed the happy Maria on her sweet lips.

A wedding was held that day. Finister was not marrying the wicked countess, but his kind, gentle Maria. It was a truly happy wedding, because true love had won. So this tale has a happy ending after all.

Flagstaff, Fatso and Big-eyes

There was once a powerful king whose daughter was so beautiful that people talked about her beauty far and wide. Many princes came to ask for her hand, but the king said he would give his daughter only to the suitor who succeeded in guarding her for three nights without losing her. Several highborn lords had tried to win the princess in this way but she always managed to escape, and the lords were beheaded by the king for their pains.

Now, there was a prince in a neighbouring country who also wished to try his luck. It is true that his father had once been in some dispute with the princess's father many years before — indeed the incident had almost led to war — but that did not daunt the prince, and he set out for the king's palace. He travelled far and long until he came to a crossroads. An inn stood at the crossroads, and as it was growing dark the prince thought he would spend the night there.

The landlord brought his supper, and the prince was eating and drinking heartily when a ragged youth came to his table and asked for alms. The prince looked at him closely and said, 'How is it that you have to beg? A strong and healthy lad like you ought to be able to work!'

'I should like nothing better,' said the lad, 'but no one will give me work.'

The prince wondered how this could be, and the lad told him, 'They call me Flagstaff and people are afraid of me because of my height.'

'Come, come!' exclaimed the prince. 'This is a poor excuse when I can plainly see that you are no taller than other folk!'

'Not now, sir,' said the lad, 'but if I wish to, I can grow immensely tall.'

'You must show me how you can do such a thing!' cried the prince, but the lad explained that the inn was not high enough. 'I will gladly give a demonstration outside,' he said. So together they went outside. Immediately, the lad struck his legs with a small whip and, before the prince's eyes, began to grow so tall that the maple tree in front of the inn scarcely came up to his knees.

At first, the prince was too amazed to speak but then he laughed and declared, 'Upon my word, the name of Flagstaff fits you well. But I like you, and I will give you a job. I will supply you with money, food and clothes, for who knows, I might yet need your services! Now shrink back to your ordinary height and let us go back into the inn. I will see that you get a decent supper!'

When the youth had shrunk back to normal, the prince led him inside and ordered him a large supper. But no sooner had they sat down to the meal than the door opened and another youth came to beg at the prince's table. The prince grew angry and shouted at him, 'Can you not find yourself some honest work? What a disgrace to see a strong lad like you going around begging!'

'Believe me, my lord,' said the youth, 'if I could find a place I should not be begging.'

'And why can you not find a place?' demanded the prince.

'Because no one will have me,' the young man replied. 'They say I am too fat and call me Fatso!'

'What nonsense!' cried the prince. 'I can see very well that you are no fatter than other folk.'

'Not at the moment, sir,' said the beggar. 'But if you will come outside with me, I will show you!'

So they went outside the inn. The youth held his breath for a moment and his stomach grew so fast that the prince was scarcely able to get out of its way.

'Upon my word,' smiled the prince, 'Fatso you are! I will take you into my service. You shall have money, food and clothes, for who knows, I might yet need your services!' As Fatso shrank back to his normal size, the prince led him inside and ordered a large supper for him.

Fatso ate a hearty meal, but no sooner had he finished than the door opened and yet another youth came in. In appearance, he was rather like Flagstaff and Fatso, and like them he came to beg for alms.

'Fancy a young and healthy lad like you going around begging,' fumed the prince, but the youth protested that all he wanted was to keep himself by honest work.

'Then why don't you?' asked the prince.

'Nobody will employ me,' answered the young man. 'They call me Big-eyes and they are afraid of my keen sight.'

'What balderdash!' exclaimed the prince. 'Your eyes are no more extraordinary than those of other folk.'

'Not now they aren't,' said the lad. 'But I can make them grow at will!' And he made his eyes pop until they filled the inn.

'Boy!' laughed the prince. 'I believe I need another freak! I will take you into my service. You shall have money, food and clothes, for who knows, I may yet need your services!' And the prince told the landlord to bring a large supper for Big-eyes. He sat talking with his new servants for a while and afterwards they went to bed in a clean and comfortable room.

In the morning the prince and his three servants went to the palace, where the prince requested the king to allow him to stand guard over the princess for three nights. He would not tell the king where he had come from, nor give his name, saying only that he would tell the king everything if he succeeded in his task.

The king agreed and introduced him to the princess who took the prince's fancy straight away. She must have liked him, too, for she gave him a sidelong glance of approval, and no wonder, since he was truly handsome.

The king asked the prince to attend a banquet in the palace and gave him the place of honour beside the lovely princess. After the feast, there was dancing until late in the evening and, when it was over, the king took the prince to the princess's bedchamber and bade him guard her well. 'If the princess escapes from you,' he warned, 'you shall forfeit your life!' The prince then asked permission to keep his three servants at his side and this was willingly given.

As soon as they were alone, the prince told his three men to keep a sharp look-out. Flagstaff stretched out on the floor across the length of the chamber; Fatso covered the door; and Big-eyes stood at the window. The prince paced the floor between them. The princess was lying in her bed and appeared to be fast asleep. Towards midnight, the prince's eyes grew heavy and he sat down on a chair to rest a little. Alas, when he awoke the princess was gone!

Flagstaff and Fatso sprang to their feet, looking ashamed, for they, too, had slept, but Big-eyes had not slept and now he said, 'Fear not, my lord, I know where the princess is! I saw her change into a wild duck. She flew out of the window and is now sitting in the middle of a lake fifty miles from here.'

'Ah, but how shall we get her back by morning if she is so far away?' wailed the prince.

'That should not be too difficult,' smiled Flagstaff. So they all left the palace. Once they were outside, Flagstaff stretched out to his full height and took the prince, Fatso and Big-eyes on his back. Ten giant steps brought them to the lake.

In the middle of the lake, the prince saw the duck, and he sighed in despair at the thought that he must capture her, for the lake was wide and deep and the duck darted like an arrow about the surface, diving below from time to time.

Without a word, Fatso lay down by the shore and began to suck up the water. Very soon he had drunk the lake dry and the duck was flapping about in deep mud. Then Flagstaff raised himself to his full height and stretched out an arm. He caught the duck easily and handed her to the prince. As soon as the prince touched her feathers, she changed back into the princess. Overjoyed, the young man took her in his arms, whilst Fatso filled the lake with water. Then Flagstaff took all four on his back, and carried them back to the palace.

Then they all took up their posts again, and the prince did not take his eyes off the princess for a second.

When day dawned, the king's chamberlain came into the room, and upon seeing the princess sleeping soundly in her bed, hurried to tell the king the news. There was great rejoicing in the palace all that day and, in the evening, the king again took the prince to the princess's bedchamber and warned him to keep a good watch. As the king had left, the prince told his servants, 'I will be more careful tonight and make sure that I do not fall asleep.'

He managed to stay awake until midnight, but upon the twelfth stroke his eyes shut and he dozed off. Sure enough, when he awoke the princess had gone.

The prince was in despair as he gazed at the empty bed.

'Have no fear, my lord,' said Big-eyes. 'I know where the princess is. She changed herself into an apple and lies at the bottom of a well a hundred miles away.'

'A hundred miles! Is that all!' exclaimed Flagstaff. 'Be calm, sire, we shall soon be there!'

Flagstaff then bade the three climb on his back and, in twenty paces, he deposited them by the well.

'Now, it is my turn!' said Fatso. And he lay down at the lip of the well, took five deep swigs of water, and the well was dry. Then Flagstaff stretched out his arm and brought up an apple which turned into the princess as soon as the prince held it in his hand.

The prince was overjoyed and the princess, too, was glad that they had found her, for she dearly wished to be won by the prince. As before, Flagstaff took them on his back to carry them homewards. Before they came to the palace, however, Fatso filled a small valley they were passing through with the water he had sucked up from the well. Once inside the palace, each took up his station, and the prince kept a close watch on the princess, but she slept peacefully until morning.

At daybreak, the chamberlain could hardly believe his eyes when he saw the princess lying in her bed. The king, too, was amazed, and again there was feasting throughout the day. That evening everything happened as before. The king led the prince to the bedchamber and bade him guard the princess well, if he valued his life. The three servants lay down and the prince paced the floor. Alas, he fell asleep, and when he awoke, the princess was gone!

Big-eyes consoled the unhappy prince, saying, 'Have no fear, my lord, I know where she has gone. She changed herself into a needle and flew as straight as an arrow for two hundred miles before coming to rest in an old oak tree.'

'It will not take me long to get there,' said Flagstaff. He sat down on the window ledge, so that his feet touched the courtyard below and lifted the others upon his back. Forty paces or less brought them under the oak tree.

Now, although Big-eyes had watched the needle fly into the tree, he had no idea where it had come to rest. So Fatso said, 'There is nothing for it but to eat the whole tree! I shall have to take big bites, of course, but you must listen well if you are to hear the needle scrape against my teeth.'

The prince wanted to help, and he began chewing some of the leaves.

'Leave it to me, my lord,' said Fatso, 'this is my job!' He started on the branches, biting and chewing them to pulp, then he devoured the trunk, but there was no trace of a needle. Finally, he tackled the roots, and only when he was chewing the last thin fibre did the needle scrape against his teeth. Quickly, he pulled it out of his mouth and passed it to the prince in whose hand it turned into the princess. How happy they were to think that they would soon be man and wife!

For the third time Flagstaff set them on his back, but Fatso was now terribly heavy after eating up the huge tree, so when they came to a deep crevice he spat out the tree and his stomach shrank back to normal again. They arrived at the palace just before dawn, and the princess had hardly lain down in her bed when the chamberlain entered the room. Seeing the princess in bed, he hurried off to tell the king the good news.

The king summoned the prince and thanked him for breaking the spell, and only then did the prince tell him his name. The king pretended that he was pleased but was secretly enraged that his daughter was going to marry the son of his ancient enemy, and he made up his mind that there should be no wedding.

Now, the princess knew very well what was going on in her father's mind, and she warned the prince to be on his guard. When the feasting before the wedding ceremony was over, the prince and princess approached the king's throne to ask the king for his blessing. There was a strange smile on the king's face as he said to the prince, 'My blessing shall be yours, of course, but not before I entertain you royally. Twenty-four fattened oxen will be roasted on the spit for you and my daughter and your three servants. They must be eaten in a day and a night. To wash the meat down twenty-four casks of wine will be provided. If you fail to eat the meat or drink the wine, the wedding will not take place and you will not leave the palace alive!'

The princess wept and entreated her father to relent, but the king pushed her aside, and ordered his servants to kill and prepare the oxen and have them roasted in the courtyard. Huge fires were lit and all twenty-four oxen were roasted before the prince's eyes.

Flagstaff took it upon himself to carve the meat and the prince and princess were given the choicest cuts, but all they managed to eat weighed less than a pound. Flagstaff himself ate up one whole ox and drank a cask of wine, and Big-eyes ate all the ox tongues.

When the prince saw how little meat and wine were gone he grew worried but Fatso laughed and said, 'Have no fear, my lord, I shall soon dispose of this little meal!' And he blew up his tummy until it rose higher than the palace roof.

Flagstaff passed him whole sides of beef and he swallowed them like peanuts, washing them down with caskfuls of wine. After a while all that remained in the courtyard were the horns of the oxen and the empty casks.

No sooner had Fatso finished the last cask than the princess said, 'Let us run away before my father thinks up another plot to destroy you!'

So Flagstaff took the prince and princess, as well as Fatso and Big-eyes, on his back and walked away from the palace.

The chamberlain went to the king and reported that the prince had succeeded in his task but that he had run away with the princess. Upon hearing this, the king grew very angry. He sent out his bravest soldiers on horseback with orders to capture the prince and princess and bring them back to the palace without delay.

The troops rode out of the palace and galloped away. The prince and princess and the three servants were resting in a wood when suddenly Big-eyes spoke up, 'My lord, there is an army of mounted soldiers on our tracks, and they are advancing fast. Indeed, they are only a mile away!'

The princess burst into tears but Fatso comforted her, 'Do not grieve yourself, my lady. Let Flagstaff carry you some distance and leave the soldiers to me.'

As the soldiers rode through the valley, Fatso lay down on the ground and opened his mouth. It gaped so wide that it blocked the valley.

All unsuspecting, the troops rode straight into Fatso's open mouth. Once inside, Fatso closed his mouth and got to his feet. As he did so, one of the soldiers, who had been delayed by his horse going lame, appeared.

'I don't intend to open my mouth once more because of one unimportant soldier!' exclaimed Fatso, when he saw him. 'You'd better turn round and ride back to your king so that you can tell him what has happened.'

The soldier galloped away so fast that sparks flew from his horse's hooves. Once in the king's presence, he reported the loss of his whole army. The king was horrified at the news. He locked himself up in a tower and admitted no one to his presence. Soon a small black cloud could be seen hovering over the tower. It grew and grew until it was a thick black thundercloud that darkened the sky until everything below was as black as midnight. All at once there was a single flash of lightning and when the cloud had scudded past, there was nothing but a heap of ashes in the place where the tower had stood! Not a trace could be found of the king.

Meanwhile Flagstaff carried the royal couple and his friends to the shores of a big lake. There Fatso lay down and released the king's army from his mouth straight into the water. The soldiers came scrambling ashore, and after they had formed themselves into ranks, the princess sent them home.

Then she went on with the prince and his servants until they came to the prince's castle.

The old king greeted his son and the lovely princess most warmly and preparations for their wedding were put in hand. After the bridal feast, news came that the princess's father had vanished and that his kingdom was now hers. The young couple united the two countries and ruled over them well and wisely. As for the prince's three servants, they lived happily in the castle for the rest of their days.

Toby and the Wolf

A young miller had a dog called Toby whom he had inherited from his father. The dog was getting on in years and had grown rather deaf, so he could no longer guard the house as well as he used to. The miller neglected Toby, and the servants took their cue from the miller. They kicked the dog whenever they saw him and often forgot to feed him.

Toby had such a hard time of it that he decided to leave the mill and try his luck in the woods. On the way he met a wolf who called to him, 'Hi, Brother Toby, where are you going?'

The dog told him what he had to put up with in the mill and that he could bear it no longer.

'Brother Toby,' said the wolf, 'for all your years you have little sense. Now, in your old age, you want to leave the mill and eke out a miserable living in the woods. When you were young, you twice saved the mill from burglars, and now you tell me you are shamefully treated. Take my advice and go back to the mill and see to it that the miller feeds you properly.'

'Brother Wolf,' said Toby, 'I would rather starve to death than go back there.'

'Don't be so hasty, Brother Toby,' said the wolf. 'We shall soon find a solution to your problem. Tomorrow, when the nursemaid comes to the field which the miller is harvesting, she is sure to be carrying the miller's baby son. As soon as she lays him down, I will creep up and carry him off. All you have to do is find my trail and follow it. I will leave the baby in the grass under the great oak tree for you to find. When you take him back to the miller he will receive you like a hero.'

The next day the maid went out to the field with food for the reapers. She also carried the miller's baby son in one arm. When she got to the field she laid the baby down on a sheaf and fell to talking and joking with the harvesters. The wolf crept up, seized the baby and ran off into the woods.

When the maid caught sight of the wolf running towards the wood with the baby in his mouth, she rushed after him, weeping and shouting for help, and not daring to go home without her master's child.

Meanwhile, the reapers had sent a boy back to the mill to tell the miller what had happened. Almost out of his mind with distress, the miller ran to get the hunter. Together, the pair went into the woods but before they had gone far, Toby appeared at the mill with the baby safely held in his mouth. The miller's wife ran out and with cries of joy she took the baby and put him in his cot. Then she stroked Toby's head and ordered that bread and milk be put down before him.

When the miller returned home and heard how Toby had rescued his son, he felt so ashamed that he had neglected the dog that he vowed Toby would have nothing but the best from then onwards.

As the story of the rescue spread Toby was given a hero's welcome wherever he went.

One day, the wolf came to see Toby as he sat in the sunshine at the back of the mill. 'You see, Brother, how well I counselled you,' the wolf began, 'you live in plenty now, so remember! One good deed for another! I have had nothing to eat all week and I need your help.'

Toby nodded. Then he said, 'Nothing easier, Brother Wolf. One of the maids is getting married tomorrow and the pantry is full of meat and pastry and other good things for the wedding feast. Let us wait until it grows dark; then we can enter the pantry by the back window and have a feast all to ourselves.'

That evening after dark, the two friends jumped through the pantry window. They feasted and drank all night until the wolf lost all caution. 'Brother Toby,' he shouted. 'I'm so happy, I feel like singing!'

'You'd better keep quiet and jump out of the window quickly,' warned Toby, 'or we shall both be discovered and punished.'

But the wolf would not listen to reason and raised his voice in a wild wolf howl which could be heard all over the house. The miller woke up and searched every room in the mill until he remembered that the food for the wedding feast was set out in the pantry. He went to look and found the wolf and Toby. Snatching a stick, he set about the two thieves, beating them until the hair flew from their coats.

The wolf managed to escape but the miller caught hold of Toby and chained him up. In the morning, the miller's wife begged her husband to let Toby off the chain, saying that he must have been led astray by the wolf. So the miller removed the chain but he warned Toby to keep away from the wolf.

Some time later, the wolf crept into the mill late one night to persuade Toby to take his revenge on the miller for the beating. Toby for his part told the wolf that the miller had a good shotgun and could easily shoot them dead. But the wolf persisted, bragging of his strength and cunning.

'Ah, Brother Toby,' said the wolf contemptuously, 'you talk like a coward. I am not going to leave here on an empty stomach. The miller has a fat old ram. For old times' sake, I want you to drive it out of the flock for me. In that way, I can kill it easily, and have a good supper without much trouble.'

Toby remembered how the miller had warned him against the wolf. He knew he had a good life at the mill, and he had no wish to throw it away. But when he saw how angry the wolf was getting, he grew afraid of him and said, 'Brother Wolf, the ram would surely bleat and the miller will come. You must wait in front of the sheep pen with your mouth open. When I drive the ram out, you must seize him by the head to keep him from bleating and drag him off to the woods immediately.'

The wolf liked this plan and took up his post outside the sheep pen. Toby jumped inside and drove the big, strong ram towards the waiting wolf. The ram butted the wolf's flank and the wolf turned a somersault and lay in the yard unable to move. He groaned and cried, 'Brother Toby, the ram has knocked the breath out of my body. I will have no more truck with him!'

The miller heard the wolf howling; he saw the ram in the yard and the wolf at the gate of the sheep pen. He grabbed his gun and fired at the wolf, but the shot missed and the wolf managed to drag himself away.

Toby lay in his kennel, pleased at the way things had turned out. He made up his mind never to listen to the wolf again. But a few days later, the wolf came again to the mill to see Toby. 'We must make the miller suffer for shooting at me,' he said. 'Three pellets are lodged in my fur, and, to get even with him, I intend destroying his favourite colt.'

Toby begged the wolf to give up his plan, saying that he would take no part in the wolf's revenge. The wolf bared his fangs at Toby. 'I will fall upon you and sink my teeth into your throat if you refuse to help me,' he threatened. 'Do as I tell you at once or you will never leave this spot alive. Drive the colt out of the stable so that I can fall upon it.'

The yard was deserted and Toby knew that by himself he could never outwit the wolf or fight him off. So he went into the stable, untied the young horse and quietly called to the wolf, 'Brother Wolf, be sure to bite the back legs first...'

The wolf obeyed, and the horse lashed out at him with all its strength which was just what Toby expected. The wolf jumped to one side, howling with pain and anger, for the colt's hooves had dealt him a severe blow. So much noise did he make that the miller heard him, and snatching up his shotgun, he rushed into the yard and shot the wolf dead.

Toby heaved a sigh of relief as he came out of the stable unharmed. Never again would the wolf bother him or lead him into mischief. For the rest of his life he could look forward to happy, contented days in the sunshine.

The Clever Cobbler

Once upon a time there lived a poor cobbler who had so many children that, try as he would, he could never feed them all. He had nowhere to turn for help and was ashamed to go begging. In time, he lost all hope and in desperation he took a rope and went into the woods to hang himself.

He selected a stout tree and was just about to fasten the rope to a branch when someone tapped him on the shoulder. The cobbler turned and saw a man in hunting clothes.

'What are you up to?' the stranger asked, and the cobbler glanced at the stranger's feet and saw that he had hoofs. He knew at once that he was talking to the devil. But he was undaunted and told the devil, 'I am going to strip bark from this tree to make a snare for devils, as is my custom.'

The stranger was taken aback for a moment. 'I can see that you have recognized me,' he said at last. 'Leave devils alone and I'll give you whatever you want.'

So the cobbler demanded as many ducats as the devil could carry on his back. The devil disappeared and the next instant a heavy sack fell on the ground at the cobbler's feet. He looked into the sack to make sure the devil had not cheated him and found it was stuffed with ducats. Then he dragged it into the bushes, thinking he would fetch his wife to help him load the sack on to a wheelbarrow and trundle it home.

Meanwhile, the devil had returned to hell where he told the story to the other devils. Now Lucifer, chief of all devils, became very angry and shouted, 'You gave the cobbler a great deal more than you need have done. Go back at once and tell him that he must defeat you in a fair fight before the money becomes his. Of course, he will lose! If you return here without the sack, I will throw you into the fiery lake!'

There was nothing left for the devil to do but to fly out of hell as fast as he could, and he caught up with the cobbler at the edge of the woods. 'Listen, cobbler,' he said, 'I gave you too much! You must join me in single combat, and whichever of us wins the fight will keep the money.'

The cobbler was wondering how best to answer this challenge when he remembered that a fierce bear had its lair in a rock nearby. He led the devil to the rock and said, 'This is where my grandfather lives. He is ninety years old and will scarcely be a match for you. But I want you to fight him first and if you overcome him, I am sure you will be able to defeat me too.'

The devil promptly crawled into the lair, and the bear came charging out at him with a roar. With its heavy paws, it knocked the devil to the ground. When the devil finally escaped he flew back to hell as fast as his wings would take him. 'I was lucky to escape fighting that Christian,' he told Lucifer. 'Why, even his ninety-year-old grandfather nearly knocked my brains out!'

'Fool!' roared Lucifer, 'you let yourself be tricked! For that I will throw you into the fiery lake!'

Lucifer then chose another devil and commanded him to fly to earth and challenge the cobbler to a race, the winner of which would keep the sack. The cobbler had scarcely moved away from the bear's rock, when he was confronted by this second devil who was certainly more cunning than the first.

'Those ducats are not yet yours!' shouted the devil. 'We must have a race first, and whichever of us is faster keeps the sack!' 'It's all the same to me,' said the cobbler with a show of indifference. 'Let us race by all means. But first you must show me how fast you can run and I will decide whether you are a worthy competitor for me!'

Now the cobbler had done a good deal of poaching in his time and so he knew where an old hare had its warren. As he spoke, he noticed the hare sitting in a furrow and told the devil, 'Look, over there in that field lies my son Janek. He was born but a week ago but he is going to be a fair runner. If you are faster than he, I reckon you will defeat me too!'

They approached the hare and the devil cried, 'Come on, Janek, get up, we are going to have a race!'

The hare leapt into the air and without waiting for the devil to take up his starting position, it raced across the field, up the slope into a thicket of thorns, and doubling in its tracks, flew down the hill and into a swampy meadow, at the bottom of which it jumped a brook and disappeared into the woods.

The devil dashed after it, his tongue hanging out. He got scratched by the thorns, fell into the bog and when he tried to jump the brook, he slipped and splash! fell into the water.

Out of breath, scratched and soaked to the skin, the devil flew back to hell and reported to Lucifer, 'I was lucky to escape racing against that Christian. Why, even his week-old son outran me!'

Lucifer was furious to find that the second devil, too, had let himself be tricked, and he had him thrown into the fiery lake in punishment.

Then he sent a third devil to earth with orders to bring back the sack of ducats. The cobbler was just making for the bushes where the money was hidden, when the third devil appeared before him.

'You got more money than you deserved,' said the third devil. 'Now you must prove that you are stronger than I am in order to keep the ducats. We shall each lift a horse upon our backs and whoever manages to carry it three times round this wood wins the money.'

The cobbler looked about him and saw some horses grazing in a field on the edge of the wood. 'There are our horses,' he told the devil, 'but you try first so that I can make sure you are not tricking me.'

The devil picked up a horse and loaded it on his back. He got twice round the wood but had to pause to regain his breath before starting again.

The cobbler was quick to take his advantage and said, 'You do not seem so very strong to me, oh devil! You had to pause for breath and you were only carrying the horse on your back. Now look at me! I will grip the beast between my thighs and squeeze it like pincers, you just watch me!'

The cobbler jumped on to the horse's back, whipped it over the rump with a hazel switch and swiftly rode three times round the wood. The devil ran after them, and when the cobbler started on the third round, the devil was wheezing with exertion, his tongue hanging out. Without waiting for the cobbler to dismount, he went flying off to hell, defeated.

He flew straight to Lucifer and reported how he had fared. 'I was lucky to escape with my life! I carried the horse on my back and had to rest to regain my breath, whereas that Christian squeezed the horse between his knees and raced it around the wood three times without stopping!'

'Fool, you let yourself be tricked!' Lucifer snarled. 'For that you shall be thrown into the fiery lake!' Then Lucifer called the oldest devils to his side and together they selected one of the younger devils whom they decided was by far the most cunning and sent him to earth.

The cobbler had taken the horse back to the pasture and was just returning when yet another devil stood before him. 'I challenge you to one last contest,' said the devil. 'Whichever of us whistles the loudest gets the money!'

'I do not know how to whistle,' said the cobbler, 'but I should like to hear you try.' The devil gave a shrill whistle and the leaves came fluttering from the trees. He whistled a second time and whole twigs broke off the trees, and at his third whistle the branches cracked and crashed down.

'Well, I can't say you haven't tried!' smiled the cobbler indulgently. 'But that will not do, of course. Wait till I give a whistle and you will see how the blast tears the trees up by the roots. You are still fairly young, as devils go, and the blast might blind you, so I advise you to cover your eyes.'

'I am glad that you warned me,' said the devil. 'Will you please blindfold me?'

The devil remained still while the cobbler blindfolded him; then the latter chose a strong branch, gave a whistle and stretching himself, hit the devil over the head with the branch until he leapt into the air and howled like a wolf.

'There you are,' said the cobbler calmly. 'Didn't I tell you my whistle would tear up the trees by their roots?'

'I don't think you need whistle a second time,' said the devil, but the cobbler told him, 'I'm sorry but I must. You whistled three times and so must I or else the contest would not be fair!'

He stretched again and hit the blindfolded devil over the head until he spun around like a top; he followed this with a third blow so fierce that it made the devil scream and fly off to hell without waiting to see if any trees had been torn up by the roots.

Lucifer was enraged when his devil made his report, but he could find no others to send to earth, so he had to let the cobbler keep the money.

Hard times were over now. The cobbler's wife bought flour, dried peas, barley and other groceries, and the cobbler went to town to buy himself a fair supply of leather. Then he set to work and, henceforth, he and his family lived in comfortable security for the rest of their days.

The Disobedient Princess

There was once a king with a lovely but disobedient daughter whom he wished to marry to a prince of his own choosing, but when the princess saw her suitor she took a dislike to him, and told her father angrily that she would not marry him, or any other! At these words, the king grew so angry that he locked up his daughter in a secret chamber in his palace, and then made it known that whoever succeeded in finding her should have her for his wife. Those who failed to discover her hiding-place would be thrown into a dungeon and remain there until the princess was discovered.

Now the king of a neighbouring country had three brave and handsome sons, the eldest of whom decided that he would try to find the princess. His father gave him a fine horse and a bag of ducats and wished him luck.

The prince saddled his horse and rode off towards the palace. When he got there, he presented himself to the king and told him why he had come. He was received kindly and invited to sit at the king's table. After they had eaten, the king told the prince, 'You had better rest today and tackle your task tomorrow. If you find my daughter, who is hidden in this palace, you will have her for your bride. Begin your search at sunrise, and remember that if you fail to discover her hiding-place by sunset, you will be thrown into the dungeon. Think well how you will dress and equip yourself, for your welfare may depend on it!'

The prince promised to do his best, saying that he would not grumble at his punishment if he failed. The king's chamberlain showed him to a splendid chamber and all that day he rested. Next morning, he got up at dawn and began his search as soon as the sun was high in the sky.

Upstairs and downstairs he went, searching every room from cellar to attic as well as all the chambers in the tower, but no trace could be found of the princess. So when the sun had set, he went to the king with a heavy heart and reported that his search had been in vain. The king had him thrown into the dungeon without further ado, and then sat down to write a letter to the prince's father, informing him of what had happened.

'Do let me go, Father,' begged the prince's second brother, after his father had read the dreadful contents of the letter, 'for I might win the princess and set my brother free as well.' The king turned the matter over in his mind and at last agreed, in the hope that both his sons might return to him safely.

He gave his second son a splendid horse and a bag of ducats and warned him to be careful. The prince rode off to the palace where he was as well received as his brother had been. Everything happened as before: the prince searched for the hidden princess from sunrise to sundown, and when he failed to find her, he was locked in a dungeon, and a letter was sent telling of his fate.

Now, the youngest prince could not rest at the thought of the terrible fate of his two brothers, and he made up his mind to set them free. He went on his knees before his father, begging to be allowed to go to the palace of the hidden princess.

'You can put that thought out of your head!' thundered the king. 'Do you want me to spend my old age deserted and alone, with all three of my sons languishing in dungeons?'

'Oh, Father,' cried the prince, 'how can I continue to live a life of ease when my two brothers suffer?' At this, the king, sorrowfully gave his consent, saying, 'My son, I give you my blessing. Go, and do what you can to rescue your brothers.'

Now, the prince was skilled at playing the concertina, having learned the art from a clever musician who was both extraordinarily gifted and wise. To this musician, he went for advice, and together they hatched a plan. The prince was to set out with his servant, a large bear skin and his concertina, and after his father had provided two horses, and a bag of gold, the prince and his servant departed.

As they drew close to the palace, they left their horses in the care of an old hermit and continued on foot. The servant disguised himself as a bear-master, leading the prince, who now wore the bear skin. One warm summer's day, they approached the palace. Sentries barred their way, whereupon the bear raised himself on his hind-legs and began to play the concertina with his front paws! This so amused the sentries that they allowed the bear-leader to pass through the palace gates, and even conducted him to the windows of the royal banqueting hall. Presently, as the bear played on, the king, who was fond of music, looked out of the window.

When he saw that it was a bear who played the concertina, he roared with laughter, and calling his courtiers to the window, he ordered a footman to bring both master and bear to the dining hall.

As the bear played and danced, the king was so charmed and amused that he rewarded his master with a handful of gold coins and ordered food and drink to be set before him, at the same time instructing that the bear too should be fed.

Later that day, the king sent for the bear and its master saying, 'I have a daughter who is ill, it might divert her to see your beast play the concertina. How much do you want to make him play for her? Name the sum and I will gladly pay it!'

'Your Majesty, you have paid me enough already,' answered the bear's master. 'It will be an honour to display my clever bear to the princess.'

The king gave him another handful of gold coins and guided him and the bear to the princess's chamber. Through his bear skin, the prince was able to take careful note of the way they were going. First, the king led them down a very long narrow passage, at the end of which he stopped. Before him was a picture of a town of many buildings with tall spires. The prince saw the king press one of these spires with his finger and immediately the picture swung aside under his touch — revealing the entrance to a spacious chamber, and there sat the princess, alone and seemingly very sad.

She started at the sight of the bear, but the king calmed her fears, saying, 'Don't be frightened, child, this bear will entertain you for a while.'

The bear's master clapped his hands and at the signal the bear raised himself on his hind-legs and began to play and dance. At the sight of the musical bear, the princess began to smile and finally begged to be allowed to keep the bear with her for the afternoon.

For a while the bear went on playing and dancing, but all at once he spoke in a human voice, 'Do not be alarmed, princess, I am a royal prince, come to set you free and win your hand in marriage!'

The princess cried out in sudden fear, so startled was she to hear a bear speak. But the bear spoke again and so calm and gentle was his manner that the princess was reassured.

'Cut open the skin,' the prince told her, 'for it is no more than a fancy dress disguise.' Smiling now, the princess obeyed and at the sight of the handsome youth, she blushed and said she would willingly be his bride if he could convince her father that he had passed the test. Then the princess helped the prince back into his bear skin so that when her father came to the chamber, he saw only the bear amusing his daughter.

'Did you enjoy the performance, my child?' asked the king, and the princess smiled and said that the bear was indeed a most amusing creature.

The king led the bear out of the chamber, locking the door behind him, and took him back to his master, to whom he gave a rich reward. Then the master and the bear left the palace.

When the town was well behind them, the prince stepped out of the bear's skin, and the servant filled it with stones and threw it into the river. Then the prince and servant recovered their horses from the hermit and rode swiftly back to the town they had so recently left.

The prince was now dressed in a splendid suit, and looked every inch a royal personage. Just on the town's boundary they stopped at an inn where they took a room for the night.

Next morning, the prince left his servant behind at the inn and rode off towards the king's palace. He was soon admitted to the king's presence, and speaking with bold assurance, he enquired about his two brothers and said he wished to search for the princess.

The king invited him to share his meal, saying, 'Your brothers failed in their task. Let us hope that you will succeed. You had better rest after your journey and tomorrow you may search for my daughter from sunrise till sunset. But if you do not find her, you will join your brothers in the dungeon!'

The prince spent the rest of the day at ease and slept soundly that night. In the morning, he rose early and began his search as the sun rose in the sky. He thought he remembered the passage the king had taken the day before, but the palace was large and full of passages and he wandered from one to another unable to find the right one. Down one passage after another he ran, until he was exhausted. The sun was just beginning to set when, more by accident than design, he stumbled upon the right passage, at the end of which hung the picture of the town. Anxiously, the prince looked at the tall spires, and once again his memory played him false. He could not remember which one the king had touched. He pressed them all, one after the other in frantic haste and not until his finger rested on the very last, did the secret door to the princess's chamber swing open.

Joyfully, the prince took the princess by the hand and together they hurried to the king, who sat waiting in his throne room. The prince bowed low before him, and the princess begged her father to forgive her former disobedience.

'I will gladly forgive your disobedience,' said the king, 'for you have suffered enough. But I must keep my royal promise. You must marry the prince who found you.'

This pleased the princess, for she had already given her heart to the courageous prince, and on seeing her joy, the king graciously set free the prince's two brothers.

All over the land, the people rejoiced to know that their king was now at peace with his daughter and himself, and many sent gifts to the princess and her handsome prince.

The royal pair lived happily together for more years than I care to remember, and in time, the two kingdoms were united, which greatly benefited the people.

As for the princess, who now reigned as queen, she saw to it that her own daughter learned quickly to love and respect her parents and be obedient in all things.

The Devil and Kate

In a certain village there once lived a young woman called Kate. She had a small cottage, a garden, and just a little money. But had she been the richest woman in the country, I doubt that the poorest farm boy would have thought of marrying her, for she was a scold and a nagger. And yet she was very sad that the boys avoided her so, and on Sundays, when there was fun and music, nobody ever came and asked her for a dance.

One Sunday, while she was sitting in the inn and watching the dancers, Kate thought to herself in anger, 'God knows, today I'd even dance with the devil, if he'd ask me.'

At that moment the door opened and in came a gentleman dressed like a hunter. He sat down, not far from Kate, and ordered a drink. When they brought him beer, he took the glass and offered it to Kate. Kate felt very honoured, and after feigning shyness for a while, she took the glass and drank. Then the man pulled a ducat out of his pocket, threw it to the bagpiper, and shouted out for all to hear:

'Now then, lads, you're playing for me!' And he led Kate into the dance.

'Whoever can *that* be?' wondered all the old men sitting round, doddering and wagging their heads. The boys grinned and the girls hid their faces, covering their mouths with their aprons so that Kate wouldn't see that they were laughing. But Kate saw no one: she was happy to be dancing, and the whole world could laugh at her if it liked.

The man danced with Kate all the afternoon and evening. He bought her marzipan and sweets, and when it was time to be going home, he took her arm and walked with her through the village.

'If only I could dance with you like that for ever,' whispered Kate, when he was about to take his leave.

'Well, that's quite easy: just come with me!'

'But where do you come from?' asked Kate.

'Just put your arms round my neck, you'll soon find out.'

Kate caught the hunter round the neck, and at that moment he became a devil, and off he flew with her to hell!

When they arrived at the gates of hell, the devil knocked and his friends came and opened up. They saw he was quite exhausted, and wanted to help him by lifting Kate down. But she clung to him tight, like a leech, and nothing could persuade her to let go. So like it or not the devil was still carrying her round his neck when he went to report to Lucifer himself.

'Who have you there?' growled Lucifer, frowning.

And the devil told him what had happened up on earth, how Kate had asked him to dance with her for ever, and how he had carried her off to hell.

'And now she won't leave me alone, and I don't know what to do with her.'

'You are an idiot, and you deserve no better,' snarled Lucifer. 'Before you start to meddle with humans, you must know what they are really like. It is true that Kate is sharp-tongued, but otherwise she is honest, and hell is not the place for her. Take her back where you found her — though how you get rid of her is *your* problem!'

The devil was dreadfully mortified. He flew back to earth carrying Kate. He promised her the keys of heaven, everything he could think of, if only she'd let him go. Then he cursed her, but that was no use either. Exhausted and miserable he reached a meadow where a young shepherd in an old sheepskin coat was pasturing a flock of sheep. The devil took the form of a human, so that the shepherd didn't recognize him.

'What's that on your back, friend?' asked the shepherd.

'Oh, help me, for I can scarcely breathe! Just imagine: I was walking along, minding my own business, and suddenly this Kate springs up round my neck, and won't let go of me for love or money.'

'Well, I don't mind helping,' replied the shepherd, 'if you'll just watch my sheep for me for a moment.'

'Gladly, sir, gladly,' said the devil.

'All right, love, come and catch hold of me instead!' shouted the shepherd to Kate.

And Kate, hearing this, let go of the devil and grabbed the shepherd by his big sheepskin coat. The boy carried her to the edge of a nearby pond. There he stopped and pulled one arm out of his coat sleeve — Kate didn't budge. Then he pulled out the other, undid one button, then another, and there was Kate swimming in the pond, along with the coat. In half a minute the shepherd was back.

'Thank you, shepherd,' said the devil, delighted. 'Truly you've done me a noble service, otherwise I'd have been carrying Kate till Judgement Day. One day I shall bring you a rich reward. But so that you know whom you have helped in need, I'll tell you: I am really a devil.' And so saying, he vanished.

The shepherd shook his head slowly and said, 'If they're all as stupid as that one, we've got nothing to worry about!'

Now, the land where this shepherd lived was ruled over by a young prince. He had immense riches but he spent them foolishly: every night the sound of noisy drunken parties could be heard at the palace. The land itself was governed by two ministers, who were certainly no better than their master. What he didn't spend, they hoarded for themselves, and the poor people of the country could hardly pay the taxes.

One day, when the prince could think of nothing better to do, he summoned a famous astrologer and ordered him to read the horoscopes of himself and his two ministers. The astrologer dutifully obeyed, and examined the stars carefully to see what the future would bring for the three of them.

When he had finished he turned to the prince, saying, 'Forgive me, your Highness, but I have discovered that your life and the lives of your ministers are in the gravest danger. I am afraid even to put it into words.'

'You must tell me the truth, whatever it is,' said the prince, 'but I give you fair warning: if these prove to be mere stories, I'll see to it that your head is chopped off.'

'Fair enough,' said the astrologer, 'I accept your conditions. Now listen! Before the second quarter of the moon is up, the devil will come for your two ministers. As soon as the moon is full he will come for you too, and he'll carry all three of you off to hell.'

The prince was much distressed by this awful forecast, and he ordered the astrologer to be thrown into prison. But neither he nor the ministers could enjoy themselves any more. For the first time their consciences started to worry them. Half dead with fear the two ministers rode off to their castles, and the prince himself tried to live a better life. He stopped holding parties, halved the taxes, and started treating his people better, in the hope that his cruel fate might yet be reversed.

Now, one day, about this time, the devil came and visited the shepherd again, and said to him, 'I've come to reward you, shepherd, for what you did for me. By the time the first two quarters of the moon are up, I am supposed to carry off the ministers of this land to hell, because they have robbed the poor and advised the prince falsely. But as I see they are trying to make amends, I am going to let them stay here at least for a while. But in doing so, I can make your fortune. Next Tuesday you must go to the first minister's castle, and there you'll find a crowd of people gathered. When I am about to take him away, come up to me and shout out roughly, "Be off with you, devil, or you'll regret it!" I'll obey you, and leave the minister lying there. That should be worth at least two sacks of ducats in reward! And then we'll do the same at the second castle. But when the moon is full, however, I really shall come and carry off the prince, so don't come and try to save him, for that would be the end of you.' Having said that, he vanished.

The shepherd took note of every word. At the first quarter of the moon, he left his flock, and went off to the first minister's castle. He arrived there just in the nick of time. The place was overflowing with people, and they were waiting to see the devil take their master away. Just at that moment a terrible shriek was heard. The gates were flung open and the devil dragged out the minister, who was terrified and as white as a sheet. The shepherd marched bravely up to them and shouted:

'Be off with you, devil, or you'll regret it!'

And the devil ran off, as he had promised. The minister, of course, was beside himself with relief, and he gave the shepherd his ducats without a word. The shepherd then went cheerfully on to the second castle, and did his job there just as successfully.

Naturally enough, the prince soon learned how the lives of his two ministers had been saved. He at once dispatched a coach-and-four for the shepherd, and when the shepherd arrived at the castle, begged him fervently to have mercy on him and free him from the claws of the devil too.

'Your highness, I'm afraid I can promise you nothing. You have been a great sinner. But if you honestly wish to make amends and mean to administer your lands justly, generously, and wisely, as befits a prince, I'll try and see what I can do, even if I have to go to hell in your place.'

The prince promised faithfully that he would do all that and more, and the shepherd went off, thinking he must work out something really cunning for the devil.

When the moon was full, the castle forecourt filled with people. They were all arguing as to whether the devil would carry off the prince, or whether the shepherd would be able to save him. And suddenly the gates of the castle opened, and everyone saw the devil dragging out the prince, now scared, and as white as a sheet. But just at that moment the shepherd pushed his way through the crowd and went straight up to the devil.

'Don't you remember what I told you?' whispered the devil angrily to the shepherd.

'You fool, it's not the prince I'm worried about, it's you,' said the shepherd. 'Kate is here and she's looking for you!'

On hearing this the devil dropped the prince, swore an oath, and vanished like smoke. The prince, of course, was so relieved that he appointed the shepherd to be his chief counsellor, and the shepherd advised him well and wisely. He was just and fair, and under his rule the people prospered and lived happily. Why, I did hear that even Kate found a husband!

Golden-curls
and How She Kept Silent

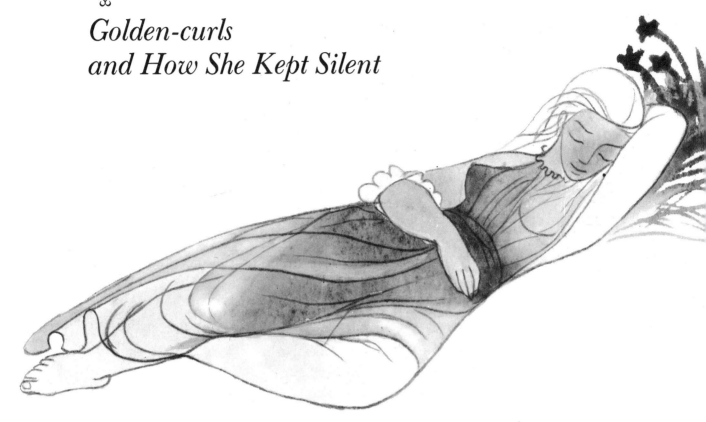

Once upon a time there was a very poor blacksmith whose worldly possessions were a tumbledown cottage, a wife, a troupe of hungry children, and otherwise nothing but seven pence. So with these seven pence he bought himself a stout rope, and went into the forest to hang himself. He found a tall tree with a strong branch, threw the rope up over it and began to tie a knot. Suddenly a lady all in black stood before him, as if she had risen up out of the ground.

'Blacksmith, stop that at once!' she commanded.

The blacksmith was so frightened that he untied the rope, and the woman immediately disappeared. As soon as she was gone he began to tie the rope round the branch again.

But the lady in black reappeared instantly, waved a threatening finger at him and snapped, 'I told you to stop that, Blacksmith!'

Again the blacksmith untied the rope, and started to make his way home. But on the way he thought to himself, 'There's nothing left for me at home but to die of hunger anyway. I think I'd rather hang myself.'

So again he found a good tree for hanging himself, and tied the rope round a branch. But the lady in black was there at once, shaking with anger.

'Why won't you listen to me, Blacksmith?' she asked.

'What else should I do?' sighed the blacksmith. 'I and my family are going to starve, anyway.'

'You will not starve,' answered the lady in black, 'because I shall give you all the money you could possibly wish for. But in return you must give me that thing which you have at home, and yet know not that you have.'

The blacksmith could hardly believe his ears, or his eyes, when he saw the sack full of gold coins that the lady handed to him. He thanked her heartily and set off as fast as he could with the heavy sack.

'But don't forget your promise,' called the lady in black after him. 'That which you have at home, yet know not that you have, belongs to me. In seven years I shall come to claim it.'

'I know everything there is in my house,' laughed the blacksmith. 'If there's anything there I don't know about you're welcome to it.' And off he went.

When the blacksmith got home he counted out the sack of gold coins into a great heap. The family was overjoyed.

'Our little Golden-curls has brought us luck,' laughed the blacksmith's wife, and she showed her husband a beautiful little baby girl with golden hair and a golden star on her forehead. It was the blacksmith's baby daughter, who had just been born that day. The blacksmith was shocked and saddened. So that was the thing he had at home, which he had not known about!

Well, the years passed and Golden-curls grew into a beautiful little girl, the joy and the sorrow of her parents. On her seventh birthday a black coach stopped outside their cottage and the lady in black stepped from it.

'I have come for your little girl,' she said, took her hand and led her to the coach. The parents and the other children begged her to relent, but the woman was not to be moved. The sinister coachman cracked his whip and in a flash the carriage was gone.

They drove for a long, long time, through barren deserts and dark forests, until at last they reached a huge black castle. 'This castle is yours,' said the lady in black. 'It has one hundred rooms, all of which you may enter freely, except the hundredth one. Do not enter that, or great evil will befall you. Remember! In seven years' time I shall visit you again.' And with that the black lady drove away.

Golden-curls lived quite happily in the great black castle. She had her ninety-nine rooms, and she never so much as glanced at the hundredth. And the seven years passed in less than no time.

Exactly seven years to the day the lady in black returned in her carriage.

'Have you been into the hundredth room?' was the first thing she asked.

'No, I haven't,' replied Golden-curls honestly.

'You are a good, obedient girl. In seven years I will return again, and if you have still obeyed me, I will make you the happiest of girls. But if you step inside that hundredth room, a fate more terrible than death will await you.'

With this threat the lady in black rode off again for another seven years.

The seven years passed quickly, and the day came for the lady in black to return. Golden-curls could hardly wait, for she was sure she would be rewarded in some marvellous way for her obedience. Then suddenly she heard strange and beautiful music.

'Who can be playing so sweetly in my castle?' she wondered. Following the sounds up a twisty stone staircase, she came to the topmost room of the castle, the hundredth room, for that was where the music was playing. Without stopping to think she opened the door, and stood there staring, horrified at what she had done.

Inside, twelve men in black cowls were sitting round a great table, and a thirteenth man was standing looking down at her.

'Golden-curls, Golden-curls! What have you done?' he cried, and his voice echoed like thunder around the stone chamber.

Golden-curls was so terrified that her heart missed several beats.

'Whatever can I do?' she murmured.

'You must never, never, tell a soul what you have seen in this room. That is the only way you may find forgiveness for what you have done.'

Golden-curls closed the heavy door and went downstairs. Almost at once she heard the lady in black's carriage rattling up.

'What did you see in the hundredth room?' the woman snapped, who knew at once what had happened.

Golden-curls shook her head and said nothing.

'Very well! If it's dumb you are then dumb you shall stay! From this moment on you will be able to speak to no one but me.' And saying this the lady in black drove Golden-curls out of the castle.

Golden-curls walked until she could go no farther. She came to a beautiful green meadow, lay down on the grass and cried until she fell asleep.

Now it happened that the young king of that land, who was out hunting, passed by the meadow and saw Golden-curls lying there asleep. She was so beautiful that he at once fell in love with her, and he didn't mind at all that she was dumb. He took her to his palace where a few days later they were married. And thus Golden-curls became a queen.

She lived very happily at the castle, and before a year had passed a little boy was born to her, who also had golden hair and a golden star on his forehead. Everyone at the palace was delighted with their new prince.

But the very first night after the baby's birth, the terrible lady in black appeared at Golden-curls' bedside, and said in a cruel voice, 'Tell me what you saw in the hundredth room, or I'll kill your little son.'

Poor Golden-curls was terrified, but she remembered what the thirteenth man had said: that she must keep silent.

So she just shook her head.

Then the woman seized the little baby, strangled him, rubbed his blood on Golden-curls' lips, and vanished with the dead child.

In the morning everyone was horrified when they saw the blood on her face, and they wondered, 'Surely she couldn't have eaten him?'

But the king did not accuse her and no one else dared to, and Golden-curls still could not speak.

Another year passed and a little girl was born to Golden-curls. She too had golden hair and a golden star on her forehead. Everyone at the palace was delighted, but they were frightened too, lest the same terrible thing should happen as last time. So the king set a strong guard round Golden-curls' room, but to no avail.

During the night the lady in black appeared again and said, 'Tell me what you saw in the hundredth room or I'll kill the girl too.'

Golden-curls was quite beside herself with grief, but she still only shook her head. The woman strangled the little girl, rubbed blood on Golden-curls' lips, and vanished carrying the dead child.

Next day the palace was thrown into dismay by the news, and the king in a rage gave orders for Golden-curls to be burned at the stake. She wept and wept, but no one now felt the least bit sorry for her.

As they were leading her out beyond the city, the black carriage appeared again, and the lady in black stepped out of it.

'This is your last chance to tell me what you saw in the hundredth room,' she cried. 'Tell me or they will most certainly burn you alive.'

Golden-curls still just shook her head and said nothing.

The executioners tied Golden-curls to the stake and lit the fire beneath her. But as the flames were starting to lick at her feet, the lady in black suddenly became dressed in white, and called out, 'Put out the fire! Please, hurry!'

Everybody was astonished, but the executioners quickly doused the flames. The lady in white went to her carriage and out of it climbed a little boy and girl, both with golden hair and golden stars on their foreheads.

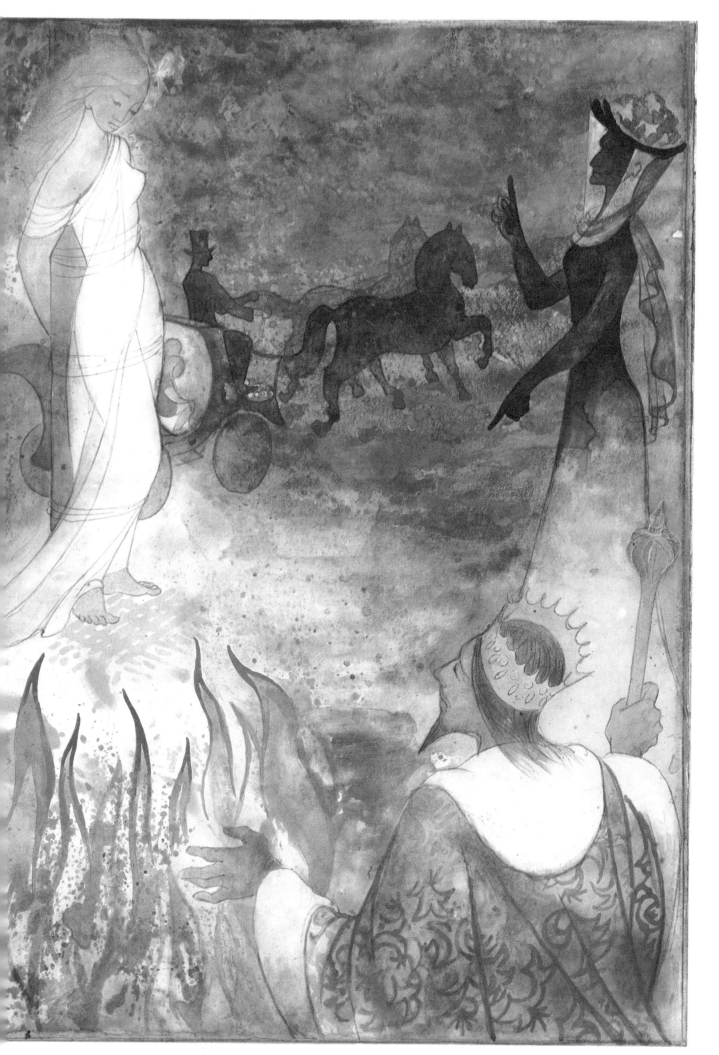

She brought them to Golden-curls, saying, 'By keeping silent so steadfastly, you have saved yourself and you have also saved me, by delivering me from a terrible enchantment.' With that she vanished.

Watching all this the king could hardly believe his eyes or ears, especially when Golden-curls finally spoke to him, and told him the whole strange story. They rode straight back to the palace, and lived there long and happily together. The old blacksmith, his wife and all his children came to live with them, and all were blessed with the greatest happiness and good fortune.

The Calf's Skin

There was once a man who had three daughters. One day he fell very ill. He asked for a glass of water from the nearby well, but the village folk had always said that this well was haunted.

'If only I could have some of that water,' he sighed, 'I know I'd get better.'

'I shall bring some for you,' said the eldest daughter, and she took a pitcher and went down to the well. But as she leaned over the edge she heard a voice from inside it say, 'You shall have no water from me unless you promise to be my wife.'

'That's absurd,' said the eldest daughter. 'I don't even know you.'

She went back and told her father, 'I'm sorry, but the well wouldn't give me any water.'

Then the second daughter said, 'Let me try,' and taking the pitcher she went down to the well. But she came back without any water either.

The father grew worse and worse, and so finally the youngest daughter went down to the well. The voice called up to her, 'You shall have no water unless you promise to be my wife.'

'I promise,' answered the girl without hesitating.

That evening a strange creature all wrapped in a calf's skin came to the house and knocked at the door. The youngest daughter opened it, but at the sight of this strangely dressed visitor she backed away in fright.

Then the stranger began to sing:

'My well is deep, my well is wide
Remember you promised to be my bride.'

So saying he threw off the calf's skin, and there in front of her stood the most handsome young man she had ever seen. He stayed until midnight, and when the church clock struck twelve he put on his calf's skin and returned to the well.

The following night he came again and knocked at the door. The youngest daughter ran to let him in, for she was already deeply in love with him. But the others hurried out of the room without waiting to see him.

When they were alone he threw off the calf's skin and again became a handsome young man. But he begged her not to tell anyone about this transformation.

However, the girl couldn't keep the secret, and she told her mother how her visitor took off the calf's skin every night and became a handsome young man. That evening the mother lit a great fire in the hearth, and, slipping into the room where the couple were, took the calf's skin and threw it into the flames. 'That'll stop him coming and going all the time,' she thought.

When the young man rose at midnight he could not find the calf's skin. At that moment the mother came into the room and explained what she had done. They pulled the calf's skin from the ashes, and although it had not burnt, it had shrunk so much that he could not put it on, no matter how hard they tried to stretch it.

Then the young man said, 'My love, I fear we must part: as a punishment I must go and live far from you, beyond the Red Sea. You will not be able to find me until you have broken an iron rod, worn out a pair of iron shoes and with your tears have filled an iron bowl.'

Sorrowfully they said goodbye, and he went away.

The girl had an iron rod, a pair of iron shoes and an iron bowl made, and then

she set off in search of her love. As she walked she wept for him, and carefully caught the tears in the iron bowl.

After a long time she came to a little cottage at the edge of a great forest. An old man was living there. 'Where are you going, my child?' he asked.

'I am looking for my true love, who lives far beyond the Red Sea. But now I am so tired that I would gladly rest for the night in your cottage.'

'My child, however did you find your way to this place? Not a bird knows it, the sun's rays never warm it, and even the winds do not blow this way. I am sorry but I cannot let you stay here, for my wife is the Moon, and she would be sure to notice.'

But the girl begged and implored until the old man relented. A few minutes later the Moon returned to the cottage. She was hardly through the door when she cried, 'Who's here? I smell a human soul.'

'Nobody special, my dear,' said the old man. 'A young girl who is searching for her true love somewhere beyond the Red Sea. You haven't seen him anywhere, have you?'

'Not I,' said the Moon, more gently. 'But she should go and find my brother the Sun. He shines everywhere and sees everything, but he lives a long way from here.'

Next morning the Moon showed the girl the way through the forest, and when she left her she gave her a nut.

The girl walked on, crying into her bowl, until she came to another great forest with a cottage at its edge. An old woman opened the door to her.

'Where are you going, my child?' she asked.

'I am searching for my true love, who lives far beyond the Red Sea. But may I please spend the night here, for I am so tired?'

'However did you find your way to this place?' asked the old woman. 'Not a bird knows it, the moon's rays never lighten it, and even the winds never blow this way. And I'm sorry, but I cannot let you stay here, for my husband is the Sun, and he spies out everything.' But the girl explained how the Moon had sent her, and at last the old woman relented.

At dusk the Sun returned to the cottage. At once he said, 'Who's here? I smell a human soul.'

The old woman said, 'It's a young girl staying the night here: she's searching for her true love, who lives beyond the Red Sea. You haven't seen him, have you?'

'No, I'm afraid not,' replied the Sun. 'But she ought to go and see my brother, the Wind. He creeps into all kinds of corners. But he lives a long way from here.'

Next morning the Sun led her through the forest, and he too gave her a nut.

She walked on, weeping into the iron bowl, until she came to another great forest with a tiny cottage in among the trees. An old woman came to the door and asked, 'Where are you going, my child?'

'I am searching for my true love, who lives beyond the Red Sea. I've already broken my iron rod, worn out these iron shoes, and filled this iron bowl with my tears. May I rest for one night in your cottage?'

'However did you find your way here? Neither the Sun nor the Moon ever shines here, and not one little rabbit has ever ventured this far. But I'm sorry that you cannot stay here, for my husband is the Wind, and he blows into every corner.'

The girl explained how the Moon and the Sun had directed her there, and the old woman relented.

That night the Wind blew in, rattling the whole cottage. 'Who's here?' he puffed. 'I smell a human soul.'

'It's just a young girl who's searching for her true love beyond the Red Sea. You haven't seen him, have you?'

'No, I'm afraid I haven't,' answered the Wind. 'But tomorrow I'll be blowing a great storm that way. I'll see what I can see.' And they invited the girl to share their supper. They had chicken, and the Wind told her to collect all the bones and keep them safe.

In the morning the Wind blew away in a great storm. When he returned that evening he was at first too tired to speak, but at last he said, 'Yes, I saw your lover. He lives beyond the Red Sea, and I'm afraid he's married. When you reach the sea, place the bones from last night's supper on the water; they will make a bridge for you to cross over safely.'

He led her through the forest, and as they parted he gave her another nut.

She walked on. On the way she met a dog, and kindly threw him a small bone. When she reached the sea she laid the bones on the water and crossed safe and dry to the other side. But at the far end she was just one bone short, the one she had given to the dog. So she cut off her little finger, laid it on the water, and safely reached the other side of the Red Sea.

At last she arrived in her true love's country. He lived in a big castle and he was married. She asked for work at the castle, and it so happened that they needed a goose-girl. One day in the fields she cracked the first nut and found in it a beautiful silver dress. The mistress of the castle, her beloved's wife, was so taken by the dress that she wanted to buy it at once.

'I will gladly give it you,' said the girl, 'if I may spend one night with your husband.' The lady agreed, but she took care to give her husband a strong sleeping potion before putting him to bed!

All that night the girl cried and whispered, 'My love, my treasure, my darling. Don't you remember how you promised to marry me, and how we stretched and stretched the little calf's skin?' But the young man only slept, and couldn't be woken.

But below the window stood a guard, who heard every word, and was most puzzled. Next morning he told his master that the goose-girl had come to him during the night, and how she had said, 'My love, my treasure! Don't you remember how you promised to marry me, and how we stretched and stretched the little calf's skin?'

The prince knew at once that it was his first love, the one who had freed him from his enchantment.

The next day the girl cracked the second nut and found in it a beautiful golden dress. Again she gave it to her mistress on condition that she might spend the night with her husband, but that night was just the same as the first. Again she cried, 'My beloved, my treasure, my darling! Don't you remember the little calf's skin, and how sad we were to part?'

Again the guard heard it all, and told his master the next morning.

On the third day, the goose-girl cracked the third nut and found such a beautiful dress inside that the mistress of the castle turned quite green with envy when she saw it. But the girl gave it to her in return for another night with her true love, and this time the young man took care to throw the sleeping potion away.

The girl came to him and kissed him, saying, 'My beloved, my darling, the one who promised to marry me! Don't you remember the little calf's skin, and how sad we were to part? I broke an iron rod, wore out a pair of iron shoes and filled an iron bowl with my tears, and yet I could not find you. And now that at last I have found you, my love, you do not belong to me any more!'

Then he opened his eyes and kissed her and said, 'From this moment you alone shall be my wife, and mistress of my castle and lands!'

And thus it was, and in this way they lived together happily for many years, in the castle which lies far beyond the Red Sea.

The Grateful Animals

In a certain village there was once a poor woman who had just one son. Each day he would go to the forest to collect wood, take it to the neighbouring town and sell it. Meanwhile, his mother would spin and weave, and what she spun she would give to the boy to sell in the town too. In this way they kept the wolf from the door.

Now each day the boy would collect a few extra branches and save the few pennies he received for them, but he never kept them long, because he could never pass by a beggar without giving him something.

One day, on his way to the forest, he saw some children dragging a dog on a lead, and beating it cruelly. The boy was sorry for the dog, so he bought it from the children for a few pence. From that day the grateful dog followed him wherever he went.

Another time, on his way to the forest, he saw some children taking a cat to drown it. He felt sorry for the cat, and bought it from the children for a few pence. From that time on the boy was never without his two faithful companions, the dog and the cat.

One day, when the boy was collecting faggots high in the mountains, he suddenly saw a burning bush. He went over to it to put out the fire, and saw that there was a snake in it calling for help.

'I'd save you,' said the boy, 'but I'm afraid that you might bite me.'

'Don't be afraid,' called the snake. 'I won't hurt you. And if you save me, I'll fulfil all your wishes and you certainly won't regret it.' So the boy held out a stick towards the burning bush, pulled the snake from the flames and saved its life.

Then the snake told him, 'Now take me to my father the dragon, King of all the Snakes. As a reward for having saved me, he will offer you a sack full of ducats, precious stones and other valuable gifts. Don't take any of them. Just ask him for the leaden ring he keeps under his tongue. When he gives it to you, hide it under your tongue and always keep it there. That ring has magic powers: so long as you have it under your tongue, it will fulfil all your wishes.'

And so they went together to the dragon, King of all the Snakes, and asked him for the ring, as the snake had advised him.

'But why do you want a cheap thing like that? I would much rather give you a sack full of gold coins, jewels and precious objects.'

'The ring is all I want,' insisted the woodcutter, so finally the dragon consented, and gave him the ring from beneath his tongue. The boy put the ring in his mouth and thought, 'I wish I was home again with my mother.'

Instantly he found himself standing in front of the cottage. He went in and said to his mother, 'Go to the tsar straight away and tell him I wish to marry his daughter.'

His mother was surprised, to say the least, but she went and did as her son had told her. The tsar was outraged.

'Get out of my palace!' he shouted. 'How can I marry my daughter to a woodcutter? Now, if he had a palace like mine instead of a cottage, things might be different.'

The woman went home and passed on this message.

Her son thought to himself, 'I wish I had a palace like the tsar's in every detail.' And there in the backyard stood a splendid palace, and it was exactly like the tsar's in every way.

The woodcutter's mother went to the tsar's palace again and told him that her son had a palace which was just as fine, and that he still wanted to marry the tsar's daughter. The tsar looked out of the window and saw in the distance the woodcutter's splendid palace. 'Why did I never notice that before?' he wondered to himself.

Then he said to the widow, 'If your son can pave with gold the road between his palace and mine, then he may marry my daughter.'

The widow went home and passed on this message.

With the help of his magic ring the woodcutter at once had the road between the two palaces paved with gold, and again he sent his mother to the tsar to tell him about it and to ask for his daughter's hand in marriage.

'That was quick,' thought the tsar, looking out of the window. Then he said, 'Your son must also build a beautiful garden round his palace, like the one I have. When the nightingales are singing there, then I'll let him have my daughter.'

The woodcutter's magic ring fulfilled this wish too: when he woke the next morning there was a beautiful garden outside, and the nightingales were singing in the trees.

So once more his mother went to the tsar and asked him to let her son the woodcutter marry his daughter.

The tsar looked at the splendid palace, the golden road and the beautiful garden, and he said, 'Well, I'm not a snob. Your son and his wedding guests may come for my daughter, but they must be mounted on snow-white horses and dressed in the finest white robes.'

The woodcutter arranged all this, and in due course led the princess as his wife back to his palace.

But the tsar had a wicked courtier whose soul was as black as his black moustache. One day he asked the princess, 'How is it that your woodcutter's every wish is granted?'

And the princess, who was awfully upset about being married to a woodcutter, even a woodcutter with a splendid palace, said, 'I have found out that he keeps a magic ring under his tongue, which carries out all his wishes.'

Then the courtier persuaded the princess to steal the ring, because, he said, the woodcutter now had everything he could wish for, and therefore didn't need it any more.

'But how can I get the ring, when he keeps it under his tongue both day and night?' asked the princess.

The wicked courtier thought a moment, and said, 'Put your little finger in water, then into a bag of pepper, and then, when your husband is fast asleep, hold your finger under his nose. He will begin to sneeze, and when he sneezes the ring will shoot out of his mouth and fall on the bed. Take it and bring it to me. I can make you far happier than any woodcutter.'

The tsar's daughter did all this, and the next day she brought the courtier the ring. He quickly put it under his tongue, and with a wicked smile said, 'Take the woodcutter's palace and place it far beyond the great river, in the mountains.

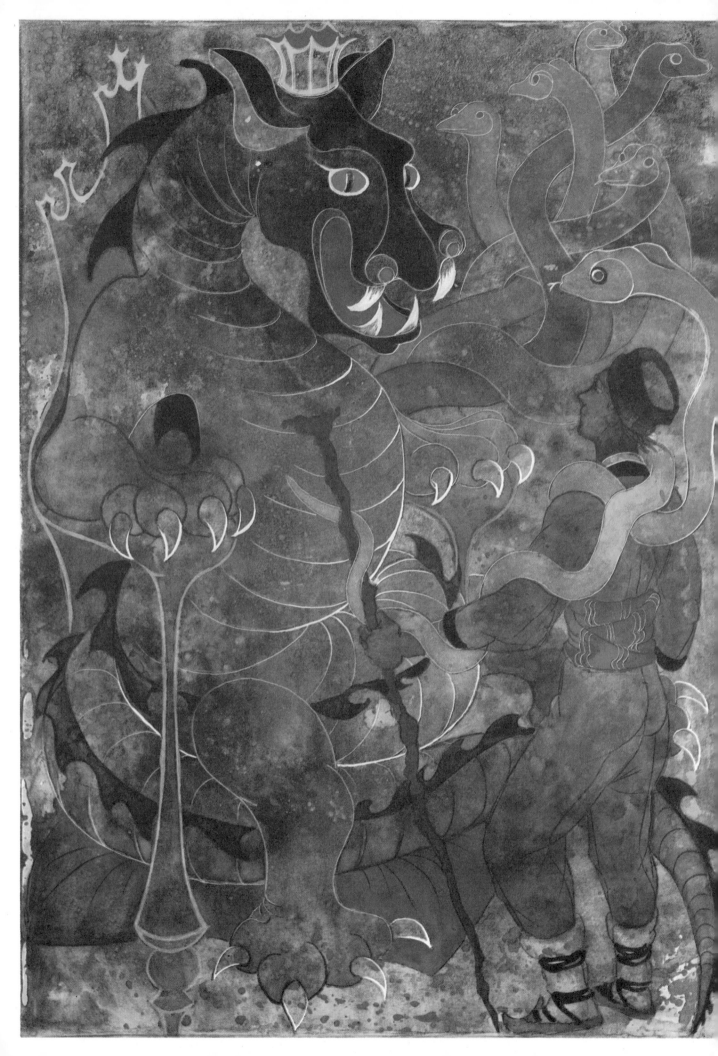

From now on it belongs to me, and the woodcutter must go back to his old cottage!'

When the woodcutter woke that morning he rubbed his eyes and realized he was back in his old cottage, and that the palace and his ring had vanished.

And he said to his mother, 'I shall take my dog and cat, and go and find where my palace has gone.' Which is what he did.

One day, he came to a wide river, on the bank of which he saw a fish that had got thrown up and was desperately tossing around on dry land. He picked it up and threw it back into the water.

Whereupon the fish thrust its head out again and said, 'Thank you, thank you, you saved my life! Here, take one of my scales, and if you should ever need me, burn it, and I'll come to your help at once.'

So the woodcutter pulled off one of the fish's scales, and then walked on along the bank. Not long after, he caught sight of his palace on the other side of the river. So he told his dog and cat to swim over, get into the palace, take the ring from the courtier and bring it back to him.

The dog swam across with the cat on his back. Then while the dog stood guard carefully outside, the cat slipped into the palace. Now it happened that just at that time the mice in the palace were celebrating a wedding. The cat arrived right in the middle of the feast, and started to chase the mice. As luck would have it she actually caught the bridegroom. All the mice ran up to the cat and promised her everything they could imagine, if only she would spare the poor bridegroom.

The cat agreed to release him, but only if they would bring her the ring the courtier kept hidden under his tongue.

'Dip your tails in water,' she said, 'then in pepper, and when the courtier goes to sleep, put your tails under his nose. When he sneezes, the ring is sure to fly out of his mouth. Quickly pick it up and bring it to me. Then I'll let you have the bridegroom.'

The mice did all this, brought the cat the ring, and she then let them have their bridegroom back. Then she put the ring in her mouth and ran out of the palace with it.

The dog was waiting for her at the gate. They ran down to the river, the cat jumped on the dog's back and they set off through the swirling water.

When they were half way across, the dog said, 'It's my turn to carry the ring now! Give it here, or I'll drop you in the water!'

So the cat took the ring out of her mouth and tried to give it to the dog. But her paws were wet, it slipped out of them and, splash! It was gone in the river!

What could they do? Sadly they had to return to their master to tell him what had happened. But the woodcutter remembered the fish, and the promise it had made. He pulled out the fish scale, burned it, and a moment later the fish appeared.

'Here I am, what do you want of me?' it asked.

And the woodcutter explained, 'My ring fell into the water in the middle of the river. Can you get it for me?'

'Why, that's easy,' said the fish. 'Wait a moment, I'll be right back.'

It swam off, looked for the ring and brought it up to the woodcutter. He put it under his tongue, wished himself back home, and at once there he was, standing in front of the cottage. Then he wished the palace back again, and lastly he wished to have his wife and the wicked courtier locked up inside it.

When all this was done the woodcutter invited his father-in-law the tsar to come and visit him.

The tsar was very interested to see the palace for himself. They walked round all the rooms, and last of all they came to the room where the courtier and the tsar's faithless daughter were locked up. The woodcutter unlocked the door, and told the tsar all that had happened.

The tsar fell into a blind fury when he heard of the treachery of the courtier and his daughter, and without any more ado he took his sword and cut off their heads. Then he told the woodcutter, 'You'd better have my second daughter instead. What's more, I think I'll make you my heir.'

And so the woodcutter married the tsar's second daughter, who was much nicer, and not long after the old tsar bestowed the tsardom on him as well.

And if you want to visit him and see his faithful cat and dog, you don't have far to go. It's just a mile or two away, there where the trees meet the sky!

Princess Purbasari

There once lived in heaven a beautiful youth whose mother was the lovely goddess Sunan Ambu. He was as restless as the breeze, as playful as a butterfly, and as affectionate as a baby monkey. He loved to go wandering, and when the gods sent rain to the earth he would travel in the glistening raindrops to the faraway isles, where he would ruffle the surface of the lakes, give the flowers a drink from his cupped hands, and dance in the women's hair. He was the darling of the gods, so that they forgave his unruliness and smiled at his mischievous pranks.

'He is still young,' they would say. 'He is only a child.'

But it came about that the divine Sunan Ambu snubbed Sang Kala, fearsome lord of the demons and jinn, who wished to pay court to her. The spiteful Sang Kala swore to take a terrible revenge. One day, he persuaded the youth to visit the forbidden chambers of the chaste goddess Luna. This time the gods were scandalized. They summoned a council to try the boy's misdeed, and he was condemned to take the form of a monkey and to leave the realm of the gods.

'Until some daughter of the Earth shall fall in love with your ugly face, you shall enjoy only the brotherhood of the gibbering monkeys! Let the trees of the jungle be your home! Let the animals and birds and human kind know you by the lowly name Lutung Kesarung — Stray Monkey!' Such was the judgement of the gods. From then on Lutung Kesarung lived among the monkeys. One day he wandered into the land of the great Rajah Indrajaya. Indrajaya was a mighty king. He lived in a palace of jasmine blossom and fiery lava. His war-elephant had four golden tusks, eight tiger's eyes and a crocodile's skin. All who set eyes on it were turned to stone. All who heard its frenzied trumpeting changed into lumps of clay. Rajah Indrajaya was invincible.

One day the rajah brought to his palace a beautiful princess from a far-off kingdom. In the daytime she cooled like the dew, while at night she warmed like the wick of the *blencong,* the sacred lamp. Her brow was an array of blossoming orchids, and tiny silver fish swam about her eyes. When she combed her hair, it was like the rustle of the rain. The rajah made her his wife. After the wedding ceremony was over, he and his young bride floated down the river on a lotus leaf for all his subjects to see. Butterflies with diamond-studded wings fluttered about their garlanded heads, and golden-shelled turtles carried delicious foods into the poorest hovels. The bank was crowded with those who had come to greet their king, and women clutched flowers in their outstretched hands. Rajah Indrajaya was all-powerful. He had only to give the word, and stars would rain down from the heavens. At his command, volcanoes spewed forth golden lava. Then the great monarch lifted his young bride high above his head to show her face to the gods.

'O gods, I commit to your protection my royal and exhalted wife, loveliest blossom of the island empire. Let her enjoy your favour!'

At that instant they heard above them the rustle of birds' wings.

'The gods have heard your plea, Rajah Indrajaya,' called one of the birds. 'But they wish you to know that the loveliest blossom of the island empire is not that which blooms in the light of your eyes, but is hidden in the homeland of the one you have raised to the throne.' The rajah frowned darkly.

'Who is this woman? I would know her name!' he called out.

'It is your wife's sister, the shy Princess Purbasari,' came the reply from afar.

'She sleeps in a parrot's nest in her royal father's gardens, so that she might not see the face of a man.'

As soon as Rajah Indrajaya heard these words, he sent envoys to his wife's land bearing rich gifts, with orders to bring back Princess Purbasari.

'I wish to see the woman whom the gods admire,' was his message to her father. 'If she is indeed as beautiful as the white birds have told me, then I shall find her a noble husband worthy of her hand.'

Princess Purbasari's father would have been only too pleased to fulfil the wish of the mighty Rajah Indrajaya, but none of his servants was able to persuade the princess to come down to the ground. It was without success that the birdcatchers spread their nets, in vain that the slender dancing-girls implored her to join them. The princess only laughed like a turtle-dove, and hid in the crowns of the tall palm-trees. When the hunters thought they had her at last, she caught hold of the legs of her friends the parrots and flew with them from nest to nest, mischievously throwing prickly nutshells down at her pursuers. Then at last one of the parrots hurt its wing on a thorny branch, and fell into the grass. At once the princess climbed down from her refuge to help the bird. In an instant the birdcatchers had her caught in a sticky net woven from the web of the spider-demon, so that in the end Princess Purbasari arrived at the rajah's palace after all.

The moment the mighty Indrajaya set eyes on the girl, he grew speechless with wonder. The sweet princess glowed like a golden honeycomb in the midday sun, and was as fragrant as the jungle in blossom. Snow-white water-lilies floated in her placid eyes, with golden fish playing in the shadow of their lashes. Instead of hair, the rays of Luna's light sparkled about her temples, and her throat was decked with climbing roses. When she smiled, jasmine blossomed upon her lips.

'Welcome to the kingdom of Rajah Indrajaya, lovely sister of my noble wife,' the rajah greeted her, and he gave orders at once that the princess be given a golden nest on the banks of a lake filled with tears, which was where the youthful beauty now went to live. She was glad to be able to meet her sister at court, but was homesick for her father's garden and her playful leaping about the palm-trees. On moonlit evenings she would sit in a boat of mother-of-pearl, singing sad songs. Not one of the dashing suitors who came to the rajah's kingdom was able to comfort her. She turned them all down courteously, without so much as looking them in the face. Her sister thought such behaviour very strange indeed, and finally she began to suspect that Princess Purbasari wished to entice the rajah himself away from her.

She grew more and more jealous of her younger sister, and planned how she might get rid of her.

One day, Rajah Indrajaya went hunting in the most distant part of the forests. No sooner was he gone, than the queen sent for Princess Purbasari.

'Dearest sister,' the queen began, pretending to be filled with sorrow. 'My royal husband, the noble Rajah Indrajaya, is angry that you should have refused to strengthen the might of his empire by marrying one of the powerful princes. He has therefore given orders that you should go to the bend in the river beside the Forest of the Monkeys, and build a dam of black stones. If you do not finish the work before he returns from hunting, you shall die,' the queen added. She was certain that Princess Purbasari would take fright and flee the realm. But Purbasari only bowed her head in resignation and set out for the river to do as her sister had ordered. All day long she toiled, heaving the huge black boulders into the water; but when the sun began to sink in the west the river was still rolling down between its broad banks as always. The princess dipped her torn and bleeding hands in the water and began to weep bitterly.

'Why are you crying, noble maiden?' enquired a voice from behind her. From out of the jungle the fearsome face of a huge monkey peered at her. The princess gave a cry of terror and took to her heels, but the monkey soon caught her up and threw his arms about her.

'Tell me what troubles you,' he beseeched her. The monkey had a voice so gentle and eyes so sad that the princess soon regained her composure and recounted her misfortune. No sooner had she finished her tale, than the monkey shouted something in the tongue of his kind. In a trice, droves of wild monkeys came hurrying out of the forest, and set to work. While some broke off huge pieces of rock from the cliff face and carried them down to the river, others used the stones to build an enormous dam. Before the sun had sunk beneath the horizon, the river's path was blocked by a high wall of stones, behind which a great lake seemed to stretch endlessly into the distance. Princess Purbasari was overcome with wonder.

'I do not know how I may reward you,' she said to the monkey.

'Look into my face,' the creature begged her. 'If you see anything there which may be loved by a human being, then take me for your husband.'

At first Princess Purbasari was horrified at this request. But then she looked into the monkey's sad eyes, and replied kindly:

'I like your glance, which is like the touch of a mother's hand. You have been kind to me — I will gladly be your wife.'

The moment she had said this, the ugly monkey changed into a handsome young man.

'Thank you, princess; your words have released me from the spell. I am the son of the purest of goddesses, Sunan Ambu, whom the gods in their wrath called Lutung Kesarung, Stray Monkey. Return to the palace of Rajah Indrajaya: your task is completed. I shall go to the holy mountain Slamet to ask the gods to take us into their kingdom. When the sun rises, we shall meet in the shade of the holy *waringin.*'

Joyfully, the princess ran back to the palace. She flew along like a bird at play and as she ran she sang the most beautiful songs the jungle had taught her. Rajah Indrajaya had just returned from his hunting.

'Woe betide you, false Princess Purbasari,' he addressed her sternly. 'Your sister, the queen, has told me how you threw in your lot with demons. She says that on your command they dammed the river, so that its waters might flood my kingdom. For this deed I sentence you to death.'

Neither tears nor explanations were to any avail. The rajah did not believe the princess's story. He ordered her to be bound and taken to the Forest of the Monkeys, where she was buried alive in a deep pit.

When Lutung Kesarung returned to earth with the morning dew, he found no trace of his lovely bride. He therefore whispered a magic spell and turned back into a hideous monkey.

'Noble nation of monkeys,' he called into the jungle, 'the eyes of your kind are sharp, and your children's ears can hear the gentlest lullaby of the palms. Where is Princess Purbasari, O monkey folk?'

In the crown of an Areca palm the oldest of the monkeys, king of them all, swung by his tail.

'Seek not among the stars, Lutung Kesarung,' he gibbered in his monkey voice. 'Seek not among the fishes, man with a monkey's face. Seek not above the ground, son of the goddess Sunan Ambu. Rajah Indrajaya has hidden the most precious treasure of the island empire deep in the bowels of the earth.'

At these words Lutung Kesarung began to scrape away the earth with his sharp claws. The monkeys came to his assistance. A whole day and night had passed before they managed to find the body of the beautiful Princess Purbasari. Lutung Kesarung took her in his arms and washed her with the morning dew. An orange butterfly settled on her lips and fanned her cheeks with its opalescent wings. The spiders of the jungle wove a cooling compress for her brow. The forest bees spread fragrant honey on her temples. All helped to bring Princess Purbasari to life again.

'Take me away to the kingdom of the gods,' she begged, the moment she opened her eyes. 'I am afraid of my sister and of Rajah Indrajaya.'

But Lutung Kesarung shook his head.

'We may enter their kingdom together only when age has turned our hair to silver. Such is the will of the gods.'

From that time on Lutung Kesarung and his beautiful bride lived with the *para wanara,* the nation of monkeys.

It so happened that one day a lone hunter brought to the palace of Rajah Indrajaya word of a beautiful princess who wandered about the treetops with the monkey folk.

'It is surely Princess Purbasari, whom the demons have rescued!' cried the rajah. Without delay he set out at the head of a mighty host to conquer the princess and her demon brethren. But the moment the warriors approached the kingdom of the monkeys, hordes of angry monkeys came rushing out of the forest, driving Indrajaya's soldiers into the river. The rajah was left alone; he, too, would have fled, but at that moment a hideous creature with a monkey's face stepped into his path.

'I am he whom the gods in their anger named Lutung Kesarung, Stray Monkey, son of Sunan Ambu, purest of goddesses, and husband of the beautiful Princess Purbasari. If you have the courage to fight with a son of the gods, Rajah Indrajaya, then unsheath your magic kris!'

Blinded with wrath, the rajah drove forward his terrifying war-elephant to attack. The fearful struggle went on throughout the whole of the rainy season. The river ran red with blood, and the volcanoes spewed forth fiery lava. When both the combatants were coming to the end of their strength, a holy man stepped forth from the jungle and placed a sprig of jasmine between them.

'Hear the will of the gods,' he ordered. 'The heavens have decreed that you shall fight no longer. Henceforth, O noble Rajah Indrajaya, your kingdom shall end at the right bank of the river. The left bank shall mark the border of the lands of Lutung Kesarung, son of the gods. All who cross from one side to the other shall be cursed. Your wife, Rajah Indrajaya, is guilty of wronging her defenceless sister, Princess Purbasari. It is the will of the gods that she go into the jungle to live with the snakes and the wild creatures. Thus have the heavens decreed.'

That was the end of the merciless struggle between the all-powerful Rajah Indrajaya and Lutung Kesarung, son of the gods. When the span of a man's lifetime had passed, Lutung Kesarung and his wife Purbasari entered the kingdom of the gods.

The Prince Who Became a Demon

When the fire gets going, and the scent of smoke enters the nostrils, the oldest of the hunters begins to tell a story.

Hunters, can you hear the cleft tree groaning? Brothers, can you hear the rustle of the leaves? Keep to the path, my bold companions, keep to the path! The demon of the hunters is calling you. That is how one tale begins.

There was once a certain prince who was a passionate hunter. He would spend the whole day in the jungle thickets, eagerly following a tiger's trail, and would return home weary and bad-tempered if he failed to find any game. One day he resolved to hunt down the biggest tiger ever seen by man. Heedless of the fact that his wife was with child, he heard only the call of the jungle, and constantly set out anew on the hunters' trail. His greed for tiger's blood had so turned his head that he often forgot to make a sacrifice to the gods. The old men warned him, but the prince would only laugh and slice through a palm frond with the blade of his knife.

'This is my friend and protector. Let he who is not afraid of his sharp claw come forth!' And the prince would rush eagerly into the *rattan* thicket towards the calls of the wild creatures. He often returned empty-handed. At the end of just such a luckless day, sitting beside his hunter's fire, he drank too much palm wine, and began to profane the jungle:

'I am calling you, cowardly rulers of the jungle; I am calling you, bloodthirsty tiger. I dare you to come within reach of my knife. Come and get me!'

At once there was the fearful roar of a tiger from close at hand, and a huge shadow crossed the jungle's edge.

'We are coming,' whispered the jungle in reply, and the thicket lit up with pairs of wild eyes. The prince was taken aback for a moment, but then he ran off fearlessly into the gloom of the jungle. Hesitantly, his companions set off after him. They called out in vain — the prince did not reply. He forced his way through the dense bamboo and the network of *rattan* stalks, tore aside the tall ferns, and stumbled over rotten tree trunks. The shadow of the monstrous tiger seemed to be within an arm's reach of him. But when he raised his hand to strike, the springy lianas wound themselves about his body so tightly he could scarcely breathe.

'Welcome, brother,' said a mocking voice beside him. The startled prince saw above him the savage face of a tiger. He tried to free himself from the lianas, but the beast growled:

'It is no use struggling, foolish one: you are in the power of the jungle.'

'Who are you?' asked the prince, anxiously. 'Your tiger's skin is false — you are no animal.'

'I am the demon who rules the spirits of the jungle. You have offended my people, profaned the jungle. Therefore I shall deprive you of your human form for ever. You shall stay here in the form of a beast until your heart is pierced by the knife of a bold hunter. Only then may you become a demon. The nation of free spirits will take you among them.'

When it had said this, the tiger disappeared. In vain did the prince call to his companions. His voice was like the roar of a tiger, and his body became covered in loathsome hair. The prince began to weep with horror.

That night his wife gave birth to a son. When she held him to her breast to feed, she heard from the jungle the voice of a tiger. It sounded like an animal's lament, and the woman went out in front of the house to listen.

'Did you hear?' she called to those who passed by. 'A tiger is weeping.' But the people of the village only laughed at her. Who had ever heard a tiger weep! But her husband did not return.

Many days passed; many times the villagers harvested the manioc and betel. The small boy grew bigger, and played with the other children. But they would whisper behind his back that he had no father. This upset him.

'Where is my father, Mother?' he asked one day. 'Everyone laughs at me.'

His mother took him to the edge of the jungle and told him the tale of the hunter who took it into his head to hunt down the biggest tiger in the world.

'He never returned; he fell into the power of the jungle,' she said, sadly. 'My son, can you hear the weeping of the tiger? It sounds like the voice of your father.'

The boy listened, and then said:

'Mother, I feel it in my blood that my father is alive. The tiger's lament calls me to the hunters' trail. I hear the call of the jungle.'

'My son, I am afraid your father may no longer be a man! It seems to me that this strange weeping of the tiger is like the wailing of demons on a moonless night. But I must not hold you back. The call of blood is stronger than a mother's love. Go and follow the trail of your father, my son!'

And she gave him their precious ancestral kris to take with him; it had been forged by an armourer who had magic powers.

'If you should meet your father in the jungle, give him back his favourite weapon. But do not forget to hand it to him blade first, otherwise you will be afflicted with misfortune!' she warned him.

The boy set off into the jungle. He went towards the sound of the tiger's weeping, along trails which the hunters avoided. In the densest thicket he came across a strange creature, bound to the trunk of a tree by lianas. It was neither man nor beast. Its body was disfigured by a loathsome yellow hair; the claws of a beast of prey dug into his palms, and a tiger's weeping came from his throat. Only his face was human. The boy took courage and addressed him.

'Who are you, unfortunate man?'

'I am he who profaned the jungle,' replied the monster, and he recounted the tale of the unhappy hunter.

'Then you are my father,' the boy cried joyfully, and was about to use the magic kris to cut through the lianas which bound the beast's body, when his father stopped him. He told the lad he must first return to the village and plant an Areca palm in front of his home.

The boy did as he was told, and the next day, when he went back into the jungle, his father begged him:

'Give me back my kris! But if your life is dear to you, do not forget your mother's words!'

With one blow the son cut through the liana bonds and then laid the kris blade-first in his father's hand. At that instant the magic knife plunged itself deep into the creature's body, and the hapless prince turned into a demon. With a burst of free laughter he flew to the top of a cleft tree, which to this day people call the demons' trap.

'You did well to heed your mother's words and mine,' he called. 'If you had handed me the kris as is the custom among men, haft-first, its blade would have pierced your own heart. May the Areca palm you have planted before your home protect you from my dark powers for the rest of your life! Go now, in peace! The nation of the spirits, my occult brethren, is calling me!'

The jungle rang with the roar of a tiger, and a lifeless tiger's body fell at the boy's feet. It was the biggest that human eyes had ever seen. The young man stripped the creature's skin and took it to the village. Because of his courage, he became the foremost among the island's hunters. From that day on no one ever heard the weeping of a tiger again. But to this day they plant Areca palms in front of their houses — to protect them from the demons of the jungle.

The Story of a Certain Hae-hae

Long, long ago, in the land of the crystal lakes, a certain youth was getting ready to join his companions and go to war. His was the longest spear of all, the sharpest knife, and the boldest tongue. Nor did he forget to visit the girl to whom his thoughts were turned, in order to impress her before he left. The dark-haired maiden was weaving a fine skirt in an alcove.

'Tell me what you like best in the whole world,' the young warrior asked her, hoping she would say his name.

The vain weaver thought most of all about how she would dearly like to adorn her hair with a *sae-sae* flower. So she replied:

'The dearest thing in all the world is a *sae-sae.*' And she began to croon a song in praise of her own beauty.

'A *hae-hae?*' said the young man, who had misheard in his disappointment. 'Very well, I shall bring you one.'

Right away he and his companions made their way to an enemy village. He fought like a tiger to fulfil his maiden's wish, and as soon as the battle was over he made straight for the alcove where the girl was wont to do her weaving.

'I have brought you a fine *hae-hae,* that which you love more dearly than anything in the world. It is yours, and yours alone.'

He had scarcely finished speaking, when the girl almost fainted with horror. The bloody *hae-hae* suddenly came to life before her eyes and went and sat down on her lap. When the young man saw this, he took to his heels. The girl began to cry.

'Do not weep, my beauty,' the *hae-hae* comforted her. 'Do you not love me more than anything in the world? I shall make you my wife at once!'

But the beautiful weaver began to make excuses.

'Very well; but first you must watch over my skirt, so that the mice may not tear it apart, dearest *hae-hae.* I shall only go to my parents' home to get some things for my weaving.'

The *hae-hae* strolled back and forth in the alcove, and trod on mice's tails to pass the time. When at last it grew impatient, it made its way to the girl's house and knocked on the door. 'Hurry up!' it called. 'It is I, your beloved *hae-hae!*'

But the girl did not reply, and in the end the *hae-hae* lost its temper. Smashing its way through the wall, it jumped straight into her lap.

'Why did you not reply, my beauty?'

'I was just moistening the yarn in my mouth,' lied the girl.

'Then why did you not open the door, my chosen one?' asked the *hae-hae,* angrily.

'I was just rocking my baby brother in my arms,' declared the unfortunate maiden. 'Wait for me just a little longer, my dearest *hae-hae*: I must go down to the rice-fields to make sure there is no wild boar digging there.'

But the *hae-hae* would not listen, and refused to be parted from her.

'You said that you loved me more dearly than anything in the world, therefore I shall never leave you.' At this the girl began crying again, so bitterly that all the little monkeys joined in.

'Why do you lament so, my betrothed?' asked the *hae-hae,* quite put out. 'Do you not like me?'

'Of course I like you, my pretty little *hae-hae*. Are you not the dearest thing in all the world to me?' the maiden was quick to reassure it. 'I am crying because my parents are not at home, and I have no food here to give to you before you go to sleep. Wait here just a moment, and I shall slip into the village for a fresh fish.'

But the *hae-hae* was angry.

'Nothing of the sort, woman. You wish to trick me again. I shall go with you for the fish.'

'As you wish,' the girl pretended to agree. 'But if you do go with me, all the villagers will run away from you, taking all the food with them. We shall die of starvation.'

The *hae-hae* thought for a while.

'Very well,' it agreed in the end. 'But none of your tricks. I can track you down wherever you go.'

At these words the girl was gone like the wind, and she did not even stop to look behind her. She ran, and she ran, until, quite out of breath, she reached the other side of the valley. At the bottom of a deep ravine the murky water of a marshy paddy field shone darkly. The girl sank into the grass and listened fearfully. When the *hae-hae's* patience gave out, it set off in her tracks with huge strides.

'Where are you, my beauty?' it called, angrily.

'Here, my dear little *hae-hae*, most precious to me in the whole world. Hurry to me!' she egged it on cunningly.

The foolish *hae-hae* wasted no time, but hop! tried to reach the other side of the ravine in a single leap; but the valley was as wide as the yawning mouth of the sleepiest of the idle Batavians, so that our dear *hae-hae* fell straight into the middle of the paddy marshes, from which perhaps only the broad-shouldered buffalo can find its way out. All the Batavian mothers say it remains there to this day. As a warning to vain Batavian beauties and boastful cowards who run away from bogies, a tree grew out of it, called the Tubung. The bottom of its trunk is a reddish colour from the blood of the *hae-hae*.

The Lama and the Carpenter

It was long ago, terribly long ago, so that no one can remember any more: in a certain kingdom there lived a carpenter and a lama.

The lama was evil and grasping. One day he said to the carpenter:

'If you will build me a house, I will pray for you in return, that the gods may bring you good fortune.'

'I do not want your prayers,' replied the carpenter, disrespectfully. 'My fortune is in my two hands and my axe.'

'Just you wait,' said the lama to himself — 'you'll not get away with this!' And he pondered day and night how he might be revenged upon the carpenter, until finally he had an idea. Going before the king, he said:

'Your Majesty, as I was visiting heaven yesterday, whom should I meet but your honourable father. All is well with him, of course, but he did mention that he would like to have a temple built. Since it is not easy to find carpenters in heaven, he asked that you send him your own, who is said to be a fine craftsman.'

'Why not, indeed?' replied the king. 'But how am I to send him there?'

'There is no need for you to worry about that, Your Majesty; we lamas have ways of arranging these things,' the lama assured him, and he explained his plan. They would have a wooden hut built, shut the carpenter inside, and light a large fire outside. When the hut caught fire, white smoke would begin to rise up to heaven, and on it, as on a white horse, the carpenter would rise up, too.

The king agreed to this plan, and told the carpenter of it.

'What am I to do?' lamented the carpenter, when he got home. 'The lama is determined to take my life.'

'I'll tell you what to do,' his wife replied. 'It's quite simple. Tonight we'll dig a tunnel from our house under the hut, and tomorrow you shall use it to escape.'

The next day they took the carpenter and shut him up in the hut. Then they piled brushwood all around and set fire to it. As white smoke began to pour from the hut, the lama started to call out:

'There you are, look! That's him! Do you see how the white horse carries him to heaven?'

Actually, no one could see anything of the sort, but they all dutifully pretended they did. Meanwhile, the carpenter had hurried home by the underground passage, and was warming his toes by the hearth. He sat there for a whole month, without so much as showing his face. The whole time he thought about how he might get his own back on the lama. In the end he went out, and made his way straight to the royal palace. Everyone stared in astonishment, particularly the wicked lama.

'You have come back?' gasped the king.

'As you can see, Your Majesty, I have come straight from heaven,' said the carpenter. 'That temple of your father's took some building — they have a very old-fashioned way of going about these things up there. But now he's got a temple he can be proud of, and very satisfied he was, too. There's only one other thing he would ask, Your Majesty. You see, he hasn't got a lama for the temple, and as you well know, sire, a temple without a lama is like strawberries without cream, so your honourable father would like you to send him one. Not just any old lama, mind you — a temple like that deserves a really special lama, Your Majesty, and your father did say he would like to have yours, seeing as the fame of his learning has reached heaven itself.'

'Why, I should gladly send him to my father,' said the king, 'but how am I to get him there?'

'The best way would be to send him as you sent me,' replied the carpenter. 'It's definitely the quickest.'

The lama turned pale, but in the end he agreed. 'If the carpenter came back,' he thought, 'so can I.' So he did not even protest too much about being shut up in a wooden hut and having a fire lit all around him.

The flames leapt high, oh so high! up towards the heavens, and a thin, black column of smoke rose from among them. With it the lama's soul, too, made its way upwards.

The Story of Broadheart

Long, long ago, when the earth was so thinly peopled that houses were miles apart from each other, a strange sign appeared in the heavens. As it drew nearer the earth, it was seen to be a flaming comet. It flew through the black night, dropping from its snaking tail tiny embers as slender as hairs. They fell upon the sleeping earth below, and wherever they came down the grass caught fire and the soil was scorched; a great conflagration swept the countryside, leaving a thousand dwellings in ashes. The once fertile landscape was transformed to a parched and smouldering desert. The land and its hapless people were afflicted by drought, starvation, and merciless thirst.

Among the inhabitants of that country was a certain young man who, because he always thought of others and was glad to lend them a helping hand, was known to everyone as Broadheart. He was indeed good at heart and sympathetic, and his eyes shone with kindness. He was happy when others rejoiced, wept for those who suffered.

'If only there was some way to rid folk of this terrible drought,' Broadheart would say to himself, and the thought stayed with him day and night. He racked his brains to find something he could do, but when nothing occurred to him he finally decided to seek the advice of an old sage who lived in his village.

When the lad had confided his troubles, the old man nodded his head gravely and said:

'Well, my boy, it is so. My great grandfather once told me the mystic secret of the eternal fire which burns deep in the cosmic void. From time to time a tongue of flame flies off that fire, and the flaming hairs of its shaggy mane fall to earth and scorch the ground. Then the only one who can save the people from their plight is he who is able to obtain the emerald pearl, which is concealed on the bed of a deep lake, in the heart of the Jade Mountains. But those mountains are far away from here, and the way to them is difficult, and fraught with perils. Nor is it so easy to get the emerald pearl when you arrive there. It is guarded by a huge black spider, whose dark web covers the lake, ready to trap all intruders.'

Broadheart listened intently. The old man paused for an instant, then went on.

'He who would reach the bottom of the lake must first go to the plateau of venomous flowers and obtain the golden sting of the wasp queen, with which to slay the black spider. The task is a fearfully difficult one, and all who have tried to fulfil it paid with their lives.'

'Come what may, I shall try,' said Broadheart and, thanking the old man, he set out on the perilous journey.

The youth wandered for a long time through the barren countryside, until at last he came to a deep forest. Suddenly, he heard from above him a plaintive cry. Glancing up, he spotted a sparrowhawk, which had grasped a young crow in its fierce claws and was carrying it from its nest.

'Let go!' he shouted, snatching up a stone and hurling it at the sparrowhawk. The stone struck home, and the bird of prey flew off, releasing the crow.

'Kwaa, kwaa — thank you for saving my son, Broadheart,' the crow croaked from above. 'If you should ever need my help, you have only to remember me.'

'How could a crow be of any help to me?' thought Broadheart to himself, and he went his way. He journeyed through the forest for a long time, until at last he emerged on the edge of a broad plain. He halted in amazement. Rising in front of him was a huge mountain, which instead of reaching a peak was cut off as flat as a table. Up the side of it led a narrow, steep path, which disappeared into thick, thorny undergrowth. Broadheart set off along this track, heedless of the fact that his feet skidded over the smooth stones and the sharp-bladed grass cut his hands. It took him three days and nights to reach the plateau. There he found himself on the edge of a broad expanse of poisonous flowers, in the middle of which was a rotten tree stump with a wasps' nest on it.

'But how am I to get there?' said Broadheart to himself, gloomily, watching a swarm of frenzied wasps as they buzzed around the tree.

'If only the crow could help me somehow,' he sighed quietly to himself. Scarcely had he spoken, when the sky darkened and a host of cawing crows appeared over the plateau of the venomous flowers.

'Kwaa, kwaa — I and my sisters have come to help you,' one of them called. Then she cawed something to her companions, at which they flew off in all directions, returning with their beaks full of wisps of dry grass. They dropped these at the foot of the tree where the wasps had their nest.

'Kwaa, kwaa — strike a spark, Broadheart,' called his black-feathered friend. The young man picked up two stones and struck them against each other until a spark flew off and lit the dry grass. The smouldering grass gave off such a cloud of choking smoke that the angry wasps flew away, leaving their nest unguarded.

Now Broadheart was able to approach the tree trunk and climb up to the wasps' nest. But before he managed to take hold of the wasp queen, she flew out of the nest and made her escape.

'Kwaa, kwaa — do not worry, I shall catch her,' cawed the crow, setting off in pursuit. She seized the wasp queen in her beak and took her to Broadheart down below. He drew the golden sting and wrapped it carefully in his scarf; then he thanked the crow, and the two of them parted.

'Good luck!' called the crow, as she flew to join the others.

Broadheart set out to find the Jade Mountains. Before his long trek was over, the moon had waxed and waned many times. He swam across nine rushing rivers and climbed across nine gaping chasms before he finally reached the foothills of those distant peaks. They seemed to breathe an icy cold, as if the sun were not strong enough to warm such enormous mountains. The higher he climbed along their ravines, the deeper was the twilight that surrounded him, until at last Broadheart found himself engulfed in total darkness, in the midst of which lay the lake he had journeyed to find.

On and around the water a deathly silence reigned, and only the tiniest patch of sky could be discerned, high, high up above the steep mountain walls that rose on all sides. The surface of the lake was so still it seemed to be under a spell. There was just one spot, right in the middle, where one bubble after another rose jerkily to break its stony calm.

'That must surely be the way to the bottom of the lake,' thought Broadheart, bending over the water. Then his heart almost froze with horror. From beneath the water, the huge, glassy eyes of the giant black spider fixed him with their stare. Slowly, it raised itself on its long, spindly legs, ready to pounce. Broadheart fumbled with his scarf, but before he could make ready the golden sting from the wasp queen, the spider rolled its horrid eyes, leapt out of the water, and hurled itself upon its prey.

It would have been the end of Broadheart, had not a stroke of good fortune come to his aid. He was bound hand and foot in the sinewy web and being carried along helpless, when the spider came to the place where the golden sting had slipped from his grasp. The monster was too intent on his victim to notice the sting, and steppend straight onto it. The sharp point pierced its black body: the spider released its prey and fell lifeless into the lake, trailing behind it a slender thread.

When Broadheart managed at last to free himself from his bonds and saw the thread left behind by the spider, he took hold of it and began to climb down it to the bed of the lake. The deeper he went, the icier was the water. The journey seemed endless to him, and he was just about to return to the surface when his feet suddenly touched the bottom. A ray of emerald light cut through the gloom. Broadheart bent down and dug out of the sand the emerald pearl, which was as cold as ice in his hand. Afraid it might slip out of his numbed fingers, he quickly put it in his mouth and set off back to the surface.

When he finally got out of the water, Broadheart collapsed, exhausted, on the bank. He slept for a long time, and when he awoke he leaned over the water to wash his face. As soon as he caught sight of his reflection in the still waters, he became speechless with wonder. He had turned into a mighty water giant, with streams of water gushing from his mouth.

He set off home with giant leaps, crossing mountains and ravines, and pouring water everywhere he went. The grass grew green where he had passed, and the fields became fertile again. When he reached his native village, he sank to his knees, and a gigantic lake poured from his body. People came running from all around, to gaze at the cool water as at a miracle. Then they set about watering the parched desert.

Since that time the people of that country need not fear the comet's fiery tail.

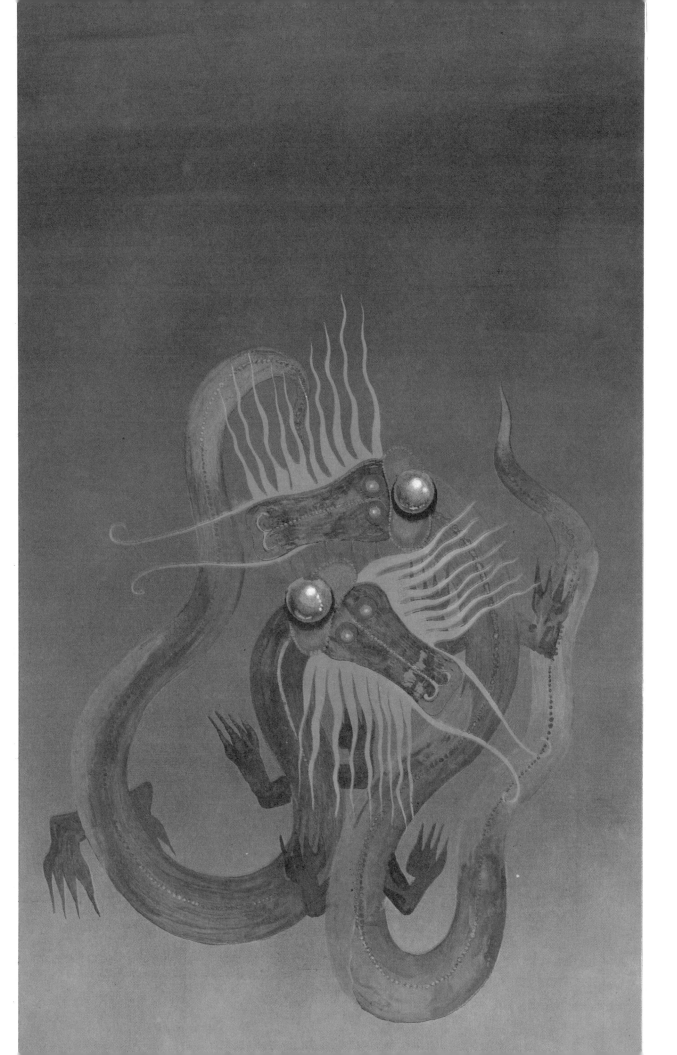

The Talking Buddha

There once lived a farmer who had an only daughter. The girl was as lovely as a jasmine flower, with sparkling eyes and raven-black hair plaited into two pigtails. And she was so good and hard-working, you simply can't imagine. When she sat down at the spinning-wheel, she forgot all about the rest of the world, and just went on spinning, and spinning. There was no other who could spin such fine thread as she, thin as a spider's yarn and smooth as silk. In the evening, when she sat down to her spinning, the boys from the village would come along and knock at the window, begging to be allowed in. Then they would all sit around the spinning-wheel and watch the spindle as it flashed through her gentle fingers, listening to her soft voice, accompanied by the whir of the wheel. Many a lad avowed his love for her, but the young woman only smiled and sent them away again.

The farmer had a shepherd-boy, a fine figure of a lad who had the strength of three. Not only that, but he also had a heart of gold, and was liked by everyone. But he was so poor he didn't have two coppers to rub together. Since the farmer's daughter had a kind heart, she was sorry for the shepherd boy, and from sympathy to love is but a tiny step. Here and there she would steal a glance at him, and a flush would come to her cheeks; now and again he would smile at her, his eyes alight with affection. So it came about that they fell in love without even knowing it. But the girl's father wanted to find her a rich husband, and would never have agreed to let her marry a poor shepherd, so they had to keep their love a secret. They were as miserable as a pair of birds lost in the mist.

The shepherd spent a long time wondering how he might get the farmer to agree to their marriage, until at last he had an idea. He set mouse-traps all around, and then waited. In a while there was a click — and there was a mouse, caught in one of the traps.

'Let me go, let me go!' squeaked the mouse. 'I am a prince, son of the mouse king: if you let me go, my father will reward you richly.'

'Very well, but first call your father — I wish to speak to him,' the shepherd ordered.

The mouse prince whistled: there was a patter of tiny feet, and there in front of the shepherd stood the king of the mice.

'Set my son free,' he said, 'and I will grant your every wish.'

'Very well,' agreed the shepherd, 'but on one condition only — within three days you must dig a tunnel from here to the temple.'

'A mere trifle,' replied the mouse king, and with a patter of paws he was gone.

Immediately the king summoned the whole royal kin and all their friends, and there was a tremendous pitter-pattering about, and whistling and scraping and gnawing, until at last, when the three days were up, the mice had dug an underground passage to the temple where the huge statue of Buddha stood. It was only then that the shepherd let the mouse prince go as he had promised.

The farmer's wife used to go to the temple where the great Buddha stood every day at cock's crow to say her prayers. She would kneel, touch the ground with her forehead, and rattle off a few prayers, until the Buddha heard her and sent her his blessing.

That day, too, she hurried off to the temple with a basket filled with good things. As soon as she got inside the door she fell to her knees and began to beat her head on the ground; then she looked at the Buddha out of the corner of her eye to see if he was smiling his celestial smile at her as always, greeted him three times, and finally added a little prayer: 'Amitabha, Amitabha, protect me and all my family, and grant that we might pass through the gates of Paradise.'

At that moment a rustling sound could be heard in the temple; the statue of the Buddha shook a little, and a stern, hollow-sounding voice broke the silence:

'You shall not pass through the gates of Paradise until you marry your only daughter to your shepherd-boy.'

The woman's blood ran cold. She was petrified. She stared helplessly at the inscrutable smile on the Buddha's face: the voice spoke again:

'You shall not pass through the gates of Paradise until you marry your only daughter to your shepherd-boy.'

'Then it was not my imagination,' said the farmer's wife to herself. 'But since when has the Buddha talked?' Frightened, she hurriedly left the temple and made her way home as fast as she could. When she arrived back at the farm, the shepherd, who had returned through the secret passage, was carelessly sweeping the yard. Quite out of breath, the farmer's wife burst into the parlour and blurted out:

'Husband, we must marry our daughter to the shepherd at once, or we shall never get into Paradise.'

'What nonsense is this, wife?' retorted the farmer. 'How could I ever marry my daughter to such a pauper?'

'Husband,' the woman replied, sternly, 'the Buddha himself told me so.'

'The Buddha?' repeated the farmer in astonishment. 'Since when have Buddhas talked?'

'If you don't believe me, then go to the temple to see for yourself!' said his wife, piqued, and left the room.

The farmer shook his head in disbelief. Though he never went to the temple himself and was no great disciple of the Buddha, he had no wish to take the celestial powers lightly: what if it were true? And when he was unable to put the matter out of his mind, he resolved to go along to the temple the next morning to see for himself.

At dawn the next day the farmer took a basket of the finest delicacies and set off. When he got to the temple he stared at the Buddha, but did not notice anything out of the ordinary. As ever, it stood there with its inscrutable smile and its eyes half-closed.

'She must have been hearing things,' said the farmer to himself. But at that moment there was a rustling sound; the statue of the Buddha shook slightly, and the stern, hollow-sounding voice began to speak:

'You shall not pass through the gates of Paradise until you marry your only daughter to your shepherd-boy.'

'Amitabha, have mercy on me: I shall do as you command,' the farmer promised, as a cold sweat broke out on his forehead. Without more ado, he spun round like a weather-cock and shot off home.

'Wife,' he gasped, as soon as he got in the door, 'we must marry our daughter to the shepherd without delay; you were right, the Buddha does indeed speak.'

The two of them did as the Buddha had commanded, and the wedding soon took place. It was attended by scores of guests, and they feasted and made merry for three whole days and nights.

'If it were not for the kindness of the Buddha in our temple, my parents would never have let me marry you,' the girl told the shepherd when they were man and wife. 'We must always be grateful to him, and must never forget him.' She told the shepherd that he must make generous sacrifices to the Buddha, revealing that her parents had only consented to the marriage because of the word of the Buddha himself.

The shepherd was not sure what to reply to this, but after a moment's silence he said:

'I suppose that it must have been the Buddha himself incarnate.' And he gave an arch smile; but he never said a word to anyone about how he managed to marry the farmer's daughter.

The Capricious Princess

Once there lived an old man who had three sons. When he realized his days were coming to an end, he called the youths to his bedside and said, 'My days are numbered. I have precious little to leave you, only this old cottage and the orchard beyond. When my eyes close for ever, divide it among you. Now I must tell you that in our orchard grows a certain apple tree and its fruit has the power of healing people.'

The old man never confided in his sons which particular tree had such magic power. Perhaps he forgot, or perhaps he thought that if they knew, they would neglect all the other trees.

When their father passed away, the brothers — the two eldest ones — divided

the orchard between them. To the youngest brother they left only one tree which stood right in the centre. It was such an ugly, crooked tree, its trunk split and cracked all over, that neither of the elder brothers wished to keep it.

One day the news reached the brothers that the only daughter of the king was seriously ill. Renowned surgeons, doctors, soothsayers and prophets were called from lands near and far. But, alas, none could cure the poor princess. She grew weaker and frailer, till she was unable to rise from her bed. The king promised her hand in marriage and half his kingdom to the one who would cure her. But no one had yet been successful.

The two elder brothers decided they too would try their luck. First the eldest prepared for the journey. Taking a basket, he picked an apple from each tree in his half of the orchard, hoping that one of them might be the health-giving fruit. Then he set off to the king's castle.

He had to travel through a deep forest. When he was right in the middle of it he met an old woman, who spoke to him kindly, 'Good day, my son! Are you perhaps carrying mushrooms in your basket?' she asked.

'It is none of your business, you inquisitive old hag,' the youth replied rudely. 'If you really want to know, it is filled with lizards and toads.'

'You are quite right, it is none of my business. Away with your lizards and toads then!' said the old woman, and she went her way.

When the eldest brother reached the royal castle, he was stopped by the guard at the gates, 'What have you there, young man?'

'In this basket I have precious, health-giving apples with which I hope to cure our princess,' the youth replied.

'It would be wonderful if you were successful. Show me the apples,' said the guard, and he raised the lid of the basket.

'How dare you make fun of the king's guard?' he shouted in fury and, whipping the youth madly with a birchrod, he chased him away from the castle.

The youth dropped the basket during the beating, and — lo and behold — frogs, toads and lizards jumped and slithered out of it!

In the meantime the second brother was preparing for his visit to the ailing princess. He too picked an apple from each tree in his part of the orchard, placed them in a basket and was off.

And, like his brother, he also met the old lady deep in the forest, who spoke to him kindly, 'Good day, my son, are you carrying mushrooms in your basket?' she asked.

'I have no mushrooms, you inquisitive old hag,' the youth answered curtly. 'Only snakes and scorpions.'

'Very well then, off with you, snakes, scorpions and all!' the old lady remarked sternly and went on her way.

The moment the second brother reached the castle, he demanded to be taken to the royal chambers of the princess, as he was bringing her magic apples.

'Let me see them first,' said the guard, his whip ready, for he could see that this youth greatly resembled the lad he had just chased away.

The second brother took the lid off the basket and gasped; all he could see were all manner of snakes and scorpions!

The guard was not surprised in the least and gave the young man a really good hiding.

'I'll give you what for, you rascal!' he said. 'How dare you try and make a fool of the king's soldier!'

With his whip he marched the youth away from the castle gates.

The youngest brother was the last one to try his luck. He picked a few apples from his crooked tree and was on his way. Deep in the forest he met the old woman and spoke to her politely.

'Good day, grandmother,' he said. 'Could you tell me the right path to the royal castle?'

'Yes, my son, you are walking in the right direction,' she replied. 'What have you in your basket?'

'There are some magic apples from my Tree of Health,' the youth replied.

'You should have them, for you are kind. I wish you good fortune,' said the old woman pleasantly, disappearing into the forest.

When the path left the forest, it led him to a river. The youth noticed a large, silver pike tossing and turning on the bank. It must have been thrown out by a large wave and now with its remaining strength was vainly trying to reach the water.

'Oh, you poor thing,' said the kind youth, and he threw the fish back into the river.

The pike raised its head above the surface and spoke with a human voice, 'One day I will repay you for saving my life. If you need me, just call and I will come immediately to your aid!'

The young man walked on until he noticed a strange moving ball in the air. An

old crow was fighting for his life against a swarm of maddened bees. Most probably they would have stung him to death in the end, though he crushed many of them with his beak and his claws.

'Stop this ridiculous battle! Look how many of you have died already! All of you, fly your own way!' the youth shouted at them sternly. And strangely enough the bees and the crow were glad to obey. In truth, they had had enough of fighting.

As they flew their separate ways, first the bees, then the crow called to the young man that they would gladly repay him for his sound advice. If he was ever in need, he should think of them. Soon afterwards the youth reached the royal castle.

'And are you, too, bringing health-giving apples?' the guard greeted him, viewing the basket suspiciously.

The youngest brother replied, 'Yes, I have magic apples, which give back health to ill people. Try one, soldier!' and he offered the guard one of the beautiful, rosy apples.

The guard, after eating it, felt as strong and happy as if he were years younger!

'These really are magic apples,' he laughed. 'Come with me, I will take you to our princess without delay, for I am sure you can help her.'

The grief-stricken king, his head in his hands, sat by the princess's bedside. The guard announced that he had brought a young man, who had special apples from the Tree of Health in his basket.

After the princess had eaten the first apple, she could raise her head from the pillow; after eating the second apple, she could sit up in her bed; and when she finished the third, she jumped out of her bed and was so happy that she danced around her chamber.

The king was overwhelmed; he was not even ashamed of the tears which fell down his cheeks. When he had calmed down a little, he patted the youth's cheeks. He liked the look of the young man, so he turned to the princess.

'Dear daughter, now we will start to prepare for the wedding; this youth has saved your life. You will take him for a husband and I will give him half my kingdom!'

The princess, however, was terribly proud. To marry a common country lad! Who'd ever heard of such a thing!

But the king would not listen to her. 'I have given my promise that whoever cures you shall receive your hand and half my kingdom. The king's word cannot be broken!' he told her sternly.

'My dear father, I want a husband who is brave and capable of great deeds,' she retorted, 'not some simple-minded country lad, who knows only how to pick a basketful of apples.'

'How do you know that this particular youth won't achieve some great deeds one day? And don't forget that he managed to cure you, and that many noble, learned men tried in vain!' answered the king.

'Very well, father,' the princess said. 'If this peasant returns to me my gold ring with the diamond stone, which fell into the sea seven years ago, he will prove to me his cleverness, and I will marry him.'

The king agreed, but unwillingly. What else could he do when he had such a capricious daughter?

The young man went to the seashore to search for the lost ring. He sat sadly on a rock, wondering what to do. Then he remembered the pike and called the fish to come to his aid.

Immediately the surface of the sea rippled. The silver head appeared and asked what the youth's wishes were. So he said, 'Seven years ago the princess lost a ring with a diamond in the sea. Now she wants me to find it. Can you help me?'

'Of course, I will help you gladly! Just a moment,' cried the pike and with a swish of its tail disappeared into the deep.

Before very long the silver head surfaced again, the gold ring with the diamond in its mouth.

The delighted youth took it, thanked the pike, and pelted back to the castle. He gave the ring to the king, who said to the princess, 'I promised your hand in marriage to the one who made you well. You promised to wed this lad if he found the ring you lost years ago. Here it is.'

But the princess was still trying to get out of it. She cried, she sulked and in the end she threatened to be ill again. The king stood firm, granting her only one more wish, one more task to set for the youth. If he could build her a castle as magnificent and as large as her father's castle within three days, she would marry him. The castle would have to shine and sparkle in the sunshine as if it were pure gold.

The king was quite embarrassed to pass on the orders of the princess, and he said, 'I know the task my daughter has set before you is an impossible one, but don't let it get you down. I will give you half my kingdom and you will find a nicer bride — one who will not be as proud and as obstinate as the princess.'

As it happened, the youth was not so worried about wealth as about the princess. So he replied, 'I want all or nothing, Your Majesty! If I cannot accomplish the task the princess gave me, I will take nothing.'

The king was most impressed by such words.

'I will keep my fingers crossed for you, dear boy,' he said and smiled.

The youth strolled into the meadow behind the castle and sat down to have a good think. He remembered the bees and called them. There was a buzzing above his head and the whole swarm of bees was present.

'What's the trouble?' the queen bee buzzed by his ear.

The youth told her about the task the princess had set him.

'Oh, that is nothing,' the queen bee consoled him. 'Go to sleep in peace ...'

In the morning, on that very spot, stood a most magnificent castle made of wax, as large and as beautiful as the royal castle. It sparkled in the sun as if built of pure gold. All the people gazed at it, marvelling at such a miracle.

The king and the princess could not believe their eyes as they stood by the window, admiring the magnificent palace built from beeswax.

'I'll stand for no more nonsense now,' said the king sternly. 'You must marry that young man. You have to admit he has achieved more than anyone.'

The princess did admit this but once again started to make excuses, insisting that she would give the youth yet another task to fulfil.

The furious king shouted at his daughter, 'If you do not wish to keep your word this time, I will turn you out of your home!'

The princess jumped into her bed, as if she were ill once again, and in a trice her pillows were soaked through with her tears.

'What is this very last task to be then?' the old king asked, beaten once again.

'If the youth brings me the oldest flame from hell, I really will marry him,' promised the princess, leaping out of bed.

The king went out, slamming the door so hard that the clock fell off the wall.

He found the youth and reluctantly informed him of the princess's latest task.

'I am really annoyed with her, and I said I would turn her out of the castle if she is not satisfied this time.'

'Do not worry, Your Majesty!' the young man replied, remembering the crow. After all, has not the crow always been called the devil's mate?

As soon as he was alone, the youth called the bird and told him what he needed.

'Have no fear,' replied the crow. 'I will help you all I can.'

Before very long the crow returned from hell. In his beak he held the oldest hell-fire, which he handed carefully to the youth.

The young man thanked the bird and ran with the flame into the castle, straight to the princess. As he ran, the flame grew hotter, till it burnt his hand. So he threw it straight into the proud girl's lap!

The princess was enveloped in a cloud of smoke. She coughed and she choked and perhaps she would have been burnt to death.

At the very last minute she jumped up and with a cry threw herself into the youth's arms, so he would save her. He, of course, gladly obliged, embracing the girl tightly, and he did not let her go again. He realized that the hell's flame had burned away all her pride.

Soon a huge, merry wedding was held.

The king gave half his kingdom to his new son-in-law, and the other half to his daughter as her dowry. He himself moved into the wax palace, where he lived happily to the very end of his days.

The Priest Know-All

Deep in the woods there once lived a poor miner. When he realized that if he continued working in the mines he would be sure to die of hunger, he went out into the wide world to look for a better living. As he was by nature a clever man, and as this time luck was on his side, he really did find happiness.

Actually, it happened as he was leaving the woods. It was a boiling hot day when the miner saw a beautiful blue lake in front of him.

'I'll have a swim, and wash away once and for all the grime and dust from the mines.'

Without further ado he dived into the water and scrubbed himself clean with fine sand. Then he made up his mind to swim across the lake. When he climbed out on the opposite bank, he found a neatly folded bundle of clothes under an alder tree, and next to it a priest's hat.

'Well, well,' he exclaimed in surprise, 'I wonder how these black clothes got here? I hope some unfortunate preacher hasn't drowned in the lake!'

He searched the bushes, calling out loudly, but there was no one about. So he tried on the elegant robe, and it fitted as if it had been made-to-measure. Pressing the hard hat on his head, the miner was anxious to see how he looked, for never had he been so smartly dressed. He ran across the dam and gazed with pleasure at his reflection, mirrored in the surface of the lake.

'You do look smart,' he praised himself. 'No one would recognize you as the grubby miner you really are.'

As he strolled along the dam, lost in admiration of his own image, a magnificent coach suddenly appeared on the road and came to a halt before him. The royal messenger opened the door, greeted the startled miner cordially, then said, 'As you must surely know, Your Grace, our king is today giving a feast for all the clergy of this kingdom. Permit me, therefore, to take you there. I can see you were already on your way. Be so kind as to step into the carriage.'

The messenger settled the disguised miner inside the coach, then sat down next to the coachman. And they were off to the castle.

'What a scandal it will be when it comes to light that I am no priest,' the dazed miner thought with dread, his teeth chattering so fiercely that his hat nearly fell off.

The castle was filled with the clergy; chaplains, vicars, canons, prelates — only the bishop was still missing. They were all deep in discussion about matters of God and prayer, and no one took any notice of the disguised miner. Some of his fear soon left him and he mingled with the rest of them. When at last the bishop arrived, they were all asked to enter the banqueting hall. Thirty-three tables, beautifully laden, were awaiting them. The king sat at the head of the gathering with the bishop at his side, and the rest sat according to their rank. The most important ones were near the king. The king welcomed them all, saying he hoped they would enjoy the feast and entertainment. Before he finished, he asked them all to forgive him for not being his usual jovial self. As it happened, just before the feast he had lost his most valuable ring, which contained a huge precious stone. If by any remote chance one of the guests could help him to find this ring, by word or deed, he would reward them handsomely.

After the king's speech there was a profound silence in the banqueting hall, as in a church. Nobody knew anything about the lost ring and so could not help. The king wasted no more time, but clapped his hands three times. The doors flew open and the royal servants, dressed as waiters, marched in, bringing delicious dishes upon silver salvers.

The disguised miner, who was used only to a diet of potato cakes and stew, marvelled at such food. His eyes grew so big they nearly fell out of his head! He sat quietly at the end of one table and when a waiter came to him with a plate of roast lamb done to a turn, he could not contain his excitement and whispered, 'This is the first one!'

He was thinking, of course, that this was his first good meal, and the first course of the feast. He did not even notice that on hearing his words, the waiter's hands trembled so much that he very nearly dropped the silver salver.

When the clergy had finished their roast lamb, another waiter entered, bringing on a gold platter a turkey stuffed with nuts. The miner was almost spellbound by such a delicacy, and when the waiter bent over him to serve, words tumbled from the miner's mouth.

'So this is the second one!' he murmured. He was thinking, of course, that this was the second course of the dinner, and one that he had never ever tasted or even seen. The waiter, however, on hearing such words, went as white as a ghost and hastily crept out of the hall.

When all the clergymen had eaten their stuffed poultry, it was time for the third course — game. Already yet another waiter was approaching, bringing an enormous pearl-studded platter of roast venison and boar.

'So this is the third,' remarked the delighted miner almost out loud, for he was enthusiastically counting all the courses, as they were brought to the table.

After the miner's exclamation the waiter's knees nearly gave way, and he trembled with fear all over. Bending over our counterfeit priest, he said in a shaky voice, 'For God's sake, Your Worship, I beg you not to give us away!'

The miner had no idea what he was talking about, but he guessed something must be radically wrong. He waited till the waiter left the hall, then followed him out.

The three waiters were standing in the passage, a stupefied look on their faces, their bodies shaking with fright. As soon as the disguised priest came to them, they admitted that they had stolen the king's ring. Afterwards the trio knelt before the miner, and with their palms clasped in supplication they begged him not to tell the king; they knew full well such a misdeed would cost them their heads.

Only then did the disguised miner realize how luck had been on his side. While

he was busily counting the dishes brought to him by these servants, their bad consciences made them think he was exposing them, one by one.

The miner played his new role cleverly and said sternly to the frightened waiters, 'For such an insolent theft our king would naturally have your three cheeky heads. And it would serve you right. But as I am your priest, it is not up to me to hand you over to the executioner, thieving rascals though you are! Give me that ring, and I will work it all out somehow.'

The three thieves were falling over themselves in their haste to hand over the king's ring to the counterfeit priest. They thanked him profusely for not giving them away.

The miner left the castle and strolled through the courtyard into the garden, where there was a lake with a fountain. White swans and black ducks were swimming about merrily. Selecting a duck with a white spot on her forehead, he gave her the ring to swallow. Then the counterfeit priest returned to the banqueting hall. Delicious honey-cakes, exotic fruit and mouth-watering cool drinks were just being served.

'I am glad I have not missed this,' thought the miner, and he soon made up for lost time.

When in the evening the feasting was over, the miner came to the king. With a deep bow, as though he were a prophet he proclaimed, 'Your Royal Highness, I know where to find your precious ring which you lost this morning. In your garden is a small lake with a fountain. In this lake swims a black duck with a white spot on her head; your ring is hidden inside her.'

The king was astonished by what he heard, but immediately issued an order for the duck to be brought into the kitchens and her stomach examined. As the miner had predicted, the ring was found inside the duck, and the king was so overjoyed he announced that he would handsomely reward this Wise Priest.

Calling the bishop to his side, he asked him to give such a clever preacher a really nice parish.

The disguised miner was given a splendid parish and became a real preacher. He was beginning to be convinced that nothing bad could ever happen to him again. But now his troubles began — with the sermons. He had no idea, of course, how to preach. And instead of conducting a proper service, he related funny stories to amuse the churchgoers.

Once, for instance, he described how difficult it was to make a goat walk across the ice, another time that you can go to fetch water with a jug only till the handle falls off, and on another occasion he told them how troublemakers often invite trouble.

One joke followed another, and though his congregation laughed to begin with, eventually the strange sermons stopped amusing them and they began to complain.

'I am only preaching the same as my predecessors,' the priest defended himself at each sermon, but the people no longer took any notice. They went to complain to the bishop.

The bishop was well aware that the Wise Priest was under the protecting hand of the king himself, so he was curt to his visitors.

'If the Wise Priest says that he is preaching what his predecessors preached, then everything must be in order and his sermons must be correct. You can go home with easy minds.'

But the people were not going to be put off.

'Your Worship, please come on Sunday and listen to the sermon of our priest,' they said. 'Then you will believe us!'

The bishop, anxious to be rid of them, promised to come the following Sunday.

When the counterfeit priest heard the news, he waited till nightfall on Saturday, then crept in secret to his church. With a saw he made a cut in both pillars under the pulpit.

As arranged, the bishop arrived at the church to hear the sermon. The priest carefully climbed into his pulpit.

'My sermon will not differ from those of my forefathers, not even today!' he stormed. 'Before I start to preach, we must all say the Lord's prayer together, for in a moment you will all witness with your own eyes a great fall.'

To emphasize his solemn words, the false priest began to chant the Lord's prayer with a particularly melodious voice, and stepped right to the very edge of his pulpit.

A tremendous rattle vibrated the church as the whole pulpit crashed to the floor. The preacher with his unfinished prayer was buried beneath the wreckage.

The frightened congregation ran to their priest's aid. They dug frantically with their hands, scattering broken beams and bricks around them, till they found him. Fortunately the preacher was not even hurt, just somewhat the worse for wear.

The agitated bishop calmed down when he saw the priest alive and well. Turning to the congregation, he said gravely, 'The Almighty God has just proved to us his power and mercy, for he has endowed your priest with clairvoyance. We have all witnessed how this chosen man has the spiritual power of being able to see into the future and to know things of which ordinary mortals are unaware.'

After this happened, all the people of the parish treated their priest with great respect; in fact, the whole region talked of him with reverence. The news of his proven prophecy eventually reached the king's ears.

The king summoned our priest to the castle and said to him in a very friendly fashion, 'You are unusually gifted, Your Grace, for you can predict things unknown to others. I recall how some time ago you discovered the presence of my gold ring in the stomach of the black duck. And now I have been told that you actually predicted the disintegration of your own pulpit.'

The false priest smiled modestly, and bowed respectfully before his king. He was really dying to know the reason he had been invited to the castle. He did not have to wait long.

'You may know already, gracious priest, that we are soon to have a child,' the king told him confidentially. 'As it will be our first born, I am naturally impatient and anxious. I would be grateful if you would fix your spiritual insight on the future and tell me whether we shall have a son, or a daughter. It is indeed most important to me.'

'I will do all in my power to oblige, Your Royal Highness, but it won't be easy. Now, with your permission, I should also like to see your wife, the queen,' the priest answered.

The king was terribly eager to find out about the forthcoming baby, so he sent for the queen without hesitation. When the priest had paid her his respects, he asked the royal pair to walk about the chamber. They were glad to oblige and as they walked, the preacher regarded them keenly.

'Something very strange is happening, Your Royal Highnesses,' he announced finally. 'On the one hand it seems that a son will be born to you, on the other hand I have a strong feeling you will have a daughter.'

Such an unsatisfactory prediction did not please the king, for he was none the wiser. In fact he felt quite annoyed as he dismissed the priest.

It so happened that some time later twins were born to the queen, a boy and a girl. The king was wild with joy and, to celebrate such an occasion, gave the command to fire all cannons. And he also immediately sent for the priest. Thanking him profusely for such an accurate prophecy, he rewarded him handsomely.

Before dismissing the priest, he thought awhile, then said gravely, 'You are far too good, Wise Priest, for a country parish; stay with me in my castle. Your exceptional foresight has been proved to me now on two occasions. If you pass the third test which I have prepared for you, I will promote you to a minister. I hope you agree with my proposition. Now come, let us take a walk through the gardens!'

'That's just fine!' thought the poor priest. 'Goodness knows what the king has in store for me! I will either win all or lose all. We'll see what happens!' Boldly he followed the king.

All the members of the court were gathered on the lawns. In the middle of the crowd stood an ordinary barrel. The king walked to it and asked the priest in a grand manner, 'Tell me, Your Grace, what is hidden in this barrel?'

The preacher's brow was wet with perspiration, for he was frightened to death by such a question.

'This is the end,' he thought to himself. Looking round him at the faces of the inquisitive, and not particularly friendly, audience, he felt like a trapped animal.

The priest was resigned now to his fate, for he felt he had lost everything. Summoning all his courage, he said, 'I knew it; there are many hunters and one trapped, frightened hare.'

The king smiled with content at such words and kicked the lid of the barrel, which flew off; a real, frightened hare leapt out. It zig-zagged amid the delighted crowd, and pelted for dear life through the half-open gates.

The same day the king promoted the priest to minister — and it was just as well, too! For since that day no one dared to rob him or the king, because it was well known all over the kingdom that the new minister was clairvoyant and could uncover any plot before it ever happened.

Lazy Lars

It is quite a tragedy when someone has a good-for-nothing, lazy child. Such a misfortune happened to a poor widow, for she was blessed with a real lay-about son
who was so well known for his laziness that people talked about him near and far.
Some felt sorry for the unhappy mother, others only laughed, saying that one day
flies would bite her son Lars to death, for he would surely be too lazy to flick them
off.

'I want to do my washing, son,' the widow said to Lars one morning. 'Take this
pail and fetch me water from the well.'

Well, of course, Lars would gladly fetch it, if only he were not sprawled on the
cosy bench above the stove. It seemed too much of an effort to climb down. Surely
his mother could fetch the water herself, instead of pottering round the kitchen?

Mother was patient, but such sheer laziness made her see red. Snatching a broom, she ran towards the stove. Lars knew his mother was really annoyed and, seeing the warning signals on her face, he climbed down reluctantly, yawned widely, took the pail and shuffled through the door.

'Things didn't have to be that bad,' he consoled himself.

Along the way he pondered how he could manage to get the pail there without carrying it. Such hard work! Especially when it would be full! How nice it would be, if the pail could run with its own pair of legs! To ease his task, Lars rolled the bucket along the path. There was such a clatter, as it rolled over the stones, that the princess herself came to the castle window.

'Hurry, Lars, or the bucket will run away from you, though it has no legs?' she laughed gaily, as she leant out of the window.

Lars, his mouth gaping wide, gazed at the princess. He would have liked to greet her properly, but it would have been such an effort to take off his hat in this heat.

'Close your mouth, Lars, or your heart will catch a cold,' the princess giggled.

She need not worry — he would shut his mouth; that was no hard work! But she didn't have to make fun of him!

At last Lars came to the well and filled the pail with water. As he bent over it, he saw a frog swimming in it.

'Please, Lars, throw me back into the well,' it pleaded with a croaky voice.

Lars would have gladly fished it out and thrown it back into the well, but it would have been such an effort. Let the frog stay in the bucket. His mother would take it out!

'Lars, if you throw me back into the well, I will make your wish come true,' the frog pleaded.

Lars thought he would be a fool to work so hard for just one little wish!

The frog grew afraid that it would not be able to persuade the lazy fellow. It promised therefore that it would fulfil as many wishes as the number of blades of grass covered by his wide hat, which was in the grassy meadow. All he had to do was to throw it back.

This seemed a better proposition. Lars squatted in the meadow, and thought and thought what wish he could make. When he was really worn out from so much thinking, he sighed with fatigue, tossed the frog into the well, and yawned broadly. 'I have only one wish,' he said. 'I would like that bucket to have its own pair of feet, so it could walk home with the water.'

The minute he voiced his wish, a pair of legs as long as a stork's grew under the bucket, and it started to march in a hilarious fashion along the path towards home.

Lars snatched his hat and followed the pail. It was all he could do to catch up with it. Threading a piece of string through the bucket handle, he held on to it tightly, otherwise it would have run away. But the pail marched speedily along on its long stork legs, so our slowcoach had his work cut out to keep up with it. In the end he put his wide hat over the bucket.

When this strange procession passed under the castle windows, the princess was still looking out. She laughed so much she got the hiccups.

'Lars, you lazy lay-about,' she called. 'I'll bet you're pretending you are in a carriage, but instead of horses you are driving a bucket!'

'It's probably you who is pretending to ride in a carriage,' Lars answered curtly.

'I don't have to pretend, I am accustomed to ride in carriages. I can see your bucket is carrying even your hat. I should put it on, if I were you; otherwise your little head might catch cold!' the princess teased. But Lars retaliated immediately.

'Be careful, or your head will catch a cold, as you keep poking it out of the window!'

'Don't worry about that!' the princess laughed again. 'My head can't catch a cold, for it is covered by a gold crown.'

'So what, I have a lot of gold crowns,' Lars boasted, patting his pocket significantly, till it rattled. As it happened, it was filled with a fistful of pebbles.

The princess knew he could not be telling the truth; where would a poor lay-about find a pocketful of money?

'Just you wait, you cheeky liar, I'll tell my father, the king, that you are making fun of me!'

'It is not I, but you who keep on pulling my leg,' the young man defended himself. But the princess just laughed at him.

'You talk like a baby,' she mocked. 'Wouldn't you like a little boy for a playmate?'

'You can have the little boy!' Lars replied crossly and turned towards home with his stork-legged pail.

What do you think happened? Before the year ended, his strange wish really did come true.

One morning, it was in early spring, the princess woke up and found next to her a tiny, naked baby boy, as beautiful as an angel.

Naturally enough, there was a terrible commotion in the palace. Everyone was astonished and whispered among themselves.

'Have you heard the news? Our princess has a baby!' they said. 'The baby is here, its mother is here, but where's the father?'

'Exactly! Who is the father of the child?' asked the agitated king.

The princess only wept, assuring him she had no idea.

The baby boy grew and grew; day by day he became stronger, wiser and more handsome.

In the meantime the king decided that a bridegroom for his daughter must be found. She had a son and must therefore also have a husband!

When the little boy was only three years old, he had the wisdom of a grown-up person. So the king summoned to the castle all the men from his kingdom. He was sure the young prince would recognize his own father, who would then have to marry the princess.

Crowds of men flocked to the castle from all directions. Some were fat and some were skinny, some were tall and some were short, some were noble and some were poor. They came in coaches, on horses and on foot.

Lazy Lars could not have cared less about all this. He lolled about on the bench above the stove, concocting all sorts of ridiculous wishes; for instance, that the flies would stop biting him without his flicking them off; or that his hair would be tidy without his having to comb it; or that his dinner would be ready — and so on.

Strangely enough, all these silly wishes were immediately fulfilled.

On this particular day his mother was cooking lunch and telling him off.

'Look at all those men going to the castle!' she said. 'It's such an important day, but my son just lies around being lazy as usual. What about you, aren't you going to the castle, too?'

No, no, he was not going to the castle. Why should he?

'Don't you know it is the king's command that all men in the kingdom must assemble there today? Are you going to wait until the royal guard comes to get you?' the mother shouted.

'All right then, I'll go,' Lars agreed reluctantly, and he sauntered to the castle.

When the king saw him approach, he called to the master of ceremonies:

'Now we can start! I am sure all the men from my kingdom are present. Lazy Lars is by the castle gates and he always arrives everywhere last,' he said.

There was a flourish of trumpets, a roll of drums and the inspection began. All the men were divided according to their rank in various forecourts of the castle: in the first court there were the noblemen and gentry; in the second, the farm owners and the wealthy citizens from the towns; in the third, very ordinary folk, servants, fishermen — in short, the people used to having both pockets empty.

The king placed a golden apple in the small prince's hand and said to him in a stern voice, 'Go, child, and examine carefully all the men present. If you find your father among them, give him this apple!'

The little boy walked through the first yard, but though he looked and looked, he did not halt in front of anyone there.

He entered the second yard. But though his little neck ached from turning this way and that as he scrutinized everyone most carefully, he still did not find his father.

He came into the third court, criss-crossed it from end to end, but still no luck. Then suddenly he saw Lazy Lars right at the very back, by the castle gates. He was leaning against the wall so he would not fall down with exhaustion, his hands thrust deep in his pockets.

The little prince ran to him and, laughing merrily, gave Lars the golden apple. The lay-about took his hand out of his pocket with a great effort, accepted the apple and swiftly hid it under his shirt, in case someone wanted to take it from him.

What a tumult followed this scene! Some men shouted, while others swore; a few threatened Lars, and many just whistled and giggled mockingly. One thing was certain: each one of them was jealous of him.

'Just think! The biggest lay-about in the kingdom gets the princess for his bride! That's what you call real luck! Our master the king will have a fine son-in-law! Ha, ha, ha!' echoed from all sides.

The king felt trapped; everything seemed even worse than it had been before. He had never dreamed that Lazy Lars could possibly be the father of his grandson. But he had given his word and as a king could not go back on it now.

'Very well then,' he decided, 'let that good-for-nothing wed my daughter, but the three of them must disappear from sight. And immediately!'

He ordered Lars, the princess and the little prince to be put in a small fishing boat which should be taken right out to sea. Let them go wherever the current might take them and if they were swallowed by the deep waters forever, so much the better!

His cruel decision was carried out forthwith and so the unfortunate trio found themselves before nightfall on the wide-open sea. First the waves tossed the boat here and there, then a strong undercurrent gripped the boat and took it far from the shore. At midnight a strong wind sprang up and carried the boat in yet another direction.

The poor travellers were lost on the waves all night long and all the next day, and they were very miserable about their fate.

The little boy was shivering with cold, the princess was sobbing silently, but as for Lars — he was sprawled at the bottom of the boat thinking quite happily that this was the very first time he was out at sea.

'Whatever shall we do, Lars?' asked the despairing princess.

Lars could not answer that one!

'Couldn't you row? Perhaps we could then reach the shore,' she sobbed.

What was the point of rowing? Where to? In which direction was the land? Lars was not one to work in vain. 'Let the boat take us somewhere,' he thought. And so their misery continued. Their son shivered with cold and cried, the princess sobbed, and Lars remained silent. Why use up energy on words, when nothing was really happening yet!

By the evening the princess had had enough and turned on Lars.

'Do something, or at least say something, you lazy good-for-nothing!' she shouted in exasperation. 'Or do you want to remain here at the bottom of the boat like a statue until doomsday?'

As it happened, Lars had had enough too. He felt he had had more than his share of the sea, and he wanted to feel firm ground under his feet!

As soon as he said this to the princess, lo and behold! all three of them found themselves standing on a delightful island, with imposing houses and kind people all around them.

The princess was astonished to see how easily all the wishes Lars made were fulfilled. And as she was very wise, she embraced Lars and smiled at him sweetly.

'Dear Lars,' she said confidently, 'wouldn't you like to be an orderly, hard-working man instead of the good-for-nothing lay-about everyone laughs at?'

Yes, yes, of course he wished this could happen! It still stung to remember how she mocked him for his laziness when he had been following the stork-legged pail.

As soon as he expressed this wish, Lars was given a new lease of life and he immediately became an upright, honest man. He also grew very handsome and very neat.

The princess then advised him to wish for a palace with all the trimmings — magnificent furniture, servants, wardrobe, carriages, horses, soldiers, the lot!

In a trice a magnificent castle appeared on the shore, with a gold roof which glittered in the sun like fire. And everything in the castle was as ordered.

The following morning the old king took a stroll along the beach. He had slept very badly, for he was troubled that he had banished his only daughter and grandson and put them out on the open ocean. He now hoped he might catch a glimpse of their boat on the surface of the sea.

But instead he suddenly noticed an island right in front of him where an enchanted castle reached to the skies, its top shining with gold. Was his sight deceiving him? He was sure the island had never been there before!

He put on his gold glasses, but it was true; a magnificent castle stood on an island about three miles out in the sea. The king could not understand it; perhaps it was an hallucination...

Swiftly he called other members of the court, and they too were dazed with astonishment when they saw the island and castle.

'This must be the work of the devil,' screeched the court jester. 'I know for sure that nothing but water was there yesterday!'

The king could not relax till he found everything out for himself. He chose the ablest sailors and, with himself as captain, sailed in his royal vessel towards the island. When they reached the shore, a long line of soldiers was there to welcome them, stretching from the castle right to the port. The king rather liked that. He was even more surprised and delighted when he was met at the castle gates by his daughter and Lars, both robed in magnificent clothes. The princess fell to her knees and on behalf of both of them begged his forgiveness.

Then she told her father how everything had happened and that she had been punished because she used to make fun of Lazy Lars. And she explained how now Lars was quite a different person and that she longed to marry him.

Lars also knelt by the princess's side and asked the king for his blessing.

'Everything is ending happily,' stated the king, well satisfied. He sent for the queen, and soon long, merry wedding celebrations were being held.

'The world is a good place after all and everything has worked out for the best,' Lars's mother remarked, quite content, as she was being driven from the wedding in the royal coach.

After some years the old king passed away and Lars sat on his throne. All the people prospered under his rule, for he was wise and just. However, he had no love for lay-abouts; in fact he had no time for them at all.

The King's Rabbits

In the region where land ends and the cold sea begins, stood a certain kingdom, governed wisely by an old king and his queen. For many years they had no children, but at last they were blessed with a daughter. She was as lovely as apple blossom, and the older she grew the more beautiful she became.

When she was a full-grown princess, scores of knights, lords and princes came to woo her from lands near and far. But the king and queen loved their daughter so much that they did not want her to marry. The old parents wanted to keep her to give them joy and pleasure in their old age! And to tell the truth, the princess did not like any of her suitors, and she was in no hurry to leave her parents.

Like all men of power, the king too had a special hobby. He reared silver rabbits in his palace, and he was very attached to them.

So that nobody could say he was against marriage for his daughter, the king sent messages throughout his kingdom. If anyone was able to take all the king's rabbits out to graze for three days running without losing a single one of them, he would gain the princess for a bride. The unsuccessful applicants would receive as many blows with a birch upon their backs as the rabbits they lost; the executioner's friend was to deliver this punishment. The king was quite sure that no one could possibly keep an eye on three hundred frisky bunnies and so was not afraid that anyone would take away his beloved daughter.

In this particular kingdom, somewhere at the foot of the mountains lived a wealthy farmer, who had three sons. The two eldest ones were strong and broad, but slack in their work and of bad character. The youngest, Esben, was rather slight. But he made up for what he lacked in weight with what he carried in his head and his heart. He was the cleverest and the kindest one.

When the news reached them that the king was prepared to give his only daughter to the person capable of minding three hundred of his silver rabbits, the eldest brother decided he would go and try his luck.

'Go by all means, my son,' his father agreed. 'I hope you'll manage to marry into the royal household, for you are useless here! At least you should be able to tend the rabbits; there is nothing difficult about that!'

The father prepared his son for the journey as best he could. He gave him a new suit, a fresh loaf of bread, a leg of mutton, and a horse. The eldest brother then rode off. He came to a deep forest and was soon lost in the dense thicket.

Some time later he came across an old coalman and shouted to him to point out the way to the palace. The coalman kindly showed him the way, and then asked for a slice of bread, for he had not eaten anything since morning.

'That's your fault,' sneered the youth nastily. 'You should have sucked your thumb, old man! You can't have my loaf; it's for me and my horse.'

'It is a shame, young man, that you are unkind, otherwise I would have advised you well,' the old man remarked, shaking his head sadly. But the youth just laughed loudly, dug his heels into the horse's sides, and before the day was over, he was knocking on the palace gates.

'So you dare to have a go at minding my rabbits?' marvelled the king, when the youth told him of his intentions. 'You can try, by all means. Just don't forget what awaits you if some of the rabbits are missing, when you return from the pasture in the evening.'

'Why should I worry,' the youth thought. 'I know how to mind a few rabbits, and getting a princess is worth that much of an effort! After all, when it is over, I'll be a man of leisure for the rest of my life.'

He drove the rabbits to pasture, but no matter how hard he tried to keep them together, the naughty bunnies pelted in all directions. It was all the youth could do to keep a handful in the meadow. When the king saw the small, sad procession returning to the palace that evening, he was so furious he did not even bother to count them.

He said to the executioner's friend, 'Give him fifty lashes with the birch on his bare back to pay him for his arrogance and his carelessness!'

The careless shepherd was paid in full; he ached so much he could hardly stand up after the thrashing. So they threw him like a sack of potatoes on to his horse, who trotted with his helpless master all the way home. He was such a sorry sight they hardly recognized him back at the farm.

'I never thought tending the royal rabbits could be such dangerous work. Why, you're black and blue all over!' the second brother cried mockingly.

'I'll be curious to see if you return from the king with the princess,' the father rejoined.

'Just wait and see,' promised the second son, and he prepared to go to the palace. He too was given a new suit of clothes, plenty of food and a good horse. He left early the next morning.

'Perhaps he'll have better luck,' thought the father, hoping secretly that he would be rid of at least one lazy idler.

This brother too got lost in the deep forest and met the old coalman who willingly showed him the way to the royal palace.

'Have you anything I can eat?' the coalman asked shyly. 'I've actually only got one tooth, but it would be nice to bite into some food.'

The youth only laughed at the old man and said nastily, 'My food is for me and my horse only. I'll give you some advice instead: pull that last tooth of yours out, then you won't be tempted to bite at all.'

Laughing coarsely, he urged his horse forward and disappeared into the thicket. The old man shook his head sadly: a shame, really, for he would have liked to give the youth some good, useful advice.

The second son fared no better in the employment of the king than his elder brother. He lost nearly half the silver bunnies, the moment he let them loose in the pasture. He was paid with one hundred lashes upon his bare back, then thrown, half-dead, across his mount, who took his master home.

'Now it is my turn,' called the youngest, Esben, and he prepared for his journey.

The two elder brothers mocked the youngest, 'What good would it do for you to go there? You wouldn't be able to stand up to such punishment as we had! Or do you think the beautiful princess is waiting for you?!'

'Who knows, maybe she *is* waiting,' Esben retorted, and putting into his sack only two slices of bread and a slice of cheese, he set out on foot to the royal palace.

Deep in the forest he got lost, like his brothers. Esben also met the old coalman, who showed him the way to the palace. Thanking him sincerely, the youth sat down upon a tree stump and asked the old man to share his meagre lunch.

When they had eaten everything right down to the very last crumb, the coalman said, 'As you are such a kind young man, Esben, I would like to give you this whistle as a keepsake. I hope it will bring you good luck.'

'Thank you very much, grandfather,' Esben said gratefully.

'I must tell you, my lad,' the coalman explained further, 'this is no ordinary whistle. When you blow on it, all living creatures that have strayed from where they belong will gather together.'

'Such a magic whistle is exactly what I shall need very shortly,' cried the delighted Esben. Thanking the old man sincerely once again, he stepped out happily towards the palace.

He walked and walked, till he reached the royal court. As soon as he had washed, freshened up and combed his hair, he sought out the king and asked him for permission to take the silver rabbits out to graze.

The king was rather surprised to hear such a request from this fragile-looking young man. But he took a liking to the lad for his good manners and courage.

'Do you know what sort of a repayment awaits you?' asked the king rather worriedly. He felt sorry for the boy when he thought of the executioner's helper.

'Of course I know,' sighed the youth, for just at that moment he glimpsed in the window the beautiful face of the princess, who smiled at him sweetly.

The three hundred silver bunnies were then placed under Esben's care. Early the next morning he drove them to pasture.

There he said to them, 'Now you can go and eat the grass until evening. But don't run too far away; stay within hearing distance of my whistle.' The rabbits, as if they understood, hopped in all directions but not too far away.

The princess was curious to find out how the new, slim herdsman, whom she had liked at first sight, was getting on with tending her father's rabbits. Disguising herself in boys' clothing, so the youth would not recognize her, the princess climbed on to a mule and trotted to the meadow. In spite of her effort, Esben recognized her from afar, but pretended not to.

'Please sell me one of the silver rabbits, shepherd. The king won't even notice it's missing. I'll give you three gold sovereigns for it,' said the disguised princess.

'No fear,' laughed Esben. 'These bunnies are not for sale! But if you insist on having one, I'll give it to you, if you embrace me sincerely and lovingly like a brother.'

'What a strange request,' thought the princess. 'But he did not recognize me, so why shouldn't I embrace him?' She did as she was asked and Esben kept his word too. He placed a bonny rabbit in her basket and soon she was trotting on the mule back to the palace.

The moment she passed through the gates, the princess looked into her basket — and found it empty. This was because Esben had whistled upon his magic whistle, and the rabbit had scampered back to him. Funnily enough, the princess was not at all sorry.

Towards evening, when the sun was preparing for bed, the shepherd blew his whistle again. Immediately, all the rabbits scooted to him and lined up beautifully, just like soldiers. Esben started to sing a merry tune and soon led his bunny regiment through the meadow to the palace.

The king was waiting for him most impatiently, and as they marched in, he counted the rabbits. To his utter amazement there was not a single one missing. 'It's not possible,' he thought, and counted again. Really and truly, they were all present and accounted for.

Such news naturally travelled fast through the palace, and everyone wanted to see the able shepherd, who had kept an eye on all three hundred rabbits without losing a single one. How many noble gentlemen had already tried without succeeding, and left, disheartened, for home!

The following day, when Esben took the rabbits to the meadow again, the king called his daughter and said uneasily, 'I don't know how the new shepherd is managing it. He must be a devilishly clever fellow. Perhaps today, too, no rabbits will escape him, and then our situation will be serious. Disguise yourself as an old farmer, harness an old cow to a cart and go to the meadow. Try and talk the shepherd into selling you one of the rabbits. Even offer him a hundred sovereigns for it. I am sure he'll let you take one for such a sum, and then in the evening he will be at least one bunny short...' The king rubbed his hands together in sheer delight at that thought.

The princess wasn't terribly proud of the fact that she had already tried to get a rabbit away from Esben, so she readily agreed.

When during the late morning an old farmer and his cart rattled into the pasture, asking Esben to sell him a rabbit, he realized of course it was no farmer who had come to see him, but the disguised princess. Again he refused, saying, 'No fear! These rabbits are not for sale! But if you really insist on having one, I will let you have it, farmer, for three kisses!'

'What pleasure could a thing like that give you — such a handsome youth as you, wanting three kisses from an old farmer?' wondered the disguised princess. 'I'll do better than that; I'll give you one hundred sovereigns for that bunny!' But Esben was stubbornly firm: he wanted no money, just three kisses. What else could the princess do? 'He thinks, after all, that I am just an old farmer,' she thought to herself, and gave the shepherd three lovely kisses.

Afterwards she was given a silver rabbit. The princess put him into a sack, tied it firmly, threw it into the cart, and urged the cow to waddle off. When they reached the castle, the king eagerly took the sack from her, but found it empty! Of course this was because Esben had once again blown his magic whistle and the bunny had returned obediently to his side.

The king was angry and he scolded the princess. But funnily enough, she did not regret even a little bit that the rabbit had escaped. On the contrary, she could hardly wait for the youth to come back with the bunnies.

When at last he arrived with his four-legged regiment, and the king counted the rabbits three times over and regretfully said none was missing, the princess heaved a sigh of relief and began to hum softly.

When on the third morning Esben drove the rabbits to the meadow for the last time, the king knew he would have to think fast and act quickly, if he did not wish to lose his beloved daughter.

This time it was he who dressed up — in the clothes of an old hag. Then he climbed on the back of a dirty grey horse and set out personally to visit that devil of a chap in the meadow.

'Hullo there, shepherd! Please sell me two rabbits; I'll pay you well for them,' the old hag said persuasively in a soft voice.

Esben recognized the king immediately, and naturally refused, saying, 'No fear, grandma, these bunnies are not for sale.'

The old hag would not give in. She pleaded, she begged, she wrung her hands in despair, till Esben gave way.

'Very well, grandma,' he replied. 'If you really insist on having a pair of rabbits, you must first kiss this old nag three times. Otherwise you can't have them.'

What else could the poor king do? If he did not give the old horse three kisses, he would have to give his only daughter to this clever shepherd that very evening. He was quite sure if he did not manage to persuade Esben to let him have the rabbits, again none would be missing. 'In any case,' reasoned the king, 'I am all dressed up and the youth has not recognized me.'

So the king obediently kissed the old mare, and took the pair of rabbits, choosing them himself. He put them in a wooden box, nailed the lid down carefully and happily turned towards the palace. Once there he quickly discarded the tattered clothes, and had the wooden box taken into the cellar. There he slowly opened the lid — and nearly fell back in a swoon, for both the bunnies were gone! It was Esben again, of course, who had whistled in time.

That evening the rabbits as usual marched in line to the palace gates, and as usual, not a single one was missing. The king could see he was cornered.

Esben bowed respectfully and announced solemnly, 'Your Royal Majesty, I have carried out the task you set me and now I should like to claim my reward. I ask for the hand of your beautiful daughter.'

The king naturally knew that he must keep his word, but he hated the idea of losing his daughter, so he started making excuses.

'Look, young man,' the king said sternly, 'I have one more test for you to pass. In the cellar there is a large barrel. If you manage to fill it to the brim with truth, the princess shall be yours.'

'Certainly,' Esben agreed happily. 'I have never lied, so to fill a barrel with truth should be an easy task for me!'

The barrel was rolled into the courtyard, and the king, the queen, the princess and all the court members gathered round. The king stood right by the barrel, as he was eager to see how the youth would fill it with truth.

Esben did not waver for long. He began, 'The first day, when I was tending the royal rabbits, some youth rode by on a mule and wanted to buy a bunny from me. I sold it to him asking nothing but a warm embrace in return. To tell the truth, it was no youth, but our princess, dressed up in men's clothes. Is it the truth?' inquired Esben, turning to the princess.

'Yes, it is the truth,' the princess admitted, and blushed becomingly.

'Let's put that truth into the barrel then,' the king grunted.

'During the second day,' Esben continued, 'an old farmer came to see me with his cow. He too wanted to buy a rabbit. I sold it to him for three lovely kisses. Again it was no farmer, but our princess in disguise. Is it true?' he asked the princess.

'Yes, it is the truth,' the princess murmured quietly. By now her cheeks were crimson, and it suited her well. She looked just like a rose in bloom.

'Into the barrel with that truth,' the king ordered crossly.

'Then, on the third day — wait a minute, how was it?' The youth purposely took a long time in remembering. 'Oh yes, now I remember! An old hag came to see me in the pasture, riding a dirty grey mare. I gave her two rabbits in payment of . . .'

'Stop, stop, it's enough, the barrel is now full to the brim!' the king interrupted Esben suddenly, wiping the sweat off his brow with his handkerchief. 'Goodness gracious, what a disgrace it would have been, if everyone here found out that I was forced to kiss that ancient nag!' And the king sighed with relief.

Esben certainly deserved to get the beautiful bride and, in all fairness, the princess had no objection to such a slim, handsome young man. The king saw he was beaten, so he ordered the wedding preparations to commence.

For three nights all the cooks and kitchen maids cooked and baked. The brewer brewed beer all day and night long, till the enormous barrel was full to the brim.

The wedding guests were busy feasting, drinking, cracking jokes. Even the king became quite jovial. One small kitchen boy wanted to look into the barrel sometime after midnight, to see how much beer was still left. He placed a ladder against it, climbed to the top and leant over. By pure chance a maid went past, tripped over the ladder and the kitchen boy fell head first into the barrel, with a big splash! The guests all became excited, but the king did not lose his head.

'Kick the tap off quickly, and he'll swim out!' he cried.

They knocked off the tap and the beer gushed out of the barrel. Everyone who had some cup or dish at hand, placed it near. But shortly all the jugs, urns, basins and glasses were filled and the beer flowed on and on, through the banqueting hall, down the stairs and into the courtyard. There it woke the silver rabbits. They licked the stairs, licked all the puddles, and became so merry that they started to hop around. It was such a crazy, hilarious bunny dance, that all the people laughed so much they thought their sides would burst. Eventually the kitchen boy swam out through the gap. In one hand he held a ladle, in the other a jug. He was shouting, 'Long live the king! Long live the king!'

The king laughed till the tears ran down his cheeks.

Esben laughed too, standing at the side of his lovely bride, and he thought gratefully of the old coalman, who had given him the magic whistle.

The Adventures of Bidjan and the Fair Princess

In the days when Persia was ruled over by the famous Chosroes, wild boars in great numbers invaded the northern regions of the land. They devoured the crops to such an extent that soon the people were faced with famine.

The shah, in despair, asked his bravest young warriors to go forth and fight the fierce wild boars. None volunteered except a young man, called Bidjan.

'Let me go,' begged the youngest of the shah's warriors. 'I promise I will do my best to rid our land of this menace.'

The shah, who was not much older than Bidjan himself, was pleased at these words, for he knew his more experienced warriors thought it beneath their dignity to fight wild boars. He gave Bidjan a handsome sum from his treasury and bade Gurgin, one of the great hunters, to accompany him on his adventure.

After long days in the saddle, Bidjan and Gurgin hit upon the trail of the wild boars. 'Take your club,' said young Bidjan to Gurgin, 'and if I miss the leader with my arrow, then you can crack its skull with your club.'

Gurgin's face suddenly burned with resentment at these words, for he was proud and arrogant and did not wish to be told what to do.

Seeing Gurgin's angry frown, Bidjan wheeled his horse round, without a word, and set off in pursuit of the boars. Like a fierce wind, he raced through the forest, and every bow he shot from his arrow found its mark.

By the end of the day, Bidjan had killed many of the boars, and taken their tusks as trophies to bring back to the shah.

In the meantime, the treacherous Gurgin was making a plan to ruin the noble Bidjan. His plan was to lure him across the border into the hostile land of Turania where he would be taken prisoner. When Bidjan at last came in sight, flushed with the heat of the hunt, Gurgin set about to put his plan into action, and turning to him, with a pleasant smile, he called out, 'You fought like a lion, Bidjan! You are a hero deserving royal honours. Two days' journey from here there is a spot where the noblest of the Turanians take their leisure. Cold, sparkling streams run down emerald-green hillsides. The air is heady with the fragrance of nutmeg, and the valleys echo to the song of the nightingale serenading the rose. Believe me, Bidjan, that amidst such delights the months pass like days and the days like hours — more especially as the charming Turanian Princess Manidja herself is at present there, enjoying the beauty with her companions.'

'Conduct me to this place — I wish to see it and the Princess!' cried Bidjan, enchanted by the vision called up by Gurgin's words. And without more ado, the pair mounted their horses and set out across the mountains.

After a long tiring ride, Bidjan saw below him a cluster of gleaming white tents and, in the centre, one decorated in gold. This was the tent of Princess Manidja herself, who saw the two riders as she emerged with her attendant.

'Who are those riders drawing nigh, nurse?' asked the young Princess. 'The younger one is as handsome as a messenger of the gods. Find out his name and to what family he belongs, and ask him what he seeks here.'

The old woman hastened away to greet the riders, and Bidjan told her how he had been hunting boars at Chosroes's command and how he had come to this pleasant spot to rest and refresh himself.

At this, the good woman hurried off to return a short while later with a message from the Princess.

'Stranger, I bring you a message from Princess Manidja, daughter of the Emperor of Turania. You are to present yourself to Her Highness without delay.'

The youth sprang from his horse's back, threw the reins to Gurgin, and with some nervousness, followed the nurse to the Princess's tent. Imagine his surprise when, at the entrance, two maidens came to loose the thongs of his sandals and bathe his feet in scented lavender water. Then the Princess herself came out to greet him, her face radiant as a spring day.

In that moment Bidjan forgot his home, the glory of the hunt, and even the waiting Gurgin. The Princess's lovely eyes held him fast.

'Are you weary?' she asked, smiling gently. And her voice and smile expressed her innermost thoughts. Already she was half in love with this handsome hero.

Music from the lutes fell softly on their ears as the two entered the tent. For three nights and three days they talked and feasted, unable to leave each other.

At the end of the third day, Bidjan bowed his head in sorrow. No longer could he delay his return to the shah.

When Bidjan told her he must return home, the Princess secretly ordered her servants to add a sleeping potion to the wine which she presently handed to the young man, saying, 'Drink this, my beloved, before you leave me.'

Bidjan raised the goblet to his lips—and the next moment fell to the ground in a deep sleep. He was borne on a sedan chair across mountains and valleys to the very heart of Turania, where the Princess had her capital. Waiting until nightfall, the bearers carried the chair into the palace under cover of darkness so that no one knew that the Princess had taken a hated Persian into her own palace.

Bidjan opened his eyes only when the Princess's faithful nurse placed a rare herb in his left ear.

'Do not grieve, my beloved,' the Princess whispered, as she bent over him. 'I could not let you go. Now we can be together for always.'

Their happiness was short-lived. One of the palace servants betrayed their secret. He told the Princess's father that an enemy of his people was secreted in the palace, and the King, filled with rage, ordered Bidjan to be brought before him in chains. Before he could pronounce the death sentence, his wisest counsellor whispered to him:

'Consider well your decision, Your Highness! The prisoner is one of Chosroes's courtiers and according to all accounts he has fulfilled his allotted tasks in slaughtering the wild boars. When the Shah of Persia learns of his death by hanging he will send a mighty army to avenge him. Must we pay the price of war on his account?'

The sovereign recognized the wisdom in his counsellor's words. Turning to the captain of his guards, he said, 'You know the spot where the evil spirit Akvan once threw up out of the sea a boulder as big as a tower? Go there with a thousand mules and a thousand slaves and have them drag the mighty boulder to a pit into which I will have this Persian cast. The boulder will act more effectively than ten prison guards. When this is done, banish the Princess Manidja from the palace. She has shamed me in my old age. Send her out as a beggar into the streets.'

And so it came to pass as the cruel sovereign decreed. Bidjan, in chains, was cast into a pit in a barren wasteland and the great boulder rolled into place. The weeping Princess was banished from the palace. For seven days and seven nights, she sought the pit where Bidjan lay prisoner. When at last, she came upon it, she used her slim, delicate hands to burrow beneath the boulder so that she might make a tiny peep-hole and talk to Bidjan.

'Oh Bidjan, light of my life,' she called. 'Be patient while I seek help.'

No one recognized her as the Princess, and many gave the beggar-maid scraps of food. These she brought back to Bidjan in his prison. From then on, the Princess kept Bidjan supplied with food, and gave him fresh courage with her words of love. At night, she laid her head on the boulder that imprisoned her beloved and slept.

What of the betrayer, Gurgin? As he set out for the shah's palace, he thought of what he would say. And when he stood once more before the shah, he had with him the trophies which rightly belonged to Bidjan. He was afraid, but nevertheless he told his well-rehearsed story with conviction. 'Bidjan,' he said, 'had chased a fine stag deep into the forest, and not returned. He had killed the wild boars himself and had brought back their tusks as proof.'

The shah did not believe his story. He took himself off to a secret chamber in the palace where he kept the most precious of all his treasures, a clairvoyant cup. This precious gem was moulded in the likeness of the legendary Senmurve—half dog and half bird with gleaming eyes of red rubies and flanks of silver embossed with gold images of the heavenly constellations.

The shah placed the cup on a round table. Then from a shelf he took a jug with a slender spout, and calling upon Ormuzda, the God of Good, he poured a potion from the jug into the cup. The surface of the liquid became as smooth as glass, ready to reveal the truth about the missing Bidjan.

Bending over the cup, the shah watched intently as in its depths the planets of the heavenly sphere began to move in tortuous patterns and magic signs glittered in the zodiac. He gazed into all parts of the heavens but nowhere was there any sign of Bidjan. Then he bent lower over the cup, his face almost touching the surface of the liquid and behold! floating up from the bottom was a picture—barren waste-land, cliffs, a plain, a huge boulder. At the sound of muffled lamentations, the shah placed his ear to the cup. Yes, it was undoubtedly Bidjan's voice! Slowly light filled the dark corners of the pit, and the boulder became transparent revealing the young man bound in chains.

The shah left the chamber, deep in thought. Was there a hero in all Persia who could go among the enemy, roll Akvan's boulder away from the pit, and rescue Bidjan? Only the bravest of the brave, the hero of heroes—Rustem! Times without number Rustem had brought glory to Persia with his magnificent deeds. Only he could perform such a difficult task!

And so the shah sent his swiftest messenger to Rustem's home, far away in the land of Seistan, to bring the hero to him. He had not long to wait. Rustem arrived, clad in armour, prepared as always to go where others feared to tread.

'Rescue a comrade from chains? There is nothing I would enjoy more, Your Highness!' he said to the shah as soon as they had exchanged greetings. 'But neither lance nor sword will be much use here. A camel milder than a lamb will accomplish far more. Give me a caravan and, instead of an army, a cargo of hammered vessels, rugs and scented ointments for which our land is famed. A merchant with these Persian wares is sure to find a welcome all over Asia. In Turania, these goods are likewise much desired as you well know. Travelling thus, the enemy will not have their suspicions aroused.'

'You shall have all you ask for,' declared the shah. 'Use cunning, strength, trickery and bravery to free Bidjan!'

Soon after this, a large caravan set out from the capital heading for the Turanian border. Rustem and his comrades, dressed in the garb of merchants, looked harmless enough. They met with no obstacles on the frontier, and continued on their way unmolested until they reached the mighty boulder. But they did not stop.

The valley resounded to the trumpeting of horns and the tinkling of the bells as the merchant and his drivers on their horses rode up and down the line of camels to see that everyone was in his place. They halted, at last, outside the town of Chotan, which was encircled with thick walls and a fortress guarding the entrance to the gates. The borders of Persia were not far off, but Bidjan's prison was closer!

In the manner of wealthy merchants, Rustem took up residence in a large house in the town together with his servants, and seven of the bravest youths from the shah's court, who had come with him disguised as camel drivers.

The next morning after their arrival, Rustem had the packs opened and the wares laid out in the market-place. News of the precious fabrics and jewels brought by the caravan from Persia soon spread far and wide. It also reached the ears of the faithful Princess Manidja.

At once, she made her way through the thorn bushes and across the rocky plain to the gates of Chotan. Many looked at the poor beggar-maid with pity when she finally stood before the house where the Persian merchants lodged. Her beauty gained her admittance and great was Rustem's astonishment at the sight of her.

'May your trade be prosperous, oh merchant,' the Princess began, 'and bring you much profit! It seems that many Persians come to our land with trinkets and bracelets greatly admired by our women. But they should come rather with armies to save the life of one of Persia's greatest heroes who languishes in a pit.'

Manidja then told Rustem the whole story and how her love had been the cause of Bidjan's downfall.

'Your words mean nothing to me. I know of no Bidjan nor of any Persian heroes. I know only about the value of my merchandise,' replied Rustem at length, his face expressionless, for he wished to put this beggar-maid to the test. Then he continued, 'Nevertheless, I will give you food to take to this prisoner you describe so piteously.' And he gave orders to his cook to bake a fat goose in a shell of pastry. When the bird was ready, Rustem secretly broke off a piece of the shell, placed his signet ring inside, and closed it up. Then he handed the baked goose to Manidja with the words, 'Take this to your prisoner. Stand by him in his hour of need. A firm and faithful love will be rewarded.'

So Manidja returned to the pit, lowered Rustem's gift to Bidjan and told him about her meeting with the merchant.

After one mouthful of the pastry, Bidjan discovered the ring, and saw that it came from Rustem.

'You have sacrificed much for your love of me, Manidja,' he whispered. 'And now, with Rustem so close, hope springs in my heart. Summon all your remaining strength and go back to the merchant. Say to him: "Oh hero and friend of the Gods, are you not Raksha's master and commander?"'

Manidja did not understand a word of what Bidjan said but she set out for Chotan immediately to deliver his message. On hearing Bidjan's message, Rustem said, 'I see now that you told the truth, oh Princess. Bidjan's life was truly in your hands and still is. Raksha is the name of my faithful horse and I am his master. I cannot, however, free Bidjan without your help. Listen carefully to what I have to say. Hasten back to Bidjan with all speed. As soon as night falls, light a fire beside the pit. Its glow will lead us swiftly to the spot.'

Manidja promised to obey, and although she was faint with weariness, she managed to drag herself back to the pit. Before the blackness of night hid the paths, she had built her fire in readiness.

Rustem and his men waited on a hillock outside the town. When black night came, they saw the glow of Manidja's fire and set out at full gallop in its direction. They reined in their steaming horses beside the boulder and, dismounting, the seven young heroes surrounded Akvan's boulder. At Rustem's command all seven strained against it. Sweat poured from their brows, the veins stood out on their necks with the effort, but the stone did not budge. Thereupon Rustem leaped down from his horse, put the handle of his mace under the stone and pressed it down hard. The boulder rocked, and then slowly lifted from the ground. With a single lunge the warrior uprooted it and cast it from him, far beyond the hills to the forests of China.

Then Rustem threw down a stout rope into the pit, and Bidjan caught it and was pulled to the surface.

'This black hole,' said Bidjan, 'might well have been my tomb, but for you, noble Rustem.' Then he turned to Manidja and held out his arms.

Rustem mounted the lovers on spare horses, and the little company galloped back to the town. Like a wise general, he had everything in readiness.

Quickly, the pair were dressed in gypsy clothes, and given stout but swift nags to ride. Then, as the town still slept, Rustem himself led them to the gates, and saw them on their way.

In the morning, the townsfolk were sad to see the last of the gay merchant-traders, and Rustem, with a show of regret, passed peaceably through the gates.

Thus did Rustem, the hero of heroes, rescue Bidjan and the fair Princess, whose love for Bidjan outweighed all family affections. They were married in great splendour and, with the shah's blessing, made their home in the shadow of his palace.

The Merchant's Son

There once lived a wealthy merchant who had an only son, the greatest wastrel in the whole of Persia. All day long he roamed the streets with his band of ruffians. They threw rotten eggs into open windows, pulled cats by the tail, and tripped up innocent passers-by. The merchant, horrified at his son's behaviour, lectured him day and night, always concluding with the words, 'You'll see how hard life is once I am dead and buried.' But his words fell upon deaf ears.

One day, the merchant decided that he must take immediate steps to safeguard his son's future, and he thought of a plan. Providing himself with the necessary tools he cut a hole in the bedroom ceiling and put a thousand pieces of gold inside.

Then he filled up the hole, whitewashed it so that the cracks were invisible, and fixed an iron hook in the centre of the patch.

'Is that hook meant for a lamp?' asked his son, when he saw it. And he began to sneer at the idea, saying that such an arrangement would look like the sanctuary lamp found in churches.

'That hook is not for a lamp but for you, my son,' replied the merchant. 'When the day comes that you find yourself in dire straits and know not where to turn for money, take a thick rope, climb up on a chair, and tie one end of the rope to the hook.'

The merchant would say no more, and the boy burst out laughing.

Shortly after this, the merchant died and the boy was now an orphan. Instead of mourning his father's death, however, he began spending his inheritance right and left. In two years' time his father's fortune was gone, and he hadn't a copper left. What was there for him to do but to sell the rugs in the house, and then the silver, and then the inlaid chests and all the furniture until nothing was left of the house but the bare walls. After that he sold the summerhouse in the garden for kindling and the kennel. Then he sold off the slaves, one after the other—first old Zarafan, next his old nurse, Masuda, then Firuza, the ostler, and last of all his own personal manservant.

Soon, as there was nothing more to sell and no one to borrow from, the merchant's son was left with empty hands and an empty larder.

One day, he was strolling along with his ragged companions when they came upon a small grove of trees. The shady grove was so inviting that the little band stretched themselves out on the soft green grass and stared up into the cloudless sky.

'A pleasant spot, this,' said the one who was the acknowledged leader of the band. Then, rolling over on to his stomach, he called to the merchant's son. 'Hi, you at the back, how about treating us to a feast? All of us here, down to the last one! And see that there's plenty to drink.'

'Agreed,' said the merchant's son without thinking. 'Come tomorrow at this hour, all of you. You know very well that it is not my habit to pinch pennies.' On his way home, however, his feet dragged and his spirits sank for he hadn't the slightest idea where to get the money to pay for the food and drink. Suddenly, he thought of his old aunt who had pampered him from the day he was born. She would surely help him now!

'Dearest aunt,' began the young man, when he was in her presence, 'I have not the means to buy food and drink for my friends tomorrow. Yet I shall be disgraced if I cannot entertain them as I promised. Will you help me?'

His old aunt could refuse her beloved nephew nothing. She took some of her clothes to the pawnshop and pawned them for quite a good sum, then she bought all kinds of sweetmeats and wines for her nephew's party.

The next day, the merchant's son, gay and carefree once again, packed all the food and wine into a large linen napkin. Then he picked up the bundle and set out, singing, for the grove where he was to meet his companions. As he went along the bundle grew heavier and heavier in the hot sun, and when he came to a date tree the young man sat down to rest a while in the shade of its branches, with the bundle on the ground near him. After some minutes, he rose to continue his journey, but before he could pick up the bundle a big dog appeared, and began sniffing at it.

'Be off with you!' cried the merchant's son in a panic, and he struggled to tie the knots more securely. Suddenly, one of the linen corners was caught fast in the dog's collar, and frightened out of its wits the dog raced off madly, dragging the bundle behind him. The merchant's son, in his efforts to catch it, stumbled and fell and by the time he had picked himself up, the dog with his bundle had disappeared.

With tears of rage in his eyes, the merchant's son made his way to the grove. Once there, he explained what had happened, but his wild companions began jeering at him, and finally they brought out what food they had with them, and turned their backs on him. Finding himself ignored, the merchant's son sat by himself and began to realize, for the first time, what a shabby, miserable bunch of friends he had been going about with.

After he had at last faced the truth, the merchant's son returned to his empty house in a state of such deep despair that he decided to take his own life.

'Never did I heed my father's advice, not a single word, but now I shall make up for it in one stroke and for always,' he said to himself. 'I shall hang myself before the day is out.'

So saying he took a strong, thick rope, went into his father's bedroom and tied one end to the hook. To test its strength he pulled heavily on the rope, and in that moment the hook came out of the ceiling and the boy fell to the floor, with a shower of gold coins and plaster raining down on him on all sides.

Almost buried beneath the great pile, the youth suddenly realized how greatly his old father had loved him. In his wisdom, he had guessed where the company of his worthless friends would lead his son and had given wise thought to the matter. 'Should my son come to the point of wishing to take his life I need no longer fear that he will squander my final gift which shall be ready and waiting for him in his hour of need. By then he will already know how to put money to good use.' So he had written in a final note which the youth unearthed among the pile of gold.

The next day, the merchant's son sought out his father's old servants and re-engaged them. Then he restored the furniture and the pictures which he had sold to keep him in wine. The shop, which he had allowed to stand empty, after his father's death, he re-opened, and stocked with new merchandise, and he repaid his old aunt to the last penny.

He became so hard-working and did so well that when one of his old companions happened to see him in the shop he couldn't believe it was the same person.

'Oh yes, I work now,' cried the merchant's son. 'Come in, come in! Don't stand there, hesitating.'

And so it was that the merchant's son began seeing his worthless friends again. To celebrate the event he invited them all to a feast in the grove where he had last taken leave of them. 'You have something to look forward to,' he told them, 'for I intend to make up for the unpleasantness I once caused you there. You can see for yourselves that neither my house nor my shop is exactly poor.' Then, with a smile on his lips that promised much, he bade his friends farewell.

On the appointed day, he galloped up to the grove on a magnificent black horse, but with no provisions. 'My dear friends,' he said to the assembled group. 'Just imagine—this morning when my cook was preparing a most savoury dish for our feast, a mouse suddenly appeared out of nowhere and made off with the mincing knife. That put an end to the cooking and so I bring you nothing. Interesting that, isn't it?' he said, dismounting from his horse.

His friends gathered respectfully around him in a circle. All nodded their heads silently until one of them spoke up in a grave tone:

'The same thing happened at our house a few days back. The cook was getting ready to make a pâté when a mouse ran up and carried off the mincing knife.'

At this a second voice chimed in:

'I know of an even more remarkable case where the mouse made off with the mincing knife, grill, frying pan and all the kitchen utensils.'

And then a third voice cried:

'May Allah forgive your father, my friend, but that's nothing at all compared to what happened at our house. Just imagine! the mouse made off with everything in the kitchen. The cook wanted to roast a leg of lamb, but into the mousehole it went; he wanted to make a fire in the fireplace to heat some soup, but all the logs disappeared into the mousehole one after another, followed by the pots and pans, lids, ladles, spoons, knives and all the rest. And when he tried to save at least one small spoon to sample his cooking, the villain mouse caught him by the sleeve and he, too, went into the hole before he could so much as scream for help.'

To all this the merchant's son listened without saying a word or changing his expression. And when they all had their say about what the mice had carried off in each of their homes, he finally spoke up.

'Some time ago,' he said, 'here in this very spot, I told you the truth about a stray dog that made off with the bundle of food I was bringing here. You all called me a liar, and turned your backs on me because I could give you nothing. You didn't even invite me to join in your fun. Today you know that I am rich again—and see how you talk! You even made the cook himself vanish into the mousehole just to show me how you accepted my obvious lie. I did not bring any food because of the way you behaved to me then. I am no longer the youth you tried to ruin and make a fool of. Truly, we learn our true friends when misfortune strikes us.'

And with that the merchant's son mounted his fine horse, and galloped away, covering his false friends in a cloud of dust.

The Melon Child

Once upon a time there was an old woman who all her life had vainly begged Allah to give her a child. 'I long for one so much,' she told her husband, 'that I would love it and care for it like a mother—even if it looked like a melon.'

And behold! One day, when she opened the door to the early morning sun, over the threshold and into the room rolled a small round melon. But that wasn't all. The melon began to tumble about at the old woman's feet. Then it whimpered like a newborn infant. It whimpered so mournfully that the old woman took it up in her arms and began to rock it just as if she were comforting a real baby. To her surprise, the little melon was soon quiet and the sound of its soft breathing filled the room.

'She's asleep, my little one,' smiled the woman, and she laid the melon in a soft cradle.

Soon she became used to looking after the melon as if it were her own daughter. Every day she would take the cradle out into the sun, soothe the melon when it wept, bathe it in perfumed water, and wipe its rind lovingly with a clean white towel.

The two would play together in the garden all day long, their favourite game being catch-and-run. The melon was as clever at dodging away as a hare, and the old woman would call out, 'You think I won't catch you, you little imp? Just you wait and see!'

With all this tender care the melon grew bigger and bigger; its coat turned a lovely golden yellow with fine stripes, and the old woman was kept so busy that she didn't know what to do first. Finally, when her melon daughter became so full of energy and impish tricks that it was almost beyond bearing, the old woman decided the time had come to send the child to school. There, its wild nature would be curbed by the stern discipline of the teacher.

The school was a short way from the padishah's palace, and the padishah's son often fled from his tutor to gaze out of the window; above everything, the boy envied the children of his father's subjects as they played and jumped around in the schoolyard.

One day, as he was standing by the window, he noticed that among the pupils pouring out of school on their way home was a fine golden melon, rolling along after the others.

The padishah's son couldn't believe his eyes, and the next day he made a point of being there at the same time to have another look. This time his surprise was even greater—and his eyes all but popped out of his head. As he watched, the melon slowed down as it reached the vineyard to let the children pass, then it stopped. Suddenly the rind split open like the shell of an oyster and out stepped a beautiful maiden, more beautiful than the moon itself.

He saw the young girl climb up one of the poles supporting the vines, pluck herself a big cluster of juicy grapes and begin to eat them with relish. When the last grape had disappeared between the two rows of pearly teeth, lovelier than any real pearls could ever be, the young girl slid to the ground, slipped inside the melon and quickly rolled away.

For the remainder of the day and all the following night, the Prince had no thought for anything but the girl in the melon, and he fell in love with her with all his heart.

The next morning, his tutor looked for him in vain. Trembling with longing and impatience, the young Prince was waiting on the roof of the vineyard cottage in the hope that the beautiful maiden would come again.

How great was his joy when she finally appeared. Scarcely had she stepped out of the melon and climbed the pole than the Prince bent over and slipped his own precious ring on her finger before she knew what was happening. But because the ring was too big for her engagement finger, the Prince fitted it on her middle finger, where it seemed absolutely right. Then he took it back. Having done this, the youth jumped down from the roof and ran to the palace straight to his mother's chamber. There he knelt at her feet, saying, 'I should like to get married, my beloved mother, but only to the girl who can wear my ring on her middle finger. Here it is.'

The Prince's mother, who loved her son greatly, gave the ring to her oldest lady-in-waiting and sent her, with a whole company of servants, to search through-out the surrounding countryside for the girl whose middle finger fitted the ring perfectly.

The lady-in-waiting spent many days going from house to house but there was no sign of a girl whose middle finger would fit the Prince's ring. At long last, she came to the house where the old woman lived with her melon, far out beyond the city. The servants pounded on the door and called out loudly, as they had been doing all these days, 'Is there a young girl living in this house?'

'Don't make fun of me!' said the old woman when she opened the door. 'All my life I begged Allah to give me a child, but he sent me a melon instead. Allah is almighty, he knows what he is about. I have come to love that melon like my own daughter and believe me, she is a source of pride and happiness, both at home and at school where she rolls to every morning.'

The lady-in-waiting and the servants burst into loud laughter at these words and bade the woman show them this unusual melon. When she did so and they saw the nice, but ordinary melon for themselves their laughter knew no bounds and they rocked back and forward, with tears rolling down their cheeks. When they had caught their breath again they told the woman the purpose of their visit, and that they had as yet not found a girl whom the ring would fit.

At their words, a girl's slender hand suddenly stretched out from the melon, which turned them to stone at the sight. The lady-in-waiting was the first to regain her senses. 'Here is a hand,' she said. 'Let us try the ring.' To their profound amazement they saw that the ring fitted the middle finger like a glove.

Without more ado, the lady-in-waiting hurried to the Prince to tell of the incredible thing that had happened. After he had heard her out, the Prince ordered that the melon be brought to the palace immediately, and when this was done, he said, 'This is the one I shall marry and none other!'

In vain his royal mother pleaded with him to give up this nonsense but the

Prince stood his ground. And so preparations were made for the wedding. After the ceremony, when the wedding feast was at its height, the groom stood up and pulling out his sword, cried, 'Come out of that melon at once!'

At these words, the melon split open, as it had done that day in the vineyard, and out stepped a maiden of such marvellous beauty that everyone gasped at the sight. So surprised were the padishah and his wife that they were unable to utter a word. The old woman was sent for that very night, and when she arrived and saw what a lovely girl had grown up in her home, the bride of a royal prince, she was filled with joy and happiness.

From that day on the old woman paid regular visits to her daughter, not minding the weariness of the long and frequent trips, and the two loved one another as only children and parents can.

One day, when she was making her usual trip to see her daughter and there was still a good way to go, she found the path blocked by a lion, who told her that he would tear her to pieces, for this was the hour when he was in the habit of taking his meal.

'Find something else to eat today, dear lion, I beg of you!' pleaded the old woman. 'I am on my way to visit my married daughter. Let me see her just once more. On my way back, you may do what you please with me.'

The lion reminded himself that he had always been magnanimous, for he was after all the King of Beasts, and so he agreed.

The old woman continued on her way but she did not go far. As she was passing a large thicket, out jumped a wolf, his eyes bloodshot from hunger and his fangs bared. The rasping voice in which he spoke to her was the only difference between him and the lion, for his intention was otherwise the same. Like the lion, however, the gaunt and haggard wolf let himself be persuaded to put his meal off until the woman had visited her daughter.

And so on she went, but not for long, for as she was going round a huge boulder that blocked the path, it suddenly changed into a terrible apparition, no less evil than the devil of the desert. His cruel smile was more horrible than the wolf's jagged teeth, and he listened with distrust as the poor woman repeated her entreaty. She begged and pleaded a long time before he consented to let her pass.

At long last, the old woman arrived at her destination. She stayed with her daughter for three days. Then came the moment of parting, and the Prince's wife saw that her mother was burdened with some heavy sorrow.

'What is the matter, mother dear?' she asked, whereupon the old woman, her voice trembling with fear, told what had happened on her way there and what lay in store for her on the way back.

'Put your fears aside. I shall help you,' said the girl. With that she ran to fetch the melon. 'Here—step inside and roll yourself home!'

The old woman did as she was told, and she rolled back along the path whence she had come until she was suddenly stopped by the cloven hoof of the Evil Spirit.

'Hi, you round, striped melon, did you see an old hag on your way?'

'No, I did not,' replied the melon. 'I swear by the soup in which the Prophet soaked his beard, and by all the skins of the onion that I saw nothing on my way that resembled a human being let alone an old hag. Push me along, now, hurry, do! I must make haste, for I have a long way to go.'

So the Evil Spirit gave her a push with the tip of his cloven hoof, and the melon rolled merrily on its way, on and on and on until it was stopped by the wolf. And since the wolf asked the same question as the Evil Spirit small wonder that he received the same answer. And so he, too, gave the melon a push with his snout, and the melon rolled on, on and on right into the lion's paws. He, too, asked the same question as the others before him, and the melon gave the same answer.

But, woe! this time the old woman should have given more thought to her reply.

The lion's mane stood up in anger at the thought that an ordinary melon should ask him to do a service. His anger was fully justified, for wasn't he the King of Beasts? And so instead of giving the melon a push, he raised the melon high and dashed it against a rock. The rind split into fragments and — horror of horrors! — out leaped the old woman, who began cursing him with an endless torrent of words.

Gone was the lion's anger, and in his sudden fright and astonishment he didn't even realize that this was the old woman he wanted to eat. Tucking his tail between his legs, he turned and fled from the thunder and lightning in her voice, into the tall grass by the wayside.

So the old woman returned safely, and when she next visited her daughter, the pair laughed loudly at the tale she had to tell.

The Magic Caterpillar

On the far side of the earth, where the sun burns so hotly that the rocks crack with the heat, there once stood a town. But the people of this town lived in houses which were protected from the burning rays of the sun by the shade of their gardens, and by the cool breeze which came from the sea. The man worked in the cotton fields, and the women and young girls worked at their spinning which they took with them into the orchards.

One day when the young girls had laid their work aside to eat the bread and fruit they always brought with them from home, Khaftvad's daughter caught sight of a lovely apple in the grass. She picked it up and was just about to bite into it when she noticed a large, fat caterpillar on the stem. The pattern on its back was as beautiful and richly coloured as a bejewelled brooch.

'You shall be my talisman,' cried the girl gaily, and she showed the handsome creature to her friends. 'From now on I shall spin three times as much. Fate did not send me such a gem for nothing!'

Loud laughter greeted the girl's joke as her friends went back to their work, and the caterpillar was soon forgotten. But that evening, when the foreman began counting the skeins, what a surprise awaited them — Khaftvad's daughter had spun three times more than the others. Gently placing the caterpillar in her spindle case she fed it the next morning with a small piece of apple, and that night she handed in three times as much work as the most skilled of her companions.

'What magic makes your fingers so nimble, dear daughter?' she was asked one day by her parents. 'Perhaps the good fairy herself has chosen you as her sister, for our house is growing rich as a result of your spinning. Tell us your secret.'

So the girl opened the case where she kept the caterpillar and showed it to her parents. It glowed a lovely blue in the darkness and the brightly coloured squares on its back resembled the rich mosaic adorning the wall of the shah's throne room.

Khaftvad and his wife were stunned at the caterpillar's beauty and they began feeding it with the finest honey, butter and milk to be had in the town. This they did every day, and so it was no wonder that soon the caterpillar became so big and fat that the spindle case could not hold it. When this happened, Khaftvad made a pretty box of cedar wood with an apple tree carved on the lid. With many prayers the whole family placed the caterpillar in its new home, and there it lived contentedly. As it thrived, so did Khaftvad's fortune.

The good man, however, kept almost nothing of his new riches for himself; instead, he spent the money on improving the lot of his neighbours. Soon he had won the love and respect of his fellow citizens and was made mayor of the town. He carried out his office so wisely and well that the fame of this town of cotton spinners spread far and wide throughout the realm. But this did not turn Khaftvad's head. His greatest pleasure was to sit by the caterpillar's box in the darkened room of his house, admiring its mysterious glow and the strange coloured patterns on its back.

One evening, as he sat thus, Khaftvad's gaze became fixed on those patterns as if mesmerized. The lines changed into letters and the letters into the words — *Wealth will bring envy and fighting.* Khaftvad's eyes started out of his head at this strange prophecy on the caterpillar's back, but in that instant the glow died, and the lid of the box fell into place with a dull thud.

The mayor thought about the caterpillar's warning a long, long time until one day he ordered that a strong fortress be built on a high promontory jutting out into the sea.

Soon there rose above the waves a building, the likes of which had never been seen before. Its towers reached to the clouds shrouding the battlements in a veil of white vapour, and it was encircled by a triple belt of fortifications. In the rock of the first courtyard Khaftvad had the men hew an opening the size of a deep well. Seven thick ropes were then used to lower Khaftvad's caterpillar inside, for it had grown so big that the cedarwood box was already too small for it; on the mayor's orders, the well was guarded by a company of sixty men who saw to the caterpillar's needs, day in and day out. They cooked its meals in a seven-eared kettle which would have served a regiment of soldiers.

Khaftvad's daughter herself presided over the preparation of the rice, honey, butter and milk for the sweet porridge which it enjoyed best of all. When the rains came and the wind blew cold the men lowered a coverlet of the finest silk to keep the caterpillar warm and happy. Without its magic — as everyone in the town knew by now — the star of good fortune would be gone forever.

And so the caterpillar thrived to everyone's delight, and the holds of the trading ships which went out to other lands were filled with mountains of white cotton skeins, the thread, firm and glossy as silk, persuading buyers to pay exorbitant prices. There was not a single neighbouring state that was not filled with envy for this flourishing town. Princes and governors of the surrounding districts tried their luck in battle against the town, and one after the other they suffered defeat beneath the walls of the fortress on the cliff. The magic power of the caterpillar protected the town like a heavenly shield and, in gratitude, Khaftvad had the caterpillar's image engraved on the emblem above the town gates.

The fame of Khaftvad's invincibility spread throughout the whole of Persia until it reached the ears of Shah Ardashir himself .

'Some cotton spinner has saddled a nag and plays at being a ruler in his castle of pigskin! I must teach him how to make war!' cried Ardashir in a terrible voice. And thereupon he began to gather an army of untold strength, as if preparing to set out against the most powerful enemy in the world.

Then off he marched from his capital, southward toward the sea. The strong wind whined through the jaws of the grotesque heads made of hammered copper and whipped the standards, making them twist and turn on the poles of their lances like angry snakes.

Horrible, indeed, was the sound made by the marching army of warriors heading for battle. Soon they sighted, on the horizon, the roofs of Khaftvad's town. The brightly tasselled sashes of his winged helmet streamed behind the shah as he galloped ahead of his army, putting his hand to his sword to raise it as a sign of

attack. But lo! his sword was suddenly stuck fast in its scabbard and his horse's hoofs rooted in the ground.

Ardashir looked over his shoulder at his men. All were turned to stone — the horsemen, the archers with their bows, the lancers with their lances, the warriors with their swords and clubs; even the banners hung limply in the breathless quiet.

In that instant, the numbed lines were struck by a gust of hot wind. The air suddenly turned a reddish black and darkness enveloped the land. When the cloud lifted, the sun burned fiercely on the backs of the men and horses, so that they might have been entombed in a fiery furnace.

Before the shah and his followers could gather their wits, a detachment of Khaftvad's armed warriors came flying across the plain on horseback. They struck like lightning, wave after wave of horsemen charging at the enemy's lines. The shah's cuirassiers, bathed in sweat in their red-hot armour, stumbled over the plain, faint from the heat and thirst. Men and horses fell to the ground; glittering swords dropped in the dust. The battle was over before it had scarcely begun.

Seeing defeat was inevitable Ardashir ordered the horns to blow the retreat. At the sound of the horns, the shah's men came to life. They wheeled their horses about and galloped off as fast as they could to a lake in the woods which promised both water and shade.

There under the trees they pitched their tents for the night. The shah sat long with his head in his hands pondering what was behind Khaftvad's easy victory. Now he began believing the rumours that he had previously scoffed at. There was no doubt that Khaftvad's town was protected by some magic force!

As he sat thus, deep in thought, the shah suddenly realized how hungry he was! Rising to his feet, he gave orders that a fat sheep be roasted on the spit, and then he invited his favourite generals to join him in the meal, so that he might learn what they thought.

No sooner had the camp cook placed the roast sheep before them, however, than they were disturbed and alarmed by a black-feathered arrow striking the ground a pace or two from the shah himself. With trembling hands, the shah stooped down and read the message which was affixed to the arrow-head.

> *'Your life is in our hands and easily taken*
> *as this arrow proves. Take your men and leave us*
> *in peace. The caterpillar within Khaftvad's walls*
> *is more powerful than any shah.'*

The shah turned deathly pale. Then with a muttered word to his companions, he turned on his heel and left them. Alone in his tent, he considered his next move. The mysterious caterpillar must be found and destroyed. A spy must be despatched immediately to report on it. But there was, in fact, no need to adopt this course, for when the shah made known his intentions, one of the men in his army stepped forward and claimed knowledge of the caterpillar.

The two talked long and earnestly together and, as a result, the shah gave orders that his army make obvious preparations to return home. But the shah's move was only a trick to deceive the watchful people of Khaftvad's walled city.

As soon as the shah's men found themselves beyond the forest, part of which stretched within a mere mile or two of the town, their leader bade them make a secret camp. He posted look-outs in some of the tallest of the forest trees and ordered them to report immediately when they saw the light of a fire on the ramparts.

'That will be the signal for a swift company of my horsemen to ride out and attack the fortress,' said the shah.

With these words, he unbuckled his sword, removed his helmet and gold encrusted armour, and donned the robe of a wealthy merchant. Then he set out for the fortress with a group of his bravest men. The backs of ten mules sagged under the weight of the silks, furs and jewels with which they were loaded, but two of the bags they carried contained lumps of lead and tin.

As dusk fell, the shah and his men arrived at the town walls and pounded on the gates. When the chief of the caterpillar's personal guard called out 'Who goes there?' he received the following reply.

'Ho there, my friend. I am a merchant from Khorasan but I come not to these walls to offer my wares. My house is not of the poorest and my family is well taken care of — just look at my six sons here! And these ten mules, you see, they are carrying gifts for you and your men. I come because I am filled with only one desire — to set eyes on the caterpillar of the mighty Khaftvad. So many wonderful things have I heard told about it that I shall not cease my entreaties by this gate until you let me in.'

Viewing the bags on the mules' backs, the guard was seized with longing for the treasures they doubtless contained. He ordered the gates to be opened and the merchant and his company admitted. The false merchant then spread all the costly gifts in front of the guard-house, and beside them five huge jugs of wine which they lifted from the back of the last mule.

The men guarding the caterpillar's well could not resist tasting the wine, and then draining the jugs dry, and it was not long before they began to laugh and joke. Finally, they began to argue among themselves as to who should go and feed the giant caterpillar.

'Why quarrel, my friends?' broke in the merchant. 'Why spoil the merry-making with needless disputes? My sons and I would consider it an honour to be able to serve the caterpillar its dinner. If you permit, we shall set to right away!'

'With pleasure!' cried the guards in unison. 'Here are the things you need and there is the fire. But take care you do not burn the porridge. The caterpillar is very particular!'

With this, they turned back to their comrades holding out their cups for more of the delicious wine that came from a fresh supply the merchant had put before them.

Thus it was that Ardashir and his men were able to go about their task unnoticed. Instead of butter, the huge kettle was filled with lumps of lead and tin which was heated red hot by the fire. Then the shah hastened with the kettle to the caterpillar's well. This was the moment the shah had planned for. He was convinced that if he could destroy the caterpillar the town would surrender.

Impatient for its dinner, the caterpillar stuck its head over the edge of the well and opened its mouth wide, whereupon Ardashir's men lifted the kettle holding the molten metal and poured it into the caterpillar's gaping mouth.

From the depths of the well there came a gurgling, hissing sound and an explosive noise like thunder. This was quickly followed by a huge column of green smoke which rose up into the sky — then silence. Khaftvad's caterpillar was no more!

Satisfied, Ardashir climbed to the highest point of the walls and with trembling fingers made a fire, while his men ran to the gates and threw them open. Seeing the glow of the fire, the shah's armed soldiers advanced on the unguarded walls and took possession of the fortress. The mayor was then found and made a prisoner while he slept.

In the morning, the shah jubilantly announced his victory, and the townspeople gloomily accepted defeat. Only the mayor guessed that the caterpillar had left them, and in the goodness of his heart he mourned the caterpillar's end more deeply than his own fate at the hands of the shah.